THE HOUSE BY THE BROOK

THE HOUSE BY THE BROOK

Grace Thompson

Severn House Large Print
London & New York

This first large print edition published in Great Britain 2005 by
SEVERN HOUSE LARGE PRINT BOOKS LTD of
9-15 High Street, Sutton, Surrey, SM1 1DF.
First world regular print edition published 2004 by
Severn House Publishers, London and New York.
This first large print edition published in the USA 2005 by
SEVERN HOUSE PUBLISHERS INC., of
595 Madison Avenue, New York, NY 10022.

British Library Cataloguing in Publication Data

Thompson, Grace
    The house by the brook - Large print ed.
    1.   Runaway husbands - Fiction
    2.   Domestic fiction
    3.   Large type books
    I.   Title
    823.9'14 [F]

    ISBN 0-7278-7431-4

Printed and bound in Great Britain by
MPG Books Ltd, Bodmin, Cornwall.

One

'I won!' Ivor called excitedly as he walked into the kitchen that June morning. 'Airborne won the Derby and I backed it!'

'Well done, Ivor.' Catching his excitement, Marie hugged him, and the fourteen-year-old twins Royston and Roger, and seven-year-old Violet ran to see the winning note he was holding.

'What'll we have, Dad?' Roger asked and was silenced by a glance from his mother. 'I mean, what are you going to spend it on?'

'Well, if I can get the clothing coupons, I need a new suit. This one is getting shabby and I can use it for around the house and get a new one for work.' He winked at Marie, then said, 'All right, we'll have a day at the seaside, that better?' Cheers filled the room and Marie looked at her husband, surrounded by the excited children, and told herself how fortunate she was. A second marriage, a man who had been willing to take on her boys, who were then only five years old, and had welcomed their daughter like the gift she

5

was, and who had created a loving relationship with them all.

She didn't ask how much he had won, she knew that even if it hadn't been sufficient to take them to Barry Island for the day, he'd add to it and make sure they enjoyed every moment.

The following Saturday, Ivor carefully selected the clothes he would wear, brushing them and pressing his trousers, as he liked everything about his appearance to be immaculate. His second best shoes were polished until they shone like glass, his socks carefully selected to match the shirt and tie Marie had placed on the washstand ready to put on. Marie smiled. His parents had taught him well, he was so particular about his appearance and noticed the slightest carelessness in others with disapproval. His manners, too, were impeccable and even her mother, who was highly critical of what she called a lowering of standards, approved of him. Marie had never met his parents, they had died when Ivor was young and he'd been brought up in a children's home. They might not have lived to see him grow up but the rules they had set had obviously been very firmly planted in the young boy.

He gave Marie the money to buy a bathing costume for Violet, who, at almost eight, had outgrown the one from the previous year. It meant using some of their precious clothing coupons but it would give Violet hours of enjoyment over the summer months ahead, she mused, checking how many she had left from the annual allowance.

The day was a great success, with Ivor arranging races for Royston, Roger and Violet plus other families who had settled on the sands near them, gathering children and making teams for ball games and rewarding the winners with a sweet. He broke an ancient tennis racquet playing beach tennis and later there was a dads' race, which he won. He was laughingly presented with the prize – the racquet he had broken. It was a day when everything was fun. Marie didn't think she could ever be happier.

The day was pleasantly warm for early June, with practically no breeze to chill the air or disturb the golden sand. They made a table from the damp sand, covered it with the cloth Marie had brought, and ate a picnic. It had been packed into a wicker hamper belonging to Ivor, which, he had told her, had belonged to his parents.

'They had a car, and we used to pack the hamper and go into the fields and woods to spend the day watching birds and admiring the flowers that my mother used to paint. She was a talented watercolourist,' he had often told her proudly. Such a pity she had never met them, although, Marie sometimes thought, his mother might not have approved of Ivor's marriage.

'I wish I'd known them – your parents sound so interesting,' she said as she began unpacking the food.

'You'd have loved them,' Ivor said fondly. 'I miss them so much.'

Sitting on the beach, as the sun rose high in the sky, Marie wondered at the life Ivor had been used to and was grateful he had settled for a widow who worked in a dress shop and her two sons. From the few things he let slip, it was clear that there had been wealth in the family, but it had all been lost when Ivor's parents had died.

Across the breadth of the bay the sand was full of families doing the same as they were and although they spoke only to those near enough to join in conversation, walk with them to the edge of the tide where they watched the children bathing, or join in with the games organized by Ivor, she felt they were among friends. They had known the nearby revellers but a few hours and were unlikely ever to see them again, yet they were close for the hours they were there and she didn't want the day to end.

Ivor and Royston climbed the metal ladder up the cliff to the café high above the beach and brought a tray of teas and cakes at four o'clock, Violet had two donkey rides, pretending to be scared as the patient animals walked around the well-worn track in the sand.

Ice-cream, which had been banned during the war years, was in demand, and the three children stood in a queue for a long time as the stall-holders doled out cornets and wafers, then ran back with their tongues busily licking around their fists to catch the drips and not waste any of the precious treat.

As shadows changed the colour of the cliffs and the tide slid quietly up across the sand, families began to disperse, they said their farewells to the friends who had shared their day and packed up to leave. Violet dragged her bathing costume off, complaining mildly about its determination to cling to her wet skin. While she rubbed herself dry, Marie held a towel to protect her from straying eyes, and the boys ran to find a suitable corner to serve the same purpose. They went home and shook the sand out of clothes and towels and unpacked the remnants of the hamper.

They were all tired and by ten o'clock they were in bed, Marie and Ivor talking softly, laughing occasionally as they reminisced about their wonderful day. They slept in each other's arms, content with life and aware of their good fortune.

Ivor worked in the offices of a wood merchant and although the yard and workshops were dusty places, he always wore a good suit. He was picking his way across the yard a few days later, trying not to get mud on his highly polished shoes, when a voice called, 'Ivor? Ivor Masters? Is that you? Well damn me, it is!'

Ivor turned slowly, dread filling his heart. He knew the harsh, loud voice instantly and it spelled disaster. The man was standing at the top of the steps near the office door. He was wearing brown overalls, dirty boots and carrying a sheaf of papers. Unless he could dissuade him and pretend not to know him, this man could destroy his life. Ruin everything he'd built. Uncover all his lies.

'Do I know you?' he asked, forcing a sharp tone into his voice.

'Yes, of course you do. I'm Jinks, Jinks Jenkins. We were at school together, surely you must remember me?'

'I'm not local,' Ivor said, still coldly.

The man stood there grinning. 'Your mam still in prison, is she?'

'You are mistaking me for someone else. My mother isn't a criminal and she died years ago.' He pointed to the office. 'If it's a delivery, ask the girl in the office to sign for it.'

'It isn't a delivery,' the man insisted, 'it's a query.' He was still wearing a wide grin, holding back laughter. 'Ivor Masters with the potty parents. Well, would you believe it?'

'If you'd go into the office I'll be there in a moment to help you. As for my parents, you're mistaken, they're both dead.'

'Your old man isn't. Saw him a few weeks ago. Your mam is probably still in prison.'

The man refused to be discouraged, and when he eventually left, having given Ivor the address where he believed his father was living, promising to call again and bring news of him, Ivor felt sick. It was all going to blow up in his face.

He tried to ignore what he had learned, in fact he threw away the piece of paper left by Jenkin Jenkins, who he clearly remembered from school, and who had been one of his many tormentors. Ivor had been small, skinny and, with parents like his, he had been a gift to the bullies, of whom Jinks had been one.

He stayed in the office for longer than usual, trying to prepare himself for what was coming. Before leaving he emptied the waste bin, rescued the torn paper on which the address had been written in childish block letters, and put it in his wallet.

Creeping through the woods and lanes, wanting to see but not be seen by his father, he was unaware that his furtive manner had attracted the curiosity of Geoff Tanner the ironmonger. Ivor found his father sitting in a woodland glade and learned that his mother – whose existence he had denied since he was twelve – was dead. Nothing would the same again – for him, for Marie or the children. By the chance visit of the hated Jenkin Jenkins, his life had collapsed like the sand castles they had built on Barry Island beach being overtaken by the tide. He needed money and he needed it fast. It was the only hope of holding on to what he had.

It was the third week in August 1946, eleven weeks since Ivor's life had fallen apart. A few days later, both Ivor and their daughter Violet would celebrate their birthdays. Ivor would be thirty-eight and Violet would be eight. Marie had planned a surprise party, although she wondered whether Ivor – this stranger who was her husband – would even be aware of the special days. She glanced at the clock for the fourth time in as many minutes. It was still only five minutes to five and there was half an hour yet before the ladies' gown shop closed its doors and she could leave. Then she'd have to dash home to prepare a meal for Royston and Roger, collect Violet from her parents and set off for Mrs Founds's house, where she had promised to paint her kitchen. It was Saturday, and while other assistants in the small dress shop looked forward to a leisurely weekend, she faced an evening and a Sunday of hard work besides preparing a birthday tea for Violet and a supper for Ivor and a few of their friends.

Avoiding the beady eyes of Mr Harries, the shop manager, she took out her notebook and went over the jobs she had arranged to do. Paint the outside lavatory and coal house door in Blake Street; she should finish that tomorrow lunchtime. Paint and wallpaper another bedroom. That would take all tomorrow and two evenings besides, she thought with a groan. And she'd fit another job in between, staining a living room floor for old Mr Greaves while she waited for paint to dry. What a life! Since that wonderful day out in June, when their lives had been so perfect, everything had inexplicably changed: Ivor was no longer a loving husband and devoted father. He was a man she didn't know.

Something had happened but he refused to tell her what had changed him. Another woman? He was unhappy with his family, so wasn't it possible he wished to be somewhere else or *with* someone else? He rarely spoke and stayed out most evenings. Gambling was no longer a bit of fun, it had become an obsession, and most of his wages were gone before they reached the house.

She went through the materials she would need, making a mental note of what she would take with her to each job, then sighed. If only Ivor would help. A small man but strong, and a fast worker when he was

13

involved with something, but as much use as a mouldy loaf. Help? Not Ivor! He'd be sitting in his chair browsing through the evening newspaper, pretending not to be searching the runners for Monday's races and probably hiding the fact that he'd once more lost most of his wages to the bookie's runner who collected bets from the wood yard where he worked. Yesterday had been Friday, pay day, only she hadn't seen a penny, her own few pounds being all she had to pay rent and feed them all. Both Royston and Roger had left school the previous Easter but no job they'd taken had lasted longer than a couple of weeks.

'Something wrong, Mrs Masters? Are we keeping you from something important?' Mr Harries asked sarcastically. 'If you could concentrate on what you're paid for it would be nice. It looks so bad when customers came in and see my assistants standing about. The stock room needs sweeping, the alteration hand never does a proper job, does she?'

Marie put away the notebook and went to brush the floor of the stock room – a task she had already done and which hadn't needed doing the first time. 'Mr Harries is always on my back,' she muttered to Judy Morris, as she reached for the brush, the bristles of which were flattened and divided into a V, like a giant moustache.

14

'He fancies you, that's why,' Judy whispered in reply. 'Fancies you rotten he does.'

'He'd be lucky! Ivor is enough for me, thank you.' Marie grinned and added, 'Too much, in fact. I'd have sent him back to his mother long ago but she won't have him.'

'Someone in his family's got some sense then.' They joked, both believing Ivor to be an orphan, who had been brought up in a children's home.

'I don't understand what went wrong. How could such a kind, loving man suddenly become a selfish stranger?'

Judy didn't reply. She thought it best not to add an opinion or to criticize, she wanted to be there when Marie needed someone to talk to, and criticizing a loved one, even one who was out of favour, was a certain way to damage a friendship.

As Marie approached 41 Hill Crescent, the noise met her before she reached the gate. The twins were arguing again and in between their raised voices she heard the louder, angrier voice of Ivor trying to calm them. She increased her speed and pushed in through the back door, her voice shrill above the rest. Violet was crouched in a corner, pale and frightened, and when she saw her mother she jumped up and ran towards her. 'Mam, stop them. I don't like it,' the little girl wailed.

Marie dropped the shopping bag she was carrying and swung her leather handbag, catching first Royston then Roger a heavy clout across the head. As she swung the bag back for a third swipe, it caught Ivor and he grabbed the bag roughly and threw it down. 'Calm youself, Marie, I've got everything under control. Just a bit of a misunderstanding, that's all, mind. Calm youself and leave this to me.'

She looked at the room, in which a serious fight had clearly taken place. A vase and several cups and saucers lay broken on the floor, cushions were torn, furniture awry. Her shoulders dropped as she hugged the tearful little girl.

'Why aren't you with Nana and Bampy?'

'Sent me home they did. Said they were going to the pictures.' She stifled a sob. 'Mam, they frightened me.'

All this, Marie thought, and I have to go out and work for at least two more hours. It just isn't fair. Although it was futile, she asked herself again, what had gone wrong? Whatever had happened to Ivor had changed them all. The boys fighting – that never used to happen – and Violet frightened in her own home.

She had changed, too, now the lack of money had forced her to find extra work to keep them solvent, juggling all the things she had to do, never having time to listen, and

16

losing patience too easily. And things were getting worse, not better. They seemed to be even more desperately short of money, yet Ivor was still employed at the wood merchants, and she worked all the hours she could. Where was the money going? It couldn't be only gambling, no one gambled away everything their family needed.

'Right then,' she said firmly as the boys stood shame-faced near the door. 'This is your mess and you'll clear it up. I have to go to work to pay for the damage. Come on, Violet, lovely, we'll leave them to it.'

'But, Mam, we're starving hungry,' Royston complained. 'What's for our tea then?'

'Whatever you can find!' Trying to hide her tears from her small daughter, she led the child out to the shed, where she picked up the paint and brushes and cleaning materials she would need and, still shaking and distressed and with an overwhelming feeling of helplessness, of being caught in a cruel trap from which there was no escape, she went to start on Mrs Founds's kitchen.

'We'll have some chips, shall we? Just you and me?' Then she remembered Ivor throwing her bag down. She'd left it there, and even if she turned and went back now this minute her wages would almost certainly be gone.

Mrs Founds might let her have a couple of coppers in advance, especially if she explained that it was for Vi. She was a kind lady and always gave her a little more than the agreed price for the work she did.

When she accepted the ten shillings Mrs Founds gave her, and returned from the shop with chips for Violet, she saw Mrs Founds watching her and at once jumped as though caught out. 'I won't be a minute, Mrs Founds. I'll just get Vi a drink of water then I'll be back on the job.'

'My dear girl, don't rush so. You know you shouldn't be doing this on a Saturday evening. After a full week at the shop you should be relaxing, having a bit of fun.'

'Fun?' Tears slipped out of Marie's eyes as she thought of the mess at home where her sons had been 'having fun'.

'You're worth more than this, dear. You really are.'

It was almost ten o'clock when Marie returned to the house, dragging a sleepy Vi and carrying the remnants of the materials and tools. The house was in darkness and she wondered whether that meant Ivor and the twins were asleep or out somewhere spending money they didn't have.

Ivor was asleep in the chair, the fire was out and when she tried to light the gas she found that the fragile mantle had been broken, probably in the fight. She fumbled in a drawer and found the new mantle, silky in its packet, and fixed it to the lamp jutting

18

out of the wall on its arched stand. She lit a match and waited while the mantle blazed then calmed to its clear light, spreading before her the chaos, which was exactly as she had left it. No attempt had been made to clear up the mess. In fact there was more: the table had been carelessly cleared by pushing things to the floor and a meal had been eaten. A loaf was down to its crust and an empty jar of fish paste with its lid and fastening band beside it.

With a deep sigh, she pulled the curtains across the windows, remembering what a pest old Watkins the warden had been not so long ago, before the war had ended; banging on doors and shouting, 'Put that flamin' light out,' enjoying the odd moments of importance. The gas mantle popped once or twice and settled into a steady glow that was oddly comforting.

There was no sign of the twins. She didn't call to find out if they were in their room, best not to wake Ivor. She was too tired for another argument. She heated some milk and gave it to Vi then led her upstairs, walking on the edge of each tread to avoid creaks. The twins slept in the front room downstairs. With only two bedrooms, the house had been too small when Vi had unexpectedly arrived and they couldn't afford to move to a larger house – and since June and Ivor's Derby win they couldn't always pay the rent on this one.

She lay for a long time, unable to sleep. Although her body ached, her mind was too active, running over thoughts of the miracles that might happen to change her miserable life. Ivor miraculously changing back overnight into a caring, hardworking husband and father was the only real hope, and while there was a racehorse or a greyhound capable of putting one foot in front of another there was no chance of that. He had not been himself since early June, less than three months ago; such a brief moment in a lifetime.

Winning the football pools was everyone's dream, but money wasn't the answer to her situation. However much they won, Ivor would lose it all. Buying drinks for friends as he did on the rare occasions when the horses performed as he predicted and gave him a win. Gambling more and more to recoup the losses that he would inevitably suffer. She remembered when Mr and Mrs Founds won fifteen thousand pounds. He'd lost it all within a year, buying a house then ruining it by so-called improvements before selling it for a fraction of what he'd paid. He'd bought new furniture and a piano no one could play, a car which he lent to a friend who crashed it into a wall. Then there were the family parties and the handouts. Perhaps that was why Mrs Founds – now widowed – is so kind to me, she mused. She at least understands.

She heard Ivor coming in, felt the slight movement of air as he pushed open the bedroom door, the staleness of tobacco and drink hovering around him like a miasma. She didn't move. With luck he'd believe she was asleep and leave her alone. He got into bed and turned, taking the covers from her, and at once began to breathe steadily. Trouble free, she thought bitterly. While I carry his burdens. Something must be done, she decided as sleep finally claimed her. I can't go on like this. Mrs Founds is right, I'm worth more.

Marie's sister, Jennie, was just creeping into bed as Marie finally slept. Unlike her sister, Jennie prided herself on being useless. She considered that working as a hairdresser entitled her to the care and attention given by her parents. She and her friend Lucy were coping alone, as their boss, Miss Clarke, was on holiday, so she felt her mother's fussing was even more deserved. Miss Clarke was a good boss, never complained, and Bill, the son of Mr James the owner, was always willing to help move heavy equipment. By the occasional looks he gave her, Jennie thought he was imagining that one day she would pay him in ways he dared not mention – although Bill had been seeing rather a lot of Miss Clarke, and Jennie and Lucy wondered whether the fact they were on holiday at the same time was more than coincidence. This was a cause for smothered laughter. Bill was the same age as Jennie and Lucy but they saw him as 'too old' for any serious consideration.

Mr James, who had owned the shop since his wife had died a few years before, was happy to leave the business to Miss Clarke, Jennie and the newest member of staff, Lucy. He rarely entered the shop and apart from a brief thank you, and a formal handshake each Saturday as he handed them their wages, they hardly saw him.

Belle and Howard Jones were immensely proud of Jennie, who had been a late arrival, eight years after Marie. They regularly told Marie how clever her sister was, and how capable and how smartly she dressed. Marie smiled and nodded agreement like an automaton, and went back to wondering how 'clever Jennie' would feed a family with the five shillings she had left until Friday. She found it impossible to smile when her father said he wanted to decorate Jennie's room, smarten it up as befitted her status as manageress of the hairdressing shop.

'Temporary manageress, only while Miss Clarke is on holiday,' Marie reminded her father with a smile. 'To hear her talk you'd think she'd been running the business for years.'

'Enthusiastic, our Jennie. She loves life.'

On Sunday morning, much to the disapproval of many who believed in respecting the sabbath, Marie took Vi and did the undercoating on the bedroom The living room was still in a mess and, apart from rescuing her purse, which had still miraculously held her wages, and preparing the vegetables for dinner, she had done nothing. She knew she would eventually clear it up, but she was becoming more and more unwilling. Once, pride would have forced her to put everything straight for fear of a neighbour walking in and seeing the state of the place. Now she cared less and less. After the past three months of increasing worry, she was reaching the point where everything would change. Pride as a housewife was less important than pride in herself.

She called at the home of her parents, the smell of a roast meal cooking reminding her of how hungry she was. If she and Vi were invited to stay then she'd accept. Let Ivor, Royston and Roger go hungry instead of her and Vi for once.

'Mam, we're starving, any chance of something to eat?' she called as Violet ran in ahead of her.

'You should be home cooking a meal for your family, not wandering about looking like a scarecrow on a Sunday,' her mother

23

reprimanded, neatly avoiding the question.
'Working I've been. Not wandering. How
could I paint and stick up wallpaper with my
best clothes on, supposing I had any!'

'You should be home getting the Sunday
joint cooked.'

'Mam, if I didn't work there wouldn't *be* a
Sunday joint.'

'Don't exaggerate, Marie.'

'Where's Jennie?' Marie asked, swallowing
the retort that she knew would be a waste of
time.

'Your sister is still in bed. She was out late
last night,' Belle Jones replied.

'I was late too. I had to take Vi with me and
we didn't get back from Mrs Founds's until
after ten o'clock. The mess left from a fight
between Royston and Roger still there, un-
cleared. I worked in the shop until five thirty
then went to paint her kitchen.'

'You do dramatize, our Marie. An argument surely, not a fight?'

'A fight, and several things got broken.
Violet was scared and I couldn't leave her
there. You don't understand my difficulties,
Mam.' She wondered why she tried to
explain, her mother only heard what she
wanted to hear.

'Poor Vi,' Belle said, proving her right. 'No
wonder she lacks colour in her cheeks.'

'Marie,' her father called as he came in
from the garden. 'Would you like some

beans and a couple of lettuce? There won't be any more, these are the last for this year. Scraggy mind, but they'll make a bit of a feed. I picked them knowing you'd call.'

While Belle went to find some newspaper to wrap them, her father asked, 'Is there any chance you can give me a hand painting the back-bedroom ceiling? Jennie never complains but her bedroom is badly in need of redecorating.'

'Why not ask Jennie?' she asked, with little hope.

Her father laughed. 'Our Jennie do something useful? That'll be the day. Helpless she is, our Jennie.' There was no dismay in his voice. In fact, he seemed to be constantly proud of Jennie's inability to do anything to help. She was pretty and amusing, how could anyone expect more? seemed to be his attitude.

Marie stifled a sigh, and she picked up the newspaper parcel. Even her father seemed to want something from her.

'I can't do anything for a while, Dad. I've promised a few people and I do work all day.'

'It's all right,' he said touching her shoulder reassuringly. 'I know I shouldn't ask, but you know how your mam is – when she wants something done it has to be now this minute. I'd do it myself but I'm not good on ladders these days.'

'I'll have a look while I'm here.' Marie

went up the stairs with her father following and went into her sister's bedroom – the room she had once shared. Peroxide-golden hair fanned out over the white pillow and a muffled greeting emerged when Marie spoke to Jennie.

'Don't worry about the ceiling, our Dad,' Jennie said sleepily as she rose from the bed. 'I can't stand the smell of paint, and our Marie takes for ever when she does a job for us. Paying customers she deals with at once, mind.' She pulled a face at her sister, then grinned.

'Don't talk nonsense, Jennie. It isn't helpful,' Howard said with a frown.

'Can't she do it later, when I go to stay with Auntie Ivy?' She gave a groan and added, 'Oooh, our Dad, imagine me lying here stiff and dead from paint poison.' She positioned herself dramatically, hanging over the edge of the bed.

Howard laughed in spite of trying not to. 'Stop your nonsense, silly girl.' Marie glanced at him, saddened by the look of affection he showed, which she never saw directed at herself.

'Is Miss Clarke back yet?' Marie asked.

'No, but I'm coping all right,' she said with a sigh. 'It's hard mind, with one pair of hands missing. Lucy's...quite good,' she said disparagingly. 'I'm trying to teach her but there isn't much time, we're so busy.'

26

Marie and Vi didn't stay long. It was useless trying to explain her situation to her mother. Belle had a safe, rather uneventful life and couldn't understand why her daughter couldn't manage to do the same. Both her parents were fond of Ivor and clearly didn't believe the little Marie had told them about the sudden change in him, and their money difficulties. Her father doted on his younger daughter and presumed that as Marie was married, with children of her own, she no longer needed his special care. Marie had believed that marrying Ivor had been a good move. Until recently it had been. Eight years of happiness and three months of increasing misery. Would she have been better staying single? Then she looked at her daughter and knew that for Violet alone it had been worth it. 'Talk about out of the frying pan into the fire,' she said aloud.

'What d'you mean, Mam?' Vi asked as she skipped along beside her mother.

'Oh, I just mean that once you've left something behind, you can't just hop back again. You have to make another jump and hope the landing is a good one, better than the last. The trouble is, where to jump and how to survive without the frying pan.'

Vi wasn't listening. She was concentrating on hopping on the paving stones without touching the lines. Girls at school had

27

warned her that landing on the lines was bad luck. Perhaps they were like Mam's frying pan, she considered vaguely.

Even through the eight happy years they had lived hand-to-mouth. No money left by Thursday and waiting for the weekly pay packet each Friday to begin a new week. Paying the rent, putting a little aside for other bills like gas and coal, and smaller amounts for the baker and milkman, never daring to miss a week thereby creating debts they'd never be able to clear. Then surviving for seven days on what was left.

Every week had been the same unless there were unexpected expenses to deal with. Only now Ivor's gambling had broken the simple pattern and made everything worse.

On Monday, Marie had the afternoon off. She and the two other assistants took it in turn to have the extra half day, and this was when she normally did a lot of extra housework. She left the house before eight and went first to the hardware shop from where she bought her materials. Geoff Tanner greeted her and offered her a cup of tea.

'Now, Marie, no nonsense about not having time. You don't need to be on duty with Misery guts Harries until five to nine. Sit down, I'll sort out your order and you can have five minutes peace. Right?'

Later, she couldn't explain why she had talked to him so revealingly about her life. It must have been the rare quiet moment in her frantic, thankless life, or maybe the friendly interest shown by Geoff, but when she started, she told him more than she had admitted to anyone before.

'What happened when you got back from your parents' house?'

'Surprisingly, the meat was in the oven, but nothing else was cooking. So it was either a long wait for dinner, or sandwiches. The twins wanted to meet their friends, so amid wild complaining they had a sandwich. Ivor was at his club and I cooked for six o'clock. It's a long day sometimes.'

'And the clearing up? The broken china?'

'Oh, I had to do that. I was afraid of leaving it any longer in case Vi cut herself.'

'And the birthday party?'

'I sent the twins around to tell everyone it was postponed.'

Geoff was silent for a while and when she looked at him he was staring at her, an expression on his face she couldn't read. It wasn't sympathy, more puzzlement and perhaps, she realized with a start, something like disapproval. Surely he wasn't another who, like her mother, believed in obedience to a husband and the marriage vows beyond all reason?

'I can't stand martyrs,' he said at last. 'I can understand people putting up with things they can't change, or dealing with sickness, tragedies and other unavoidable troubles, but I don't understand how someone like you, clever, hardworking, honest, can lie down, day after day and allow yourself to be treated like a doormat.'

'I have to keep everything going for the children. It's all very well to have dreams of getting out, changing things, but I have two fourteen-year-old sons and a daughter who is only eight. What do you think I can do? Run away? Leave them to it?'

'One day, I think that's exactly what you'll do. You'll take Violet and walk away.'

Her hand was shaking as she replaced the cup and saucer on the table. She was angry, most of the night had been spent thinking of ways of doing exactly that, and all she had come up with was the realization that there wasn't one.

Jennie went to see her sister, and to Marie's surprise and irritation, she talked about how miserable *her* life had become. 'Staying away another week, that Miss Clarke is! There's me running the hairdressing shop, expected to do the accounts and see to the ordering of shampoos and all that, employing a cleaner – I put my foot down when Mr James asked me to do that! – I'm worn to a frazzle.'

'Shame,' Marie said. 'Poor put-upon you.' Her sarcasm went unnoticed.

'And our Dad's getting more useless by the

day, our Marie. I have to get up on chairs to reach things he needs, and he's so slow. You'll have to help more, it shouldn't be down to me all the time. They're your parents too. And Mam doesn't cook like she used to.'

'Jennie, you know how things are for me, I can't do any more. I'm doing two jobs as it is, or haven't you noticed? And as for Mam cooking, haven't you heard of rationing?' Marie said irritably.

'People still cook, don't they?'

'Mam and Dad are getting older. Nothing stays the same. Except that for me they get much much worse,' she added bitterly. 'Ivor is gambling and you can imagine what that means with five of us to feed. He won't talk about it or explain why he's changed so much. He's useless and the twins are still looking for work.'

'I thought they were working for the farmer.'

'That was two weeks ago. Since then they've been at a builders, supposed to be learning the trade but I think they fool around most of the time. Whatever, they've been sacked again. Fourth job they've had in as many weeks. They fight and avoid doing what they're asked, and no one will put up with that and pay for the privilege.'

'What are you going to do?'

'Until now I've left it to Ivor, but, as usual,

31

it ends up with me having to sort it. I'm going to see Mr Harris in the wholesale fruiterers and Mrs Flint in the chip shop. Whatever Ivor says, they have to work separately or they'll never keep a job.'

'They won't like it,' Jennie warned. 'Neither will Ivor.'

'That's too bad.'

By the end of the day, her precious half-day off, Marie had found work for the two reluctant boys: fruit and vegetable wholesalers for Royston and the behind the scenes preparation at the chip shop for Roger.

Although it was August, it was cold, with an evening breeze rustling the leaves of the trees in the park and those lining the pavements, and blowing hats askew, as people hurried home. She had brought Vi to the playground and was dreaming as she pushed her on the swing. A couple of evenings this week, and one more weekend, then she would have caught up with her list of decorating jobs. Perhaps, with Royston and Roger actually bringing in a wage, she could take a few weeks off from her second occupation. Her heart leaped as an alarming possibility occurred. She had to make sure to tell the boys to hand their wages to her and not their father, or she wouldn't see a penny of it. Today she and her friend Judy Morris were going to the pictures – a rare treat. Jennie had agreed to stay in with Violet. But, she thought with irritation, her presence was mainly to make sure the boys didn't fight and hurt themselves or break furniture.

Jennie leaped up from the tea table before being asked to help clear up, having eaten her fill of the sandwiches and a few cakes her mother had prepared. 'What time's supper, our Mam?'

'Usual, about half past nine,' Belle replied. 'Poached egg on toast all right?'

'Leave mine till I come in. I might be late. Lucy and I might go to the pictures.'

'I thought you were looking after Vi, so Marie could go out?'

'Oh no! I forgot! I'll have to cancel. She won't mind, she was only going to the pictures with Judy Morris and they see each other all the time at the shop, don't they?' Jennie shut her mind to her mother's mild disapproval and ran upstairs to get dressed. Twenty-eight she might be but she was still young enough to enjoy a bit of fun.

She and Lucy had a double date with two RAF boys they had met at the Saturday dance. A good laugh they'd been. The promise of a few drinks, a dance, followed by supper somewhere, had filled her mind all day. As if she'd give up on this to sit with boring little Vi! Fat chance of that!

She hurried down the road, pulling an un-seen face at Watkins the ex-air raid warden as he strolled with his pompous walk through the streets. He had been unable to discard the cloak of importance the war years had given him, and people teased him, something of which he seemed unaware. Waving frantically at the approaching bus, she pushed her way to the front of the queue, then settled down to dream of the hours ahead.

She was a pretty young woman with fluffy blond curls, the result of hours of discomfort sleeping on curlers, and regular perms and treatments at the shop where she worked. She had heard, and firmly believed, that gentlemen preferred blondes and one day, when she was too old for fun, a gentleman was what she hoped to find. Rich, of course, and with eyes only for her.

The bus stopped at the town hall and she was first to alight, pushing her way through the other passengers as though it was her right, ignoring the few who complained and smiling sweetly at those who did not. Lucy was waiting, huddled up in an imitation fur, high heels tapping an impatient tattoo as she approached.

'Late you are, Jennie Jones, and there's me standing here like a tart waiting for you.'

'Sorry, Lucy, but I had to make myself presentable, didn't I?'

'Your hair's nice,' Lucy said grudgingly.

Chattering and planning their evening,

34

they went into the dance hall and straight to the ladies' room. Lucy took off the scarf she had been wearing and waited for Jennie's comments.

'Not bad. Here, let me open out a few of those sausages at the front. Soften it a bit.' She fiddled and eased the heavy rolls, which were exactly as they had been when taken out of the dinkie curlers, and moulded them skilfully into a nest of tiny curls. Lucy thanked her. 'A marvel you are, Jennie Jones. A real marvel.' Silently she wondered whether Jennie would ever fail to criticize her efforts or she would ever be able to disagree. Their friendship was based on admiration given by one and accepted by the other.

It was some time before they found their dates. As they walked in, two young men in navy uniform asked for a dance and the girls – Lucy coaxed by Jennie – accepted. They had been around the floor several times before seeing their dates waving. 'Don't want them to think we're desperate,' Jennie said as she insisted on them dancing a second dance with their partners.

'They're a bit young for you, aren't they?' one of the sailors remarked.

'Say that again – if you want your face slapped,' Jennie said, a smile taking the sharpness from the words. She spread her arms as much as the crowd allowed and greeted their dates with, 'Here we are, you lucky lads, your

35

dreams come true.'

Laughing, they allowed themselves to be led onto the dance floor for a lively foxtrot.

As the evening wore on, and the melodies became slower and more romantic, Jennie began to feel a little uneasy. The way her partner was pressing himself against her, and the words he uttered in her ear, were giving a clear warning. The young men had bought them a few drinks, and had promised supper – always a treat – but there were expectations of a payment she was unwilling to give. She signalled to Lucy and pointed to the ladies' room.

'I have a feeling they want more than a goodnight kiss,' she whispered when they were touching up their make-up.

'Me too. Pity, mind. I was looking forward to going out for supper.'

'Perhaps we can have supper then belt for home before they realize we've gone?' Giggles and whispered plans kept them there for longer than planned and when they went outside the swing doors both their dates were waiting.

'We thought you'd gone home,' one of them said.

'What, and miss the best part of the evening?' Jennie said with a wink.

'Let's go now, there's no need to wait till the end.'

'Supper first, mind. Where are you taking

us?' Lucy asked.

'The Spinning Wheel is open till eleven, we'll have to hurry.'

'That suits me,' Lucy said, with a glance at Jennie.

The meal was simple but to the young people it lacked nothing. An omelette using dried egg and filled with an assortment of vegetables followed thin soup, and the meal ended with a serving of stewed apple rings and watery custard.

The bill paid, the two men, excited after several hours of teasing and hints of the best yet to come, stood and asked for their coats. Lucy took hers and Jennie's under her arm and pointed to the ladies'. 'Won't be long.'

'Oh come on, you've already been there twice,' one complained.

'Don't be impatient, boys,' Jennie said, smiling a promise.

Laughing, they ran to the door that led to the lavatories and also to the back entrance, now standing open as rubbish was being placed outside ready for the morning's collection. They walked quickly, keeping to the shadows until they reached the bus stop, then leaped on the bus that had just pulled in and ran up the stairs.

'Lucky they don't know where we live,' Lucy panted.

'Oh that was a fantastic evening,' Jennie sighed. They began singing one of the melodies to which they had danced. Passengers smiled tolerantly at their high spirits.

'Keep your head down,' Lucy warned, 'they could be out there looking for us.'

They alighted from the bus, and from a car parked behind the bus two men got out.

'Hello, girls, did you think you'd lost us?'

'Oh, hello again.' Jennie knew her voice sounded trembly.

'Sorry, but we just realized the time. It was awful late, and—' Lucy began

'We girls have to be in before midnight,' Jennie said.

'Girls! Too old for that title. Old slags more like. Tarts like you can't afford to be choosy. Old floozies. Fit for nothing better than what we had in mind. Don't pretend that isn't what you do.'

As the bus disappeared and they were left in the silent empty darkness, the two women began to be afraid. Arm in arm, they tried to walk away. Both were grabbed roughly and at once the men began to hit them. Insults hissed through tight lips, and the words became one continuous sound, the pain of each blow melding into a panic-filled agony. When they were dragged and dumped into a shop doorway, they lay for several seconds, disoriented and stunned.

'Have they gone?' Jennie asked in a voice she didn't recognize as her own.

'There's a toilet down the next street, we

could clean ourselves up before we go home,' Lucy whispered, through split lips.

Arms around each other they made their way to the stale-smelling building and, avoiding the mirror, washed their bruised faces.

'How old are you, Lucy?'

'Twenty-eight, same as you.'

'It's time something changed. I don't want to live like this any more.'

'Nor me.'

'When I think of the chances I let slip by, of marriage and a home, well, I'm not going to let another chance pass me by.'

'Nor me.' Lucy began to cry softly. 'But who'd have us? Got a reputation we have.'

'I don't know why. We've never done – that – have we?'

'No, but it was fun pretending we had, to shock a few people. And now we're paying for it.'

'I'll wait a while so Mam and Dad are asleep,' Jennie said, stifling a sob. 'The fewer people who know the better.'

'I'm so cold.'

'Here, come and *cwtch* up to me.' She opened her coat and they sat there, on the cold cement floor, in the sour-smelling building for an hour, before rising stiffly and walking towards home.

Marie lay unable to sleep. She was angry

39

with everyone at that moment, but mostly with her sister. Once in months she had asked her to stay with Vi and she had let her down. Something had to change. For a start she would tell Jennie exactly what she thought of her and the idle way she lived. She knew her resentment towards Jennie wouldn't last, she loved her and that would never change, but having a target for her anger soothed her, and, once she had imagined all she would say, sleep gradually overcame her.

The knock on the front door woke her almost immediately. Who could it be? She lit a torch and shone it on the alarm clock. One o'clock in the morning. Something terrible must have happened. Mam? she wondered. Or Dad? She slid out of bed and, reaching the landing and closing the bedroom door, she switched on the torch and went softly down the stairs.

'Who is it?' she hissed, her hand on the latch.

'Oh, Marie, open the door, it's me, Jennie.'

Alarmed, Marie opened the door. 'What's happened? Is it Mam?'

'Oh, they're fine. Let me in can't you? I'm in trouble.'

'And I'm supposed to be sympathetic? When did you care about me and my troubles?' Woken from sleep and following a hour of imaginary argument with her selfish sister, Marie was in no mood to be concerned about Jennie's concerns.

'Put the light on,' Jennie whispered, her voice strangely muffled.

'We'd better go into the kitchen.' Feeling her way in the darkness, Marie reached for matches and lit the gas light in the small cluttered kitchen where the table was neatly laid for breakfast. 'What is it? Tell me quick, I have to be up in about five hours,' she snapped. Then she turned to look at her sister, who was slowly removing a scarf from her face, and she cried out in horror.

'Jennie! What happened to you?' Jennie's face was already swelling from the man's fists, and dried blood that had trickled from her nose and distended lips made her face into a grotesque mask.

Confused, shocked, Marie turned and lit the gas under a kettle then turned back to her sister. 'We'll get that face washed first, then a cup of tea, I think, while you tell me exactly what happened. I want the truth, mind.'

'Flirted and ran off once too often, didn't we? Me and Lucy met these airmen, see, and when we thought they were expecting more than a goodnight kiss, we got them to pay for supper and a few drinks then ran off. They caught up with us and...' She began to cry. 'They said we looked like a couple of tarts, and it was obvious how we earned

41

our living.'

With difficulty, Marie declined to retort that that was what many people believed, and hugged her instead. 'What will you tell Mam and Dad?'

'I don't know. I thought of saying I fell. Lots of people have tripped over kerbs and fallen down steps. But if they see Lucy in the same state they might not believe me.'

'They'll believe you.' Marie tried to avoid sounding cynical, but failed.

'What d'you mean? You make it sound as though I lie all the time and I don't! So of course they'd believe me! I'm honest about myself and what I am! And I never pretend to be Miss Holyness like you do. Miss Perfect, with a wayward husband, two idle and useless sons and a daughter who's scared of her own shadow. I'm not ashamed of what I am!'

More tears, and, as they subsided, Marie asked, 'Aren't you, Jennie?'

They stared at each other until Marie stood to turn off the gas under the furiously boiling kettle. She made tea, then prepared a bowl of water to wash Jennie's ravaged face. She pulled some cotton wool off the roll but Jennie snatched it from her and threw it to the floor. 'I don't need your help. I can manage, thanks!'

Ignoring her, Marie pulled off another wad and this time Jennie allowed her to wash away the blood.

As though seeing the scene in her head, Marie said slowly, 'You and Lucy saw a fight starting. You didn't want to be involved so you tried to get out through the back door but had to push your way through an angry mob of drunks. Thinking you were part of the argument they attacked you. Right?'

Tearfully, Jennie nodded. 'You'll have to go and see Lucy, mind, to make sure she says the same.'

'I'll go on the way to work,' Marie promised.

'I'm sorry I came here and woke you,' Jennie said, as she took the tea her sister offered.

'Where else would you go? I'm your big sister and I love you.'

'It's got to stop. I can't continue carrying on like a—'

'Eighteen-year-old prostitute?'

'But I'm not! You know I'm not! We never did more than flirt and make promises. Promises we never intended to keep. I couldn't risk having a baby, could I? Mam and Dad put up with a lot from me but I'd be on my own if that happened. No, I'm taking this as a warning of what could happen if I don't change my ways. They could have...' Her voice dropped to a whisper. 'God 'elp, Marie, we could have been raped.' She tried to sip her tea, twisting her lips to

43

avoid the damaged area. A tear slid down her cheek spreading mascara in its wake.

'People think the worst of you because you're behaving as though you're ten years younger. Eighteen-year-olds have fun teasing men and they get away with it because it's part of growing up, but you're old enough to make people think the worst.'

'My life's a mess.'

'You're able to start again. My life is in a mess too, but I don't know how to change it for the better.'

'It's different for you, you're married. As you say, I can start again, alter things, but you can't. You're stuck with it.' Sympathy was intended but the words came out wrong. She touched Marie's hand affectionately.

The bald truth was a shock, but Marie knew Jennie was right. 'I know. I've thought about it, but there's nothing I can do unless I leave Ivor and the twins, and I can't do that. Even if I did find the courage to move out, where would I go with Vi? Just nine she is. It's certain Mam and Dad won't help. Everything was wonderful until last June. Three months and everything's changed. I'm so tired of fighting to keep a roof over our heads, all alone, no one to support me. But what can I do except continue in the same miserable way?'

She glanced at her sister, who was staring at herself in a handbag mirror and applying powder to the shining bruises. She wasn't interested. She wasn't even listening. Sadly she realized that the one remark about her situation, stating the impossibility of her changing anything, had begun and ended the discussion on Marie's problems. For Jennie there was only herself. She couldn't help it, that was the way she was. Her face was hardly recognizable, lumps enlarging and bruises already showing colour. She reached over and put an arm on her sister's shoulder to comfort her.

A knock on the back door startled them both out of their reveries. Jennie leaped from the table and shrank back behind the half-open door leading to the hall. 'It's them! They followed me. Oh, Marie, don't let them in.'

Marie went to the door, but before she could ask who was there their father's distressed voiced called, 'Let me in. For heaven's sake open the door, Marie. It's your mam, she's fallen and hurt herself.'

Jennie didn't reveal herself at once. Her thoughts were still on her own injuries and the excuses she would give. She had decided to slip out through the front door and run home and into bed. She could pretend to be asleep and leave explanations till morning. But her father's words changed her mind.

'You've got to come,' their father almost shouted. 'She went outside looking for

Jennie, who's very late home, and she fell down the steps. The doctor's been and she's broken her arm. Worried sick about Jennie she was. Gone midnight it was and no sign of her. Where can she be?'

'I'm here, Dad.' Covering the worst damage to her face with her scarf she stepped out from behind the door.

He didn't notice her injuries at first. 'Thank God you're all right. We were so worried.' Then she opened the scarf a little and he gasped. 'What the – how the – Jennie, love, what happened?'

'Quite a night for accidents, eh, our Dad?' In a childish tone, interspersed with sobs, she went on. 'Lucy and I were leaving the dance and got involved in a fight. Marie has bathed the damage and I'll be all right. Don't worry about me. I'll—'

'Forget *your* bruises, Jennie! What about Mam?' Marie's sharp tone startled Jennie into silence.

While Marie wrote a note for Ivor, and they discussed what had happened, Jennie sat and thought about the future. If she wasn't careful she'd be stuck with looking after her parents until she was too old to have a life. A broken arm meant that Mam would need a lot of help. What a night this had been. But it had taught her something. She would have to get married and leave home before it was too late. Leave the caring

46

to Marie, it was what she was good at. Today was the turning point. She was happily unaware that the same decision was filling Marie's mind.

Two

With no one to open the hairdressing shop
apart from themselves, Jennie and Lucy
braved the comments about their ravaged
faces, prepared their lies and opened as
usual. Mr James was horrified when he saw
the full extent of bruises already showing a
variety of colours. They told their prepared
story tearfully, Jennie adding embellishments to the more prosaic descriptions from
Lucy, thereby receiving more sympathy.

'Don't ask us to go to the police, Mr James,
we've had all that from our parents and we
aren't going to make ourselves look fools. We
were going out through the back door,
through the kitchens, see, to get to the bus
stop first, and it isn't allowed. So it's our own
fault really.'

'You shouldn't be here, you need rest after
such a shock. I'll go round and tell the
clients that you're unable to open,' he said,
guiding them to chairs. 'Sit there for a while
before you go home and I'll get you a cup of
tea.'

Bravely, Jennie choking back tears, they

insisted on carrying on as usual. The last thing Jennie wanted was to be at home. Looking after her mother could so easily become a habit. Dad was quite capable, albeit untrained and undomesticated, but he'd have to learn to cope.

At nine o'clock their first client arrived and they had disguised their damaged faces with make-up and were ready to begin. The sympathy and extra tips made it well worthwhile.

They closed at a quarter to one and when Jennie reached home, hoping to find at least a snack waiting for her, she was pleased to see her sister there, mashing potatoes to accompany sausages and tomatoes.

'Thank goodness, our Marie, I'm starved.'

'Best you enjoy it because tomorrow it's your turn.'

Jennie ignored that fearful reminder. While they ate she talked about her morning, making them laugh at some of the comments she and Lucy had received. She stood up and hugged her father. 'You'll cope, won't you, our Dad?' You won't expect me to give up my job and let Mr James down, not while Miss Clarke is on holiday. Pity 'elp his customers if *he* did their hair, eh?'

'I'll make a couple of sandwiches for your tea,' Marie said. 'Then you're on your own. I'm working tomorrow all day and in the evening.'

'Don't worry about sandwiches for me.

49

Lucy and I will be going to the pictures straight from the shop. Save me some supper, though, I'll be starving when I come in.'

'As usual,' Belle said fondly.

Marie was irritated by her sister's selfish attitude. 'Jennie! You'll have to come straight home tonight. Mam can't manage without help.'

Jennie spread her arms to encompass the tidy room. 'What's there to do?' She winked at her father. 'I don't think Mam and Dad want me moping about with a sympathetic face, do you? Make the place untidy, wouldn't I, our Dad?' She put on a freshly ironed cardigan, grabbed her handbag, patted her hair and, with a chirpy wave, left the room.

'We'll manage between us, love,' her father said as he walked with her to the door, but he looked full of doubts. 'Getting older we are, Belle and me. And so lucky to have you still at home.'

The words stayed with her all the way back to the shop, terrifying her with their implications.

Marie and Jennie both finished work at five thirty and, a few days later, when Marie left Ladies Fashions, her sister and Lucy were waiting outside.

'How long before Mam's better?' Jennie

asked at once. 'It's been a while and she's still not able to do much around the house.'

'I don't know. Weeks rather than days. She won't be able to lift anything for a while, even after the plaster's removed. Why?'

'It's what Dad said the other day about them getting older, things like this might happen more often.'

'What, breaking her arm? Don't be daft!'

'Falls do happen, and there are other things, illnesses. I can't leave my job to look after them, whatever they think. You don't know what it's like being the youngest. So much is expected of you.'

'I hope you don't think I can do more. You know what Ivor's like these days. I need my wages to keep us fed. I'm responsible for five of us, remember, not just myself.'

'I hope you don't think I should give up my job? Hairdressing's valuable work. Morale and all that. Besides, you've got a husband.'

'Who isn't supporting us!' In her exasperation Marie was shouting. Lucy was standing uneasily near by.

'Perhaps if you weren't so damned clever and efficient, and left more to Ivor, he'd be more inclined to take responsibility!' Marie was startled by the reprimand and she stared at her sister's face, a pretty face that so rarely showed such anger. 'A man doesn't like to be bettered by a woman. I might not be married but I do know that!' Jennie went on. 'And if it was me, I'd—'

'Stop! Now, this minute! You know nothing. How long d'you think we'd last if I left everything to Ivor? He tells lies and he gambles money his family needs. Do you have any idea what that means?'

'If you trusted him to look after you, and not go gallivanting off working for strangers, showing him up, making him feel a failure, he might stop.'

'You're talking nonsense. As usual!' They were both raising their voices. 'I didn't do extra work to keep the bills paid until he let us down.'

'Always right, aren't you, Marie? It's never you in the wrong.'

'Are you all right, Jennie?' a voice called, and Mr James appeared. 'Not feeling worse, are you?' He was wearing a dark suit and a trilby, his black shoes shone impeccably. He looked older than his forty-eight years, partly because of his pale skin and heavy eyes, and partly because of his formal dress and manner. 'Once Miss Clarke gets back you and Lucy can have a few days off, one at a time of course, she can't spare you both at once.'

'Thank you, Mr James. It's just our Mam, broken her arm she has and we have to share responsibility for looking after her,'

'I'll leave the appointments to you, so you can arrange them to do what you have to at home.' He lifted his hat politely and walked away.

'Thank you, Mr James,' Jennie said, with a slight bend of the knee.

'Thank you, Mr James,' Lucy echoed, the chant similar to the responses of children at school.

'Stuffed shirt,' Jennie whispered to Marie. The sisters stifled laughter and their quarrel, like so many others, ended as quickly as it had begun.

Marie collected Violet from her parents, went home to change her clothes and put out food for Royston and Roger and Ivor, fed her ever patient daughter, then went straight out to prepare a floor for staining. Sanding was hard work and, once the job was finished, nothing showed for all the effort. Vi sat with the owner of the house and read 'Sunny Stories', the Enid Blyton magazine for children, reading out pieces occasionally to her mother. Marie thought about her sister's words and wondered. If she hadn't asked Geoff Tanner to find her some extra work, what would have happened? If she'd allowed them to reach the point where they couldn't pay the bills, would Ivor had been less willing to gamble away his wages? Somehow she doubted it. They would have been in such debt by now that there would have been no way out. There wasn't now, if she stopped accepting the work Geoff

Tanner found for her, unless Ivor miraculously returned to being the devoted family man he had been for almost nine years. Since his sudden transformation from loving husband to stranger, she no longer believed in miracles. What had gone wrong? Why hadn't he been able to talk to her?

Even after these difficult weeks had turned to months without an end to their problems in sight, Marie occasionally had dreamlike moments when she forgot them.

One morning she woke early. The late-August sun creeping into the bedroom spread around the room and touched her face. She was glad she had opened the curtains before getting into bed. At this time of the year it was a joy to be woken by the sun. She stretched out a hand, but Ivor wasn't beside her. Sleepily she roused herself, stretching, enjoying the few moments of peace before starting her hectic day. He was probably downstairs, drinking tea, smoking and listening to the wireless. Idly she imagined him coming up the stairs with a cup for her.

Then the shock of memory hit her. That was a fanciful dream. Ivor wasn't that sort of husband. Not any more. He had forgotten all the loving and caring he had lavished on her. Ivor was a stranger, sharing their house but no longer the focus of their life, their home. No, he would walk up the stairs soon, but only to remind her that he was hungry and demand his breakfast.

She pulled on a dressing gown and, shivering in the early morning air, went downstairs. To her surprise Ivor wasn't there and the kitchen was as she had left it the night before. Where on earth could he be? He wasn't the type to go for a walk, however wonderful the morning. She prepared a tray for tea, her mind sleepily going over explanations for his absence. While the kettle boiled she opened the back door and stood for a moment or two listening to the calming sound of birdsong. They were quieter than in the spring, hiding their shabbiness as they began their moult, and it seemed to her they too were subdued by the unhappiness that had taken over her life.

As she poured milk into a jug and waited for the water to reach its irritable boiling point, she heard voices. Going outside again, she saw Royston and Roger coming across the field towards the house. She waved then took two more cups from the dresser. They had been fishing again, walking across the fields to the beach, where they would have fished the incoming tide.

'Morning, Mam,' Royston called as he threw his rod and bag on the floor.

'It isn't fair,' Roger complained, throwing his equipment to join that of his brother. 'He gets all the luck.'

Royston laughed and began teasing. 'Casting into a tree won't catch many fish. Fancy, our Mam, he's so hopeless he lost yards of line, bait and a good hook, all tangled in the hedge.' Too late, his brother pushed him to shut him up. 'What am I talking about, trees? I mean an old boat on the beach.

Hands on hips, Marie glared at them. 'Poaching you've been!'

Both boys took the tea she had poured and hid their faces in the breakfast-sized cups.

'Don't think I'm paying your fines if you're caught. You'll have to pay out of your wages. And,' she asked as an afterthought, 'where's your father?'

'He wasn't with us,' Royston said. 'We went out at five o'clock. Had to catch the tide, see.'

'Did you catch anything, except the tide? Although what tide there is in Farmer Jones's river I'd like to know!'

'Only a couple of trout too small to bring home,' Roger admitted.

'Sorry, Mam,' his brother added.

'Did anyone see you?'

'There was someone down there, near the old barn. Some ol' tramp sleeping rough probably. I don't think he saw us. In fact he seemed anxious for us not to see him. Creeping about, hiding behind the hedge he was.'

'If you land up in court I won't pay your

56

fine. You'll have to do that.'

'We can't, we lost our job on Friday.'

'Again?' She glared at them. 'My first day off for weeks and this is how it starts. Where's your father?'

'Here I am, love,' a voice called and Ivor stepped out of the hall doorway and reached for the teapot. 'Damn me it's cold, make another pot will you, Marie. Gasping I am.'

'Where have you been?'

'Nowhere! What you talking about, woman? Only now this minute I've come down, to a smell of fishy clothes and cold tea.'

'You weren't in bed,' she accused. 'Where have you been?'

'In the lavatory.'

'You weren't. I went in there.'

'Looking in on our Vi then. Stop making a mystery when there isn't one, for heaven's sake!'

'Catch anything?' he asked the boys as Marie turned to reboil the kettle.

'Nothing. The river's too flat. Rain we want to liven it up a bit. We saw a water vole, though. Pretty little thing. I bet he had better luck than us.'

They began to discuss the wildlife to be seen around the river until Marie interrupted.

'Tell your father about losing your jobs again. And perhaps you'll explain what happened.'

'Lost your jobs again, have you?' Ivor asked almost conversationally. 'What happened this time?'

'Mam got us separate jobs and we hated it.'

'So it wasn't fighting?'

'We mitched off to go fishing, didn't we?'

Marie saw the glimmer of a smile on Ivor's face and said, 'I keep telling you, Ivor, they'll have to find jobs far apart from each other. I understand that being twins and close they want to work alongside, but they can't spend every moment together and we have to face the truth, that individually they stand a better chance of keeping a job. Trouble they are, one leading the other into scrapes. I'll go to the employment exchange with them and make sure they are separated. One each end of the town, if necessary, if that's the only way they'll keep a job.' She glanced around and saw the wink he gave the boys. Irritated she banged the teapot on the table and asked, 'Ivor. When are you going to take this seriously? Employers are crying out for workers, 'specially in the building trades, and these two idle their way through the weeks and there's us keeping them. Fourteen they are, not four!' She poured tea and pushed it towards Ivor.

'Why are you wearing your best suit? Where have you been? You don't wear that first thing in the morning.'

'It's for work. I'm going to see a supplier. I've just been up to change.'

'But I didn't see you upstairs, and you came in from the garden.'

'Oh, don't keep on, Marie. Give it a rest.'

The door to the hall pushed slowly open and Violet stood there. 'Stop shouting,' she said, tearfully. 'Always shouting you are.'

'Sorry, Vi, love. It's your lazy brothers that's the trouble. Out of work again and that's the fourth job they've been given. Mitching from school day after day and now they've left and can't keep a job.'

Ivor held out his arms and Violet climbed on to his lap. He offered a sip of his tea, tipping some into a saucer to cool for her.

'And I still want to know where *you* were,' Marie demanded of her husband.

'All right, I was very late. A card game at Trevor Williams's if you must know.'

'If I must know? Don't you think I'm entitled to know?'

'We had a few beers and I fell asleep.'

'How much did you lose this time?'

'Now come on, why presume I lost? Here, buy yourself something.' He fished in his pocket and gave her a ten shilling note.

They were interrupted by the back door opening and Marie's sister walking in.

'Jennie? What's up?' Jennie's face looked pale, the bruises still visible, and the lack of make-up making them more alarming. Her blond hair was wildly untidy, as though she had just risen from bed. Her eyes were wide with shock. 'I just heard, there was a road accident last night and Emily Clarke was killed.'

'Emily Clarke?' Marie queried.

'Our Miss Clarke, manageress of the shop. There's been talk that she and Bill, Mr James's son, were getting engaged at Christmas and now she's gone! Dead on the road she was, tucked up in her coat all tidy, and pushed under a hedge. The car didn't stop. Someone called an ambulance but didn't give a name and didn't wait for the help to arrive.'

'Oh, the poor woman. Poor Bill. And Mr James will be devastated,' Marie exclaimed.

'And what about me?' Jennie wailed. 'Mr James will probably close the shop and I'll have no job and there's only the enamel factory and I can't stand the thought of working in a place like that. An artiste I am, not a factory hand!'

Marie flinched at the selfishness of her sister. She loved her, but there were times when she wanted to slap her.

'You'll have to go to work as normal until you find out what is going to happen to the shop,' she said, biting off the retort that sprang into her mind. Her sister had always been self-centred, she shouldn't have been surprised that Jennie's first thought was how the poor woman's death would affect her. 'And don't talk nonsense. Work in a factory? When have you ever done something you didn't want to do? If you have to find another job it will be as a hairdresser. You do dramatize everything. Think of poor Bill.'

'What d'you mean, poor Bill? He'll get over it, this will be his third "real thing", and once the girls start filling their bottom drawer, planning a wedding, they quietly fade away.'

Ivor began cutting bread awkwardly, the slices thick at one end and tapering off to nothing at the other. Marie took it from him. She saw him give Jennie a sympathetic glance and pat her shoulder comfortingly, putting Marie in the role of unreasonable sister.

She lit the grill on the gas cooker and asked Jennie to stay. They ate toast as they talked, using a loaf and a half, a pot of home-made blackberry jam and most of the margarine ration with it, while Jennie complained about the lack of butter.

'This is awful, our Marie, eating margarine instead of decent butter,' she sighed, taking another slice and spreading it liberally with margarine and jam. 'The war's been over almost a year and there's us still being told we can't have any more than two ounces of butter.' All concerns for the death of Miss Clarke were forgotten.

When Jennie had gone, Marie went up to make the beds and noticed for the first time that Ivor's side of the bed was unruffled, the pillow smooth and obviously unused. He hadn't been late; he hadn't come home at all.

It wasn't the first time he had stayed out late recently playing cards. Gambling was his life now, and when he played, or followed the horses or dogs, nothing else mattered. Thank goodness it had been a Saturday night. At least she'd got some money from him. If he went out on a Friday before she got back from work, she risked having to cope without a penny for housekeeping.

She frowned deeply as she wondered again what could have happened to change him so. Was there a debt he had to repay? Or had he borrowed money and was trying to pay it back? When Airborne had won the Derby and they'd spent that wonderful day on Barry Island's golden sands, that was the last time they had been truly happy. At the time there had been no shadow over their lives, no hint of what was to come.

Later that day, as she began preparing the dirty washing ready for the following morning, putting it into piles, some for washing in the big galvanized bath Ivor carried into the kitchen and another for boiling, she found his jacket. The front was stained and to her untrained eye it looked at first like oil. Then, finding a similar stain on his shirt, she realized it was blood. She looked again at the jacket and found several holes, torn as though it had caught on something and had been dragged free, tree branches perhaps.

That kind of damage didn't happen during a card school. She called Ivor, wanting an explanation of what really happened the previous night, but he didn't reply. Her mind filled with what she would say to him when she found him, she went to pick some vegetables for supper. If she didn't have a decorating job to do they ate late on Sundays to make the day easier.

Ivor was in the garden, reading the paper in the last of the sun.

'There's blood on your clothes,' she said in a hoarse whisper so the children couldn't hear. 'What happened last night? You have to tell me. I can deal with anything as long as you're truthful. Heaven knows I've had plenty of experience in dealing with things, living in this family recently!'

'My shirt got messed up when I was chopping firewood, that's all. A splinter sprang up and cut my arm and I wiped the blood on my shirt. Sorry, love, but I couldn't find anything else. Not a bad cut, though, don't worry, it soon stopped bleeding.' He looked to her in the hope of seeing a sympathetic expression.

'What about your jacket? There's quite a

lot of blood on that, too.'

'No, that's grease, sure to be. I drive the firm's van sometimes, remember. Give it to me and I'll clean it with some white spirit.'

'But you don't wear those clothes for the office.'

'I did yesterday. I knew I'd be getting a bit messed up and didn't want to spoil my good suit.'

'And the scratches and tears? Was that chopping wood too?'

'Walked home through the fields, didn't I?' His explanations were slick. Not so long ago she would have believed him, wouldn't have given the situation a second thought, now the glib replies filled her with dread. She sat on the ashbin and felt her whole body droop in despair.

'Tell me what's wrong, Ivor, please. Once we were a normal family, now we've no money, the boys are encouraged to break the law, losing their jobs is a joke. Why won't you tell me why everything has changed? I'll listen, Ivor. If you tell me what's wrong I'll listen and do all I can to help, whatever it is.'

'There's nothing wrong, you're imagining things. I just need a bit of fun now and then, that's all, a bit of male company.'

'Fun? Stealing from your family?'

'It's my money too, I can decide how I want to spend it.'

It was such a stupid remark she didn't try

to answer it. She dug a root of potatoes for their supper, and when she went to find the jacket, it was gone. Something stopped her asking Ivor its whereabouts, she had again that inexplicable feeling of unease. Without understanding why, she washed her hands repeatedly as though washing away the memory of the stains that weren't grease, and denying the violence shown by the torn fabric.

All the time in the back of her mind was the news about the accident that had killed Emily Clarke, the hairdresser. Apparently no one saw the accident and whoever was responsible had dragged the poor woman into the hedge and hidden her, presumably to allow himself time to get away and build an alibi. Could Ivor have been involved? Common sense told her no, that if he had hit someone he'd have sought help, called the police, not dragged a body away from the road and hidden it. Rumours hinted that the woman had been alive when she had been hauled off the road and placed under the hedge; that a call for an ambulance might have saved her. To have become an obsessive gambler, someone who could steal from his own family, didn't mean Ivor was also capable of such a cold-blooded act.

Bill and his father were talking about the accident to a couple of policemen, one of

65

whom was taking notes. When they were told the woman might have lived had she not been moved, Bill gave out a wail of distress. The policeman looked at him. 'Did you move her, sir?'

'I wasn't there. I knew nothing until you knocked on my door this morning. She was just back from Tenby and I hadn't seen her since she got back. I was going to marry her. She was precious to me. If I had been there I'd never have moved her, I know it's the wrong thing to do.' He combed his fingers through his hair, a gesture of despair. 'I can't imagine how you'd think I'd have risked moving her. I loved her.'

'I'm not accusing you of anything, we just need to know all the facts. Perhaps you thought she would be safer off the road while you ran to the phone box for help. Another car might have come around that rather nasty bend and—' He allowed the thought to hover. Bill stared into space as though seeing her lying there, utterly still, then being carried to the grass verge and, later, as Jennie had described, being tucked under the hedge.

'I didn't move her, I didn't know she'd been hurt until you came and told me.'

'Another of your fiancées lost her life in an accident, didn't she, Mr James?'

'I was in London at the time, on a training week, and I could account for my whereabouts then as now.'

'An amazing coincidence, though. And I'm a man who doesn't like coincidences, Mr James.'

They took away most of his clothes and left him sitting as still as a statue, his father trying to coax him to drink some brandy. He regretted lying to the police but it was too late to change his story now.

He had been waiting for her to arrive and, impatient, he had walked a part of the way to meet her. He had a ring in his pocket in a jeweller's velvet-lined box, and wanted to suggest they didn't wait until Christmas before announcing their engagement.

At first, he had been aware of a slowly approaching vehicle, then, as the small figure appeared around a bend in the lane, the engine revved, the brakes squealed, making him jump out of its path, then the vehicle had raced past him, swerved and hit her. Up in the air she had flown, before landing, with a sickening thump he kept reliving, in the centre of the lane.

Ivor had been coming home from a card game. He heard the car and the squeal of brakes, but hedges hid the scene from view. Fearing an accident he ran to where Bill was bending over the still figure in the middle of the lane. He could see from the unnatural angle of her neck that she was dead.

'Oh no,' Bill had chanted repeatedly. 'It

can't be happening again.' He called Emily's name, whispering to her, telling her it would be all right, but he knew there was no hope of her coming back to him.

Ivor placed fingers on the pulse point but shook his head, she was quite dead. 'We can't leave her here, Bill,' he said. 'Another car might come along, and...' Ivor's sentence remained incomplete as the horror made Bill wail in distress. They lifted her as gently as they could on to the kerb.

'I'll go to the corner, there's a phone box there. I'll dial 999. We need an ambulance and the police,' Ivor told him.

'Who'll believe I'm innocent this time?' Bill whispered. 'It's happened again. In exactly the same way. First Gloria and now Emily. They won't believe me.'

'What are you talking about?' Ivor asked, thinking the man was in shock. 'Sit there beside her while I call for help.'

'I was engaged before, to Gloria, and she was killed by a hit and run driver too. Just like now. How will I convince them I'm innocent a second time?' he wailed softly. Then he took off down the road, leaving Ivor staring after him in disbelief.

Finding himself alone with the dead woman, Ivor panicked. He pushed her further into the hedge and neatened her clothing in a respectful gesture before running away in the opposite direction from the one

Bill had taken. He paused only to make the emergency call.

As he left the lane and hurried across fields, pushing through hedges, he knew he was being foolish, leaving the scene of an accident, knowing the woman was dead and he had witnessed or at least heard it, and had seen Bill there immediately afterwards. Out of breath, he slowed down, bent forward with hands on his knees and asked himself why he was running away. Panic was contagious and Bill's fear had trapped him, caught him in that unthinking instinct for survival that was stronger than the needs of the poor woman he'd left, lifeless, under the hedge.

Too late now to change his mind, the police would be there and he was best out of it. If he told them he'd seen Bill and Bill denied it he'd be accused of covering up the truth, and if he said he wasn't there and Bill told them different the result would be the same.

He was shaking with the shock of it, unable to consider going home, and some time later – he had no idea how long – he went to Bill's house and, seeing a light burning, knocked on the window. They didn't stay together long, just enough time to agree to say nothing at all.

Bill felt he was living through a nightmare. Now, with his father putting the brandy glass

69

to his lips, it all seemed like a dream, something he'd half imagined, made up of bits of films he'd seen, not really true. In moments of sanity he knew that by moving her, running away, not calling at once for an ambulance, he had created trouble for himself and Ivor that might be serious. All this was racing through his mind and it was several minutes before he spoke to his anxious father.

'Dad, why did she die? What happens to make becoming engaged to marry me such a risk? Two engagements and both ended in death. You see, I don't believe in coincidences either.'

Marie usually visited her parents at least once a day. Sometimes she would call on the way to or from work and occasionally, when there wasn't shopping to do, she would use her lunch hour. Today being Sunday, during late afternoon she left the small roasting joint in the oven. She put the water for the vegetables on low and ran to 1, Rock Terrace with Violet.

In her parents' house the table was laid for tea, with a few thin slices of bread and butter, the ration being a Sunday treat, and dishes of jams, a fruit cake and some cheeses. Six years of war hadn't altered her mother's insistence on a properly set table. There were hand-crocheted doilies under the cakes and sandwiches, a napkin beside

70

each plate, all a bit worn but neatly ironed. A second tablecloth was across a corner where Belle usually sat, with a tray set with tea cups and sugar and milk, awaiting only the filled teapot.

'Will you and Violet stay?' her mother asked. 'I wish you would. I'm that worried about our Jennie. Up in her bedroom she is, crying.'

'Because of the accident?' Marie asked, surprised. 'I didn't think she was that fond of Emily Clarke. She complained about her most of the time.'

'Different now she's dead.'

'You mean she suddenly realizes she liked her after all?'

Her sarcasm caused her mother to frown. 'Don't be so unkind, Marie. Jennie's sensitive, you know that.'

Stifling a sigh, Marie asked, 'What can I do?'

'Talk to her, cheer her up. Get her to eat something. She hasn't eaten a thing all day.' Marie declined to tell her mother about the rounds of toast Jennie had enjoyed when she had come with the news. Instead she said, 'I'll try, Mam.'

She went upstairs to see Jennie and as she entered she mimicked her sister's voice, saying, 'Oh, Mummy, I haven't eaten a thing all day, I'm so distressed about poor Miss Clarke.'

71

Jennie tried to look offended but the humour was too strong and the girls hugged each other and gave in to it.

Bill James sat staring at the photograph of Emily. How could she be dead? She was only thirty, the same as himself. Yesterday she was on her way back from holiday filled with stories about her visit to Tenby. A car driven by a mad man and in moments she was gone.

He had visited her while she was in Tenby. Working shifts on the railway it was easy to go there for half a day, using his father's car, and spend time with her. They had talked about their wedding and planned their future.

Why she had died? The road was a quiet one and there had been nothing to cause the driver to run into her. He tried to convince himself it had been an accident, but remembered all too well the way the sound of the engine had increased, the vehicle speeding up, swerving towards her. Emily's death had been deliberate.

The frightening thought, and one that was keeping him awake, was the similarity to the death of his previous love. Could there be a connection? Was there someone who hated him enough to ruin his life? He shook the fearsome thought away. What nonsense even to consider that for a moment. But he decided to talk to the police and see whether anything had been learned about the car or its driver.

He put down the photograph and wandered through the connecting door to the hairdressing shop. Nothing more than the front room of the house, but his mother and Emily had built up a successful business there. He smiled, remembering how she had tried to persuade customers to call it a salon, but it had never caught on. The hairdressing shop it had always been. What would happen to it now? His father could hardly sell the business and have a stranger running it, using a part of his home. He touched the pink overall hanging behind the door, the towels neatly stacked, all clean and ready for Monday. His mind drifted back to Emily. Trying to accept that she was gone was exhausting him. Trying to think of something else was impossible.

At one o'clock his father, Ernie, set the table for dinner, a scrappy meal which neither of them wanted. Cheese on toast was not the usual Sunday fare but Ernie's housekeeper didn't come on Sundays and they usually ate at an hotel. Today they were too stunned to think about it.

A knock at the back door startled them as they were about to eat, and Ernie stood to answer it. Barbara Lewis from next door was there, carrying a tray on which two dinners were steaming and sending out appetizing smells.

'Thought you'd like a bit of a hand, just for today. Custard and apples for afters. I'll send our Johnny round with it in a little while, right?' Hardly giving them time to thank her she was gone. Appetites suddenly returned, they ate with gusto.

It was late afternoon when the front door-bell rang, the tenth time that awful day. Bill went to the door and invited their visitors in.

'It's Lucy and Jennie from the shop,' he called.

'So sorry we are, Mr James,' Lucy said. 'We called to tell you that, and to ask should we open the shop as usual once – once everything's, you know, all over.'

Jennie said nothing. She smiled at Bill and wondered whether he could possibly become more than the son of her employer. She wasn't really interested, she liked younger men with a stronger sense of fun, but couldn't resist a bit of flirting, even at a time like this. After all, she was desperately looking for an escape from home. An excuse to get away from Mam, Dad and tedious domesticity. From the way Bill and Ernie lived, with a housekeeper and a cleaning lady, she might consider it one day. Tearing herself away to concentrate on Mr James, she listened to Lucy's suggestion that they run the shop after the funeral, to give him time to make a decision.

'Pity to let it all go, Mr James,' Lucy was saying, 'Nice little business it is. And valued by the local ladies. Miss it they would. We could manage, couldn't we, Jennie?'

Jennie put on a brave smile and said, 'It wouldn't be the same, mind. Not without Miss Clarke, but we'd do our very best.'

As they left, it was Bill who showed them out and Jennie turned at the gate for a final wave, then winked at her friend. 'Pity Bill's so old, don't you think, Lucy?'

'Thirty he is, not much older than us!'

'Hush!'

'And don't be so unfeeling, Jennie. Grieving he is. Terrible losing a fiancée like that.'

'She was the third hairdresser he'd been courting, did you know that? There was a small, shy girl, can't remember her name, but she vanished and no one's heard of her since, then Gloria and then Emily, two who died on the road. Strange, eh?' She gave a shiver of apprehension. 'Ooer, thinking about it like that, perhaps I don't want to be a fourth!'

'Don't frighten me, he asked me out once, remember.'

'I like men younger than Bill. And so do you, which is why you refused his invitation.'

'Thank goodness I did or I might have ended up under a car!'

'Odd though. I'd forgotten about the one

before Gloria. What was her name? I wonder what happened to her.'

'You can't open until after the funeral, Dad,' Bill said, later that evening. Ernie nodded.

'I know that and customers will understand. Will you write a sign for the front window to tell people the shop is closed for a week? Then go and tell Jennie and Lucy to come in a week from Tuesday. We've always closed on Mondays for half day, hardly worth reopening for a few hours. They can let people know. And I'll pay their wages as usual.'

'If I hurry I'll catch them up.' Bill grabbed a coat and ran into the street.

Bill James was a big man like his father, under six feet tall but powerfully built so people thought he was taller than he actually was. His features were large, a nose spread and slightly flattened as though by a blow, rounded cheeks and full lips that in repose made him appear bad-tempered. It was the calm expression in the eyes that took away the impression of an aggressive man.

He stopped when he saw Jennie and Lucy and called to them. He waited until Jennie walked back and instead of giving her his father's message, invited her to meet him to discuss what would happen to the shop. 'Dad doesn't know much about the business and I need you to clarify a few things. He left

76

everything to...' his voice faded away as he tried to say her name.

'A date?' Lucy asked with a grin when Jennie explained. 'With an old man of thirty?'

'It might be, if I decide to make it one.'

'You've got no heart, Jennie Jones.'

'Neither has Bill if the looks he's giving me are anything to judge by!'

Marie was at their parents' house when Jennie returned home.

'How is poor Bill? Marie asked.

'More boring than usual,' Jennie hissed so her mother wouldn't hear.

'What's happening about the shop?'

'I'm not out of a job. Yet! We offered to run it for him while he makes up his mind. After the funeral of course. Oh, why aren't we rich?' she sighed. 'Lucy and I could buy the business if we could afford premises. I know we'd be able to buy the equipment cheap, but I haven't a bean and neither has Lucy.'

'I'd start looking around for another job if I were you, love. Or you'll end up in the dreaded enamel works,' her father teased.

'Not on your nelly! Work in that noisy place? I'd get married first!'

'We're having tea as soon as the kettle boils. Will you stay?' Belle Jones asked Marie.

'Better not, Mam. I have to feed my lot soon.'

'Not for me either, our Mam,' Jennie said. 'I'm going out.'

'Where can you find to go on a Sunday evening?' her father asked.

'Not church, that's for sure,' Jennie retorted with a laugh. 'Hang on, Marie, and I'll walk with you.'

She went to her room and put on a new outfit she had bought. A skirt, the length of which made her mother frown, and a Hungarian-style blouse that was alarmingly transparent. The drawer string was loosened to reveal a great deal more than the designer intended, and with nylon stockings and high-heeled shoes she couldn't have made more of a contrast to her sister. Belle said nothing but she tutted a lot.

Jennie was silent for a while as they headed towards Marie's home. Marie was conscious of her glancing at her from time to time and was uncomfortably aware of her over-long coat and down-at-heel shoes. She could never dress like Jennie but she wished she were more presentable.

Then Jennie asked, 'Marie, don't you feel uncomfortable walking the streets dressed like that? And on a Sunday too? Everyone we pass has best clothes on, and there's you, hair hanging down like an unironed scarf, not even a bit of lipstick, a coat that's seen better days too long ago to remember what colour it was when it started out.'

'Who cares?' Marie said with a shrug.

'*You* should. You need to make your husband proud of you, everything doesn't stop once you get married, you know. Men can get tired of women who don't seem to care.'

Visions of Ivor creeping back into the house hoping no one would be aware of his overnight absence flooded through her mind. What was Jennie trying to tell her? Was Ivor seeing someone else? Had he been with a woman? Had the blood on his clothes been the result of a fight with the woman's husband? Her imagination went wild. The fact that he still had a ten shilling note to give her made her seriously doubt the 'card school' story. From the rumours that reached her he rarely gave up until he was broke. She stopped and turned to her sister. 'You know something, don't you?'

'Know what? That my sister is dressed worse than some tramps I've seen and should do something about it? I certainly know that!'

Continuing to stare at Jennie, with her glamorous golden hair and blatantly provocative dress, her carefully made-up face, her slim feet in fancy summer sandals, Marie felt drab. She forced herself to ask the question to which she dreaded to hear the answer. 'He isn't seeing someone else, is he?' Her stomach lurched as Jennie looked away before answering, unwilling to meet her gaze.

'Your Ivor? Not as far as I know. Although he did try it on with me once. I soon told him what to do with his—'

'Jennie! You're lying! Ivor wouldn't. Not with you!'

'Oh, all right, I was joking, trying to lighten your life with a laugh. You rarely smile these days and – I'm sorry, sis, but you do look a mess. Men like to be flattered. They like being proud of their women, wearing them on their arm like a trophy. And what about poor little Vi? She can't like seeing you like this. Children can tease and for those looking for an excuse you're a gift.'

'Don't talk rubbish. She's happy at school.'

'Even if she isn't being laughed at because of you, she's bound to compare you with other mothers. Clothes rationing isn't an excuse for giving up. Honestly, sis, you should look at yourself.'

'I know I'm a mess,' she retorted, fighting back tears. 'There's no need for anyone to tell me that! I've no money for clothes, even if I had coupons to spare. It's all I can do to manage to keep our heads above water. I work all day at the shop selling beautiful clothes, and when I get home I take off my best things and change into these. Clothes for working. I spend evenings and weekends decorating other people's houses, not going to dances and having fun. So what chance do I have of looking like you?'

'Sorry, Marie. I really am. I thought I was being helpful. I thought you hadn't realized how you've let yourself slip. Are things really that bad?'

'Worse than you know.'

They were approaching Steeple Street where Geoff Tanner's warehouse-cum-shop filled both angles of the corner. Marie had known Geoff all her life and had recently become a regular customer, buying paints and wallpapers and all the etceteras for her second job.

Geoff was washing his van as they passed.

'I'll be calling in the morning on the way to work to put an order in, Geoff,' Marie called. 'I'm papering a bedroom for Mrs Ricky Richards.'

'Good luck, then. You'll need it. Never pleased, that one, whatever you do for her.'

'Another happy social evening. I wonder should I wear my fur?' she whispered to her sister. She was self-conscious as she passed Geoff, Jennie's words reminding her harshly of the contrast between her dowdy self and her glamorous sister. Just this once she wished she had worn her best coat, the one she wore to work.

She would have been surprised to know Geoff Tanner's thoughts as they passed by. He saw Jennie as a flighty, over-dressed woman who was too old for the clothes she wore and the men she spent time with. Too much make-up gave her a harsh, almost brazen look, and many accused her of being worse than she actually was.

To his eyes, Marie was beautiful. Kind, caring, her expression was soft and gentle. She had a full, generous mouth that was always ready to smile – a smile that lit up her eyes. Yet, in repose, he could also see the sadness there. One lived her life for fun, the other had discarded all hope of fun when she had tied herself to a man who had become a gambler and cheat.

The police were searching for the vehicle that had hit Emily Clarke, and two constables went to the woodyard where Ivor worked and asked to examine the firm's fleet.

'Fleet?' Ivor laughed. 'One ancient van and two decrepit lorries.' He pointed across the muddy yard to where men were loading the lorry with lengths of two-by-two timber. He glanced at his watch. 'The second lorry will be back in about twenty minutes, fancy a cup of tea?'

The constables examined the van, taking photographs and measurements. Doing the same to the lorry, it was sent on its way. After they had drunk their tea the other lorry returned and was given the same treatment. Ivor explained that the lorries were used for heavy loads, and the van was a run-about,

taking small orders and sacks of sawdust to
the local butchers for them to use on their
floors.

'And you drive the van, Mr Masters?'

'Sometimes, when I need to see a customer. And I move it around the yard when the
lorries need a bit of space.' That information
was written down with the rest. After a
thorough search they went away, giving in-
structions that the van was not to be touched
until it had been properly examined. An
anxious Ivor checked his keys and wondered
whether the person responsible could possibly have been driving that scruffy old van.

He'd heard the engine and his blood
chilled as he remembered it revving up
before the squeal and the awful thud when
the woman had been hit, but apart from
guessing it hadn't been as heavy as a lorry he
had no idea what kind of car it had been. But
surely not the firm's van? It didn't look
reliable enough. And with the wire fence and
the gate it wasn't possible for someone to
have stolen it and returned it without someone seeing them. There would have been
better choices on any street.

As soon as Marie reached home after seeing
Jennie to the bus stop she searched again for
the bloodstained jacket, but it was gone. A
bonfire in the garden smouldered and when
she investigated she recognized part of the

sleeve that hadn't burned away. Harris tweed that jacket had been. Good enough for quite a few more years. Ivor was proud of it, so why had he burned it? She was frightened by the implications of his uncharacteristic act.

Honesty was something she had always taken for granted, hardly needing to give it a thought. But the new Ivor seemed to lie as a matter of course, and now this. Disposing of evidence, wasn't it? Evidence of what? A fight? He showed no bruises. An involvement in something worse? A road accident and the death of a young woman?

Shaking the ashes with a stick to encourage the fire to revive and burn what was left, she went inside. She wouldn't say a word. Tomorrow she would shovel up the bonfire ashes and carry them to the far end of town and put them in someone else's ashbin. Ivor couldn't have been involved in Emily Clarke's death; she couldn't, wouldn't believe it, but she knew she had to cover his tracks in case she was wrong. She had to protect him and their family.

Jennie and Lucy had had what some would call a 'good' war. Plenty of young men around to partner them at dances, men far from home and grateful for someone to talk to and flirt with, and even, when they were in a mellow mood, someone to listen to them as they talked about their families and the girls they loved. With a camp not far away, there were still servicemen around the town. These young soldiers didn't have much money, but a ticket to a local dance costing a shilling or two gave Jennie and Lucy enjoyable evenings, a few kisses, and a feeling of youth and desirable beauty.

Marie's only benefit from the war years was more recent. The loss of local decorators who had been conscripted into the forces, some killed, others returning with plans to build a different career, had created a need and now gave her opportunities to earn money to compensate for Ivor's inability to support them.

Geoff Tanner found work for her and promised to help if ever she was in difficulties. He had been widowed several years before and filled his time helping out wherever he found a need. She had thanked him but had no intention of accepting his help, although there were times when she would have been glad of it. Rushing from one job to another, fitting in housework and shopping when she could, she wondered how long she could keep it up.

The paint and paper she had ordered from Geoff Tanner were delivered to Mrs Ricky Richards and she went there as soon as tea had been eaten and supper prepared. Two coats of paint and the wallpapering meant at least three visits and she knew that Mrs

Richards would find an excuse to delay payment and argue about the previously agreed sum.

Ivor wasn't in when she got home. Violet was in bed and a surly Roger was sitting beside the fire. 'It's not fair, our Mam,' he began.

'When is it ever?' she said with a sigh. 'Did your father bring in some firewood ready for tomorrow?'

'No, I did,' he said, as though the task was huge. 'He said that as we weren't working we ought to help him.'

'Help *him*? What about me?' She laughed then. Tiredness and the futility of expecting anything better overcoming her anger.

She went to the sideboard, where the payment books were kept, intending to put the money into the insurance book ready for the collector the following morning, but she noticed the books had been rearranged. Staring in disbelief she saw that the books were all empty. Money for the gas and the electricity, the coalman, the milkman, the baker, it was all missing. There should have been more than one pound and ten shillings there.

'Roger, have you touched these books?'

'No, Mam. Not me, honest.'

'But you know who did?' It took a long time but Roger finally admitted that Ivor had 'borrowed' the money, 'just till pay-day'.

Marie set her alarm for six o'clock. She might be able to do the second coat of paint before work. That way she could hang the wallpaper that evening if she was careful. The money would be paid a day sooner and might just save them receiving a final demand. She hated those, shaming they were.

She wondered why she didn't hate Ivor. She longed to leave him, forget she had ever been his wife, but hate was never in her thoughts, even at times like this. Just disappointment. 'For better or for worse' had been the only time in her life she had gambled, and she had lost.

Three

Marie had been to her parents' to collect her daughter, but they didn't go straight home. She had a small job to finish at a house in Steeple Street and, giving Violet a bag of chips to ease her hunger, even though she had eaten with her grandparents, she worked until the job was finished. Sizing the walls ready for papering and painting the skirting boards with primer were tiring tasks, and her muscles were stiff with fatigue when they reached home at nine.

Marie had promised herself that, if she could stay awake long enough for the washing boiler to heat the water, she'd have a soak in the bath before bed. She filled the boiler and lit the gas under it, and dragged the galvanized bath from where it hung on the coalhouse door. Fighting sleep she sprinkled some scented crystals into the bath and prepared to wait. As she walked through the hall with her night clothes and a towel, an official-looking letter on the hall table caught her eye. It must have come by second post. She was curious but she settled Violet into bed and dealt with the dishes before sitting down to read it. The contents made her gasp. The rent was in arrears and if they weren't cleared in four weeks they would lose their tenancy.

Quickly swallowing the fear, confident there had been a mistake, she went to the sideboard to find her rent book – the book she left on the window sill every week for the rent collector to take the money and mark the book. Nothing had been paid for weeks. Foolishly she never checked the book for receipt and signature. Someone must have taken the money before the collector arrived.

'Ivor!' she said aloud. The twins wouldn't dare. Not the rent. Only Ivor would be foolish enough to believe he could gamble with it and return it before it was missed!

What could she do? There was no spare money to clear it. There was barely enough to pay the weekly bills. She would have to take time off work and go to the town hall and plead for an opportunity to pay off the arrears week by week. There was no sign of either the boys or of Ivor and, turning off the gas and forgetting about her luxurious bath, she ate a sandwich of marmite and drank a cup of cocoa and went to bed.

She couldn't sleep, her mind was too active, stimulated by all that had happened. Several times she went down to see if the boys were home. She tried not to think of where Ivor might be. Spending their rent money on another woman? Visions of a young woman a cross between her sister and Rita Hayworth came to mind but somehow it no longer hurt. She had to get away and make a home for herself, the twins and Violet. She knew the twins wouldn't want to go with her. They were not yet fifteen and to them Ivor, with his easygoing ways, was sure to be a more attractive prospect than her with her apparently futile attempts at guidance.

She had to face the fact that, if she decided to leave, Royston and Roger would almost certainly choose to stay with their stepfather. These days he seemed to take a pride in their idleness and consider their escapades a joke, convinced they were nothing more than childish devilment. He often said that he couldn't criticize them as he had been worse at their age. It had been a joke, given the comfortable life he had led until the death of his parents, a privileged life. He'd have had no need to steal or poach fish. But perhaps Jennie was right, and he would change if the finances became his own responsibility. The thought of leaving was frightening. She knew the twins would give her a hard time, and how could she leave the home where she and Kenneth, her first husband, had been so happy, the house in which the children had been born?

She gave a huge sigh that seemed to come from the very depth of her being. It was hopeless. Leaving her home and starting again without Ivor was nothing more than a foolish dream. How could she leave, wash her hands of him and pretend not to care? 'Better or worse' wasn't a mindless promise, no matter how many times she pretended that it could be broken. Besides, with no money and in debt how could she begin to look for a fresh place to live? What landlord would trust her?

She heard the boys come in at eleven o'clock and went down to see them. 'Where's your father?' she asked, the oft-repeated phrase seeming to echo in the air around them.

Both boys shrugged. 'We had a row and went out, he was here then.'

'What did you row about? You haven't lost your jobs again, have you?'

They looked at each other rather sheepishly and she demanded to know what had happened. 'The day can't get much worse, so tell me.' They glanced at each other again but still said nothing. 'I worked all day and then most of the evening,' she told them then. 'I came home to find the house empty, no note to tell me where you were. No idea where your father is, and then I found that the rent money has been stolen. Not just this week, but for more than six weeks. So come on, let's have it. Nothing you can tell me can be worse than all that.'

'We got caught shoplifting,' Royston said. 'It's not fair,' Roger predictably wailed, tears not far away. 'We were only looking.'

Marie sank into a chair and stared at them.

'Fool, wasn't I, to think it couldn't get worse. Well swallow this, you stupid, stupid boys. Two weeks and we'll be homeless. And that, with all the hours I work,' she said glaring at Roger, 'is definitely not fair!' She walked around the small room, pushing chairs under the table, bringing them out again. 'And where's your father?' she demanded again of no one in particular.

'We don't know,' Royston muttered. Both boys looked stricken, staring at her as though she were a stranger. 'Is that true? We'll have to move out?'

'We'll be homeless?' Roger whispered.

'Where will we go? Where will we sleep?

She regretted blurting it out so suddenly the moment she had spoken, but decided that, having done so, she had to tell them the full story. 'And so,' she finished, 'we'll probably have to leave here, and with nowhere to go, *you* tell *me* what we should do. Fourteen you are, finished with school and supposedly a part of the adult, working community. Assuming responsibilities, capable of contributing to the household, of keeping a job. So you tell me, where should we go? What should we do?'

A sound outside made her stop and listen, and they all looked towards the back door. The handle turned and a bedraggled Ivor came in. His jacket and trousers were creased and bits of straw and foul-smelling stains were spread over them. He tried a nonchalant smile. 'Bit late for a family conference, isn't it? What's new then?'

'Where have you been?'

'Nowhere special, just out, talking to Jack Harris and Morris Fender.' He thumped Roger on the shoulder light-heartedly. 'Got sacked again I hear, you stupid boy. You'd have done all right with Jack Harris. A mate of mine he is.'

'Royston has lost his job too.' Marie spoke softly.

'I've got to get out of these filthy clothes or I'll be sick,' he said, his face a mask of horror. 'I can't bear dirt and this is stinking.'

Another time it might have been funny, Ivor, who was so particular about the tiniest mark on his clothes, who was offended by a stray thread of cotton spoiling his immaculate appearance, standing there covered in dirty straw that smelled of manure.

'That's not all. There's something else,' Marie said.

Ignoring her he glanced at the boiler, from which steam drifted up like a miniature cloud. 'Hot water, thank goodness.'

'That was for me,' Marie said, but she shrugged and added, 'Your need is clearly greater than mine.'

Saying the words was going to be hard. Telling him that the rent money had been stolen had to be said without sounding as though he were accused. His need for a bath was a reprieve that she accepted with relief.

Ivor hoped he could avoid her asking how he had got in such a mess. He could hardly explain that he'd left his tidy clothes hidden, changed into old ones and returned to find that his good clothes had been stolen. Otherwise he would have returned as clean as when he'd set out. He couldn't explain the reason for the complication either. That was something she must never find out, however many lies he needed to tell.

They moved from the kitchen and no one offered to help him fill the bath from the boiler, bucketful by bucketful. No one moved. He closed the kitchen door and they listened to the sounds of his washing himself singing cheerfully, then the swish of pailful after pailful gushing down the outside drain and the scraping sound as he dragged the bath back outside.

The twins yawned but were unable to go to bed until they knew what Ivor had to say about the missing rent money. Hopefully he would reassure them that they were not about to be thrown into the street to sleep in doorways like some sad, injured and confused ex-soldiers they had seen. A family being driven from their home, protesting wildly, with their pathetic collection of furniture piled haphazardly around them on the road outside, was something they had witnessed once and the memory still frightened them.

When Ivor emerged from the kitchen wearing underwear and carrying the rest of his clothes delicately in an outstretched hand, he saw the line of anxious faces and began to pass through the room and head for the stairs, humming nervously.

'Something's happened and you have to help us deal with it,' Marie began. She didn't want to start with a challenge, there might still be a mistake. An error at the rent office, or even a reason for the money to have been moved. She desperately wanted there to be a simple explanation, although none of the more and more unlikely thoughts whizzing through her mind gave her much hope.

'Let's get to bed,' he said with exaggerated patience. 'Now isn't the time for serious discussions. It's almost midnight and I'm tired.'

'We might as well hear it now. Waiting till morning won't change anything, Ivor.'

Ivor glanced around the room, at his solemn-faced wife, at his sons, who were uncharacteristically subdued, their blue eyes wide, their faces white. Ignoring her quietly

95

spoken remark he returned to the subject of the boys and their inability to stay in employment. 'It's only a job,' he said, clouting Roger softly on his head. 'Plenty more for strong lads like you two.'

'It isn't about the boys.'

'Oh come on, love, I'm tired and I want to get these clothes off. Fell I did. Right into the chickens' coop, sneaking home through the farmer's yard. That'll teach me, eh?' He looked at the boys, expecting them to smile, but their faces were numb. 'All right, what's happened?'

All her intentions of taking it slowly, treading carefully, vanished. 'You! That's what happened. You've been stealing the rent money and we have little more than a month to find the arrears or we're being evicted.'

Ivor tried a laugh but it vanished from his face the moment it appeared. 'What d'you mean, I stole the rent money? That collector must be a thief. Yes, that's what happened, he took it and didn't hand it in. I always thought he had shifty eyes.'

'When have you seen the collector? He comes when you're at work, or have you been sacked too?'

It took a while but he eventually admitted that he had borrowed the money. 'There's these deals, see. Some cigarettes at half price, and I bought them and sold them with a bit of profit. I'd have put the rent money

96

back in time for the next week, no trouble. But then there was the chance of some food-stuff, tins mostly, and that went all right. That's why I've been out so late at night. Had to be careful not to be caught, see. Then I got some off-ration bacon, ham and some meat and it went wrong. I hid it in the barn near the river and someone found it and I lost the money. I wasn't worried, though, I knew there'd be another chance.'

'So you "borrowed" more money, but once more you couldn't pay it back?' Marie was feeling sick. Until she had spoken to Ivor she'd held on to a faint hope that the situation could be retrieved, and hope was fading with every word he spoke. 'What you've said accounts for a couple of weeks. What happened before that? Where did it go before these "deals"? Treating your friends? Handing it over to the bookies?'

'Tonight I'd arranged a meeting with a couple of restaurant owners who were going to buy the last batch of stuff, a good deal it would have been, sorted out all our troubles, but when we got there the farmer had filled the barn with young chickens and they'd ripped open the packets and, well, it's all ruined.'

'And so are we,' Marie whispered in a voice that trembled. 'So what are you going to do? Where will we live?'

'Don't worry, I'll find us a place. Better

move if we can, no point paying off the arrears when we can leave and make a fresh start.'

'Moving won't cancel the debt!' Marie's voice rose to a scream. 'The cost of moving will just add to what we already owe!'

'Hush, love, we don't want to wake our Vi, do we? If we move all quiet, at night, and tell no one where we're going, we'll get away with it.'

'Oh yes, hide away, not tell Mam and Dad and Jennie. Or d'you intend involving them in your lies and fraud? And what about Vi? Hide her away? Keep her out of school? Brilliant that would be.'

'Let's go to bed. Tomorrow we'll sort it.'

'*We'll* sort it? You'll do nothing, as usual. It will be me having to sort it, but this is the last time, Ivor. One more disaster, one more mess that I'm expected to retrieve us from, and I'm leaving you. Did you hear that, boys? One more chance for you as well. This is the end. Right?'

She ran upstairs and threw down bedding and a pillow. 'Use the couch, Ivor Masters! I'll be awake all night wondering what will happen to us, and I hope the broken springs do the same for you.'

Marie went downstairs the following morning at six o'clock, having struggled to stay in bed, certain she wouldn't sleep but knowing that to walk around downstairs wouldn't help solve the difficulties that faced her. Her mind was made up. She would try to arrange a regular repayment to the council, or borrow the money somewhere. There was no shortage of work for her, but how could she possibly work longer hours than she was doing already? Tears threatened but she forced them away. The time for tears and self-pity was long gone. Now action was needed.

Moving wasn't a possibility. Where would they go? To find somewhere cheaper would mean living further from town or renting somewhere very run down. Typical of Ivor to think of doing a moonlight flit, running away, leaving everything they owned, covering their tracks in the hope of leaving no trail for the debtors chasing them. What about her beautiful furniture, things she had chosen with Kenneth, gifts from his parents, valuable pieces that she had treasured?

She walked to school with Violet and wondered how she was going to get through the day, smiling, advising people with apparently charmed lives about the best gown to buy. Would the police call regarding Roger and Royston's shoplifting? They were well known already because of their poaching. Again her thoughts turned to her first husband. Disloyal thoughts or not she knew none of these things would be happening if he had lived. Then, as always, she reminded herself that she and Ivor had been happy for all these years, until the day Airborne won the Derby, and she wouldn't have had Violet. She put an arm around the little girl and hugged her tightly. 'I love you, you know that, don't you?'

'Of course, Mam, and Daddy loves me too.'

'Yes, he does.' But he loves gambling more than either of us, she thought sadly. Dealing in illegal meat was only slightly different from betting on the speed of a horse, it was a gamble against being caught, losing everything or making a profit. The excitement was much the same.

Ivor was an orphan, she knew nothing about him. From what he'd told her he'd been born into a moneyed background. His parents had been wealthy people, but their money disappeared when they died. There was nothing to suggest a weakness for gambling. Perhaps that wasn't his only problem. Perhaps he was involved with another woman, even taking these risks to keep two homes. Had her sister hinted at it when she had reminded her to take more care about her appearance? Was she working at two jobs, struggling to keep them out of debt, to finance another woman? Sadly, that made sense. If it were true, what could she do except leave?

★ ★ ★

Roger and Royston were worried. Both decided they had to help.

'We'll have to stop fooling around and keep our jobs for a start,' Royston said.

'We could ask Gran and Gramps to help. They might have enough to pay off the arrears.'

'No. Our Mam doesn't want them to know.'

'Why?'

'Pride I suppose, although what's pride if we're sleeping on the pavements?'

When Marie left the shop at lunchtime they were waiting outside.

'We've decided to get a job in the factory, making saucepans and things,' Roger said at once. 'It's better pay and you can have all of it.'

'Thank you,' Marie said, hugging them, to their embarrassment. 'But I'd rather you stay where you are, if Gwennie Flint and Jack Harris will give you one more chance. Just until you've decided what you really want to do.' She put a hand on their shoulders, pulling them towards her. 'I love you and I'm proud that you want to help. Whatever job you take, do it well. Get a reputation for being good workers, that's the best way you can help.'

'You'll still have all we earn,' Roger said tearfully. 'No pictures or treats.' She waited

101

and, as expected, he added, 'It isn't fair.'

'No, but we'll deal with it, together.'

Jennie and Lucy were happy sharing the management of the hairdressing shop. Mr James didn't interfere and, apart from when they handed over the appointments book and the takings every evening, they rarely saw him. Their wages had increased generously, and it was this that gave Jennie the idea that they should find a couple of rooms to share.

'Leave home you mean?' Lucy asked, as though her friend was joking. 'We can't do that.'

'Why not? We're old enough. Time we unfastened our mothers' apron strings. Just think, Luce, we'll be able to please ourselves what we do and when we do it, invite friends around, it would be great. And I'd get away from Mam and Dad taking me for granted as a live-in nurse.' She gave a low groan. 'Imagine it, Luce, at Mam's beck and call all day every day. Heavens, I'd not only leave home to avoid that, I'd leave the country!'

'I don't know,' Lucy said doubtfully. 'It would be a lot different. Going home and having to cook a meal for ourselves. Do our own washing, and cleaning and shopping, managing the rations.'

Jennie hadn't thought deeply about that side of the independent life, but she shrugged it aside as unimportant. 'What's a bit of washing?' She grinned and said, 'We can always take it home to Mam! And as for cooking, what's wrong with fish and chips? We'll be able to afford to eat out now and then and there are always men willing to treat us, eh? Come on, Luce, it'll be a gateway to freedom. After all, girls have been going into the forces, haven't they? Living away from home? Most of them a lot younger than us. Old Mr James was married with kids when he and Thelma were younger than we are. Come on, it'll be fun.'

Lucy knew her friend well enough to remind her that, 'We share the work, mind, both taking turns at all the jobs, nice and nasty?'

'Of course. Shall we start looking then? Get the evening paper and see what's to let?'

'All right, but not a word to anyone. If we can't find anything suitable it's best our parents don't know we've tried.'

'We'll find something.' Jennie waved a hand, brushing away the mild concern as an irrelevance. 'I'll ask our Marie. She knows a lot of local people and we can ask our customers. Bound to find something we are. Oh, Lucy, it'll be great.'

Jennie took the appointments book and the takings to Mr James. Bill was there and he looked on with amusement as his father asked politely what the girls were doing that

103

evening. 'Pictures? I go now and then, but it was dancing I used to enjoy.'

'Why don't you start again, there are plenty of –' she had been about to say old people but checked just in time and said instead. '– Plenty of all ages. You'd find a partner. I'll dance with you myself, I'm really quite good.'

'That's something to think about,' Mr James said with a laugh. 'Can you see me on a dance floor, Bill?'

'Why not?' Bill was looking at Jennie with a curious expression. 'Jennie would give you a few lessons in...whatever you wanted to learn – wouldn't you, Jennie?'

'Of course,' she said, wondering exactly what he meant. 'Any time, Mr James, just ask.'

'I think Mr James almost invited me out on another date,' she whispered to Lucy as they put on their coats.

'He never did!'

'Yes. He said he used to like dancing and might try it again.'

'Oh yeah? In his navy suit, collar and tie and his trilby stuck on his head?'

'Now Bill-the-lovelorn, he might be a different proposition,' Jennie said with a wink. They went out singing 'In the Mood'. 'Mister what you call it what you doin' to-night...'

A few days later, Bill was at the cemetery. He laid the posy of late marigolds and corn-flowers he had brought on the grave of Gloria, the first of his fiancées who had died after being hit by a car. The more recent grave of Emily was not far away and he had already placed a bouquet of Michaelmas daisies, one of her favourite flowers, on the harsh, freshly disturbed earth. How could this have happened a second time? And why hadn't the police found the vehicle? He had been devastated when Gloria had died so tragically, but the death of Emily was far worse, haunted as he still was by the possibility that if they hadn't moved her she might have lived.

Why had Ivor and he panicked? He was innocent but he'd been afraid the police might have been able to prove different. Guilt swept over him as he stared at the new grave, returning to the moment he saw her lying there in the road. It had been so reminiscent of the last time. The sudden realization that Gloria's death was being repeated made him fear for himself. Both had been engaged to him, and there was nothing else, no one else, connecting the two women.

He sat for a long time staring into space, seeing in his mind the two women in the road, Gloria, then Emily, until the two scenes melded into one and it was as though

105

he were standing there watching the car come and smash into them. The shock was repeated time and again, the sound of a car approaching and suddenly increasing its speed, intent on murder. Both were dead and somehow he had been the catalyst. But why?

As he walked away, stooped and sad, grieving for the young lives destroyed, a figure stepped out of the line of trees and bushes on the perimeter of the quiet place. The flowers on both graves were snatched up, shredded and strewn wildly across the wasteground outside the wall. A spray of Michaelmas daisies escaped and fell near her feet and she kicked it and stamped on it until it lay in ruins.

Taking a couple of hours off work was frowned upon by Mr Harries, manager of the dress shop, but when Marie told him it was important business he reluctantly agreed. Dressed in her smartest clothes for work, she presented herself and asked to discuss rental arrears. An hour later, humiliated at having failed to admit to a sensible explanation for the lapse, she had been given an alarmingly short extension. They would accept additional payments each week but the book had to be brought up to date by the middle of December. 'So we could be homeless by Christmas,' she said, after sarcastically thanking them for their cooperation.

'I'm sure we won't do that, Mrs Masters.'

'No, perhaps you'll wait for the January snows. How kind.' Alarmed by the implication that that outcome wasn't excluded, she glared at the poor man. She knew the newly appointed clerk was not to blame, he was stating the facts, doing what the rules stipulated. No, the fault lay with Ivor, but that hadn't stopped her treating the young man as though he were the cruel landlord in a Victorian melodrama.

On her way back to the shop she decided to risk an extra few minutes and call in to place an order for lino paint. Mrs Ricky Richards again. This time she was painting a linoleum floor in a back bedroom. She was tempted to ask for more money, knowing how the woman forced her payment down with a tirade of excuses, but she couldn't. However she found the money it wouldn't be by cheating, even on people as difficult as Mrs Richards. She didn't want to copy any of Ivor's tricks.

She had written to both Jack Harris, the wholesale fruiterer, and Mrs Gwennie Flint at the chip shop asking them to give the boys another chance. She wasn't very hopeful and wondered whether the boys were actually looking for work as they had promised, or had sneaked down to the river to poach a few more fish. What a life!

She hoped the fear of losing their home might have given them more determination to find and hold down a job, but suspected that, at fourteen, as time passed they had persuaded themselves it was less serious than she had implied, that neither she nor Ivor would allow it to happen.

'You look worried,' Geoff said as she went to the counter. 'Anything I can do?'

'Tell me how to win with the football pools when I can't even afford to play?'

'Surely you aren't seriously worried about money – you work all the hours of daylight and more. Is it the thought of Christmas?'

She laughed then. 'Oh yes, it's Christmas all right.' Unless something amazing happened she would be homeless, but how could she tell anyone that? Admit that her husband had been so stupid? That he had risked prison for a small profit and lost the lot?

Loyalty in some circumstances was foolish, and an openness, an honesty, especially to friends, could sometimes offer a solution, but loyalty was a strongly held principle. Loyalty to a husband was not easy to forgo, even when that husband had been as disloyal as Ivor. She had told Geoff too much already. She was glad when another customer came in, and she hastily put down her list of requirements, waved goodbye and

108

hurried back to work.

Over the next day every moment seemed filled with disasters. The farmer knocked her door and held out Royston's donkey jacket. 'This belongs to your son, I believe.'

'Oh, well maybe, it looks a bit like his.' Marie spoke warily. She didn't want to say something that would incriminate him. 'I wondered where it had got to.'

'The next time it walks on to my land and settles down to do a bit of fishing, I'll walk it to the police station. Right?' He pushed the jacket into her arms. 'I won't this time, I know they're in enough trouble at the moment, but you'd better warn them. No more. Right?' He stormed off and if he heard her 'thank you', he showed no reaction.

Two policemen called a few minutes later and told her that the boys had been charged with shoplifting by three shops in the town. One ticked off on his fingers. 'Poaching, trespass and now shoplifting. Unless you're fortunate and have a very generous judge, Mrs Masters, your boys could be sent to a remand school for this little lot. What were they thinking of? They have a decent home, they aren't deprived and certainly not stupid, so why do they do these things?'

'Us losing our home. That's what they were thinking of. And, like their father, they've only made things worse.'

'You'd better explain,' he said kindly. 'It

might help if there are extenuating circumstances, Mrs Masters.'

'Oh,' she said airily as though it was hardly important enough to mention, 'there's been a mix-up and the rent hasn't been paid.'

Marie had no one to talk to. She had never felt more alone. Ivor would *have* to take their situation seriously. The twins' behaviour could no longer be treated as a joke. She sat at the table unaware of time passing, the arrangement to whitewash a garden wall and outhouse forgotten. A remand school. The very words made her shiver. How could two boys, hardly more than children, cope with prison? There was another knock at the door and she snatched it open, expecting more trouble, prepared to shout her anger and rage to whoever stood there. Her anger subsided when she saw Geoff.

'I've brought the white paint for you,' he said. Then, 'I saw two policemen leaving. Is everything all right?' He stepped inside, put the box he carried on the table and took her hands in his. He led her to a chair and coaxed her to sit. 'Where's the kettle, you look as though you could do with a hot drink.'

'It's outside. I was washing the drains with soda,' she murmured.

He fished around in cupboards and found tea and sugar, and when he had made a pot of tea and poured a cup he sat down and faced her. 'Are you going to tell me what's happened?'

'I can't.'

'Marie, we're friends. We've known each other all our lives. I was at your wedding, you were at mine. You can trust me to help if I can, and not interfere if I can't.'

She looked at him and slowly began to explain. 'Ivor has never been very good at managing money, he can't help it, it's the way he is,' she said, trying to make an excuse for him. 'I've always known that. He makes grand gestures we can't afford. Although he was brought up in a children's home he seems to have the wealth of his parents and his early years indelibly marked on him. He spends money we don't have, a tendency I've always had to curb. But something happened in June, I've no idea what, and since then everything's got worse. Far less money and there are weeks when I don't have any housekeeping at all, and I've learned to cope, and, thanks to you finding jobs for me, work to compensate for his weaknesses. A week ago all the money put aside to pay the coalman and the rest was gone and then I had a letter.' She opened her handbag and showed it to him. 'He's been taking the rent money, trying to make more cash to put things right, and of course it didn't work. Weeks we owe. And unless I pay what's due we'll be out of here by Christmas.'

'I'll lend it to you.'

'No, Geoff. I can't let you do that,' she said at once. 'And if you repeat the offer I'll never talk to you again and I really need someone to talk to. I really, really do. I'm telling you as a friend, not to beg for money.'

'Very well.'

'I can't tell Mam and Dad. They don't have the money to help and there's no point in worrying them unnecessarily. Although I'll have to tell them about moving out, make up some story I suppose. Lies create lies and more lies, don't they?'

'Only if you let them. Sometimes the way to deal with things is to face them honestly. The offer still stands, and I know you don't want to talk about it,' he added, holding up his hands as she half stood and glared at him, 'but facing it is usually the best way, believe me.' He picked up the cup and offered it to her. 'Drink this, there's plenty of sugar. Sod the rations for once, eh?' She sipped and he waited to hear the rest.

'The twins tried to raise the money we need by stealing, they have to appear in court and it seems likely that they will go to a remand home.'

'What? Stealing a few fish can't be that serious.'

She told him the rest and he listened in silence until she had finished.

'Where are their brains?'

112

'So you see, Geoff, whatever I do it's never enough. As soon as I get straight, Ivor and the boys do something to ruin everything again.'

'I came to tell you about a job that's going. Decorating four flats in a house in the main road. They're all empty and before they're re-let the owner wants them all painted and re-papered. I recommended you for the job. But now I don't think it's a good idea. You should be doing less, not more. It sounds a contradiction, but money problems aren't always helped by money. It has to be a complete change of attitude, and I can see how Ivor's behaviour convinces the twins that it's all right to cheat and steal. They're at the age for hero worship and the danger of being caught – even though they think it will never happen – adds to the sense of adventure. He's the one who has to change and I don't know how you'll accomplish that with someone like your Ivor.'

'Those flats, that job would put everything right, we'd have a fresh start. If Ivor would help...' There was a gleam of hope in her eyes.

'Let me help and if you can persuade Ivor to join us that's great. We'd get it finished in a week or so. Plenty of time to settle the arrears and well before you have to start worrying about the court appearance.'

He discussed the work with her for a while

and Marie decided that decorating the flats was something she had to do. But how? She could hardly work through the night and there wasn't time to finish them in the time she had before the arrears were due. Ivor would have to help.

'I'd be able to work later into the evening if Jennie would sit with Vi,' she was saying, when there was another knock at the door and she felt her heart leap.

What further problems would this visitor herald? The door burst open and her sister walked in carrying a small gaily wrapped parcel. 'Happy birthday, sis,' Jennie said, pushing the gift towards a surprised Marie.

'My birthday? I'd forgotten.'

'It's for tomorrow, you daft thing. But I thought you'd better have it now as I'm busy tomorrow.'

'Thank you. Where are you going tomorrow then? Aren't you working?'

'Oh yes, but in the evening Lucy and I will be looking at places to rent. We're going to share a flat, or at least a couple of rooms. Exciting, eh? Honestly, Marie, we can't wait. But don't tell our Mam. Not yet. Not till we've found somewhere and it's definite.'

Marie was so bemused at the reminder about her birthday that she didn't remember to ask Jennie about sitting with Violet. Although as she was planning to move she would have an excuse not to help. Good at finding excuses, Jennie was, but surely when she knew the trouble Marie was in she'd spare her some time? Hope didn't burn with a bright flame: she knew her sister too well.

When Geoff and Jennie had gone, Marie sat thinking about what lay ahead. She was stunned by Jennie's news about moving out of their parents' home. Besides meaning that she would have to spend more of her fractured time checking on their parents, gone was her hope of asking Jennie to look after Vi. Her only hope was Ivor.

When Ivor came in later he laughed at the idea of helping. 'Me hang wallpaper? Get on with you! I'd be useless. Damn me, you know that. Besides, I hate working for other people, having them look down on me as though I were their servant.'

'You don't mind if I do?'

'Of course I mind. I hate it, seeing you going around dressed in shabby working clothes. I wish you'd stop.'

Ignoring his useless protests she said, 'Then you'll have to stay in with Vi. This time I insist. It's your mess I'm trying to sort out and you'll have to help.'

'Have to, will I? You insist, do you? You're getting stroppy aren't you?'

'Help or get out!'

'Come on, Marie. You're overwrought.'

'We're losing our home! The boys are facing prison, I'm exhausted and you're

115

useless!'

Instead of adding to his guilt, her reaction increased his anger. The impossibility of explaining made him want to run away, put miles between them. He calmed himself, then turned the complaint on her, saying quietly, 'You're worried about the boys, I understand that, love.' His voice was soothing but the tautness of his jaw belied the comforting words. Ignoring her further outburst, pretending to put it down to anxiety, he touched the teapot to see if the contents were drinkable. 'Uh! Stone cold. What about a fresh cup of tea for your old man, then, eh? They'll be all right, Marie, they won't go to prison – that was said to frighten you.'

'What frightens me is the conviction that we'd all be better off without you. I'd cope with everything better on my own. You only drag us all down.'

'Don't be stupid.'

'I can't help being stupid. I promised to love, honour and obey, for better or for worse and all that stuff. Well, I've had the worse for long enough. I have to decorate those flats if we're to keep our home. Help me, or get out.'

'I don't give in to threats, so you can stop talking like that. I'll help, but only this time. I'm not going to make a habit of working for other people. And I think you should stop too. You don't seem to mind what people

116

think of us but I find it degrading. Leaving us to fend for ourselves while you grovel to inferior people for a few measly shillings, it isn't right.'

'But it's to pay off your debts!' Exasperation made her shout.

'Don't raise your voice to me, woman. And ask yourself why I go out to meet friends and have a laugh. It might be because you're never here and there are no laughs when you are.'

She calmed down, put the kettle to boil and set a tray for tea. 'Then you'll help, if I take on the flats? To pay the arrears? I can't do it on my own, Ivor. I really can't.'

'I don't know if I can, but I'll try. Right? I'll try!' Anger fizzed in the air around him, and Marie felt her spirits drop lower. Reluctant help would be worse than no help at all.

'I have worries too,' he said.

'Then tell me, help me to understand.'

'I can't.'

His handsome face was moving as he sifted through ideas to escape from his promise. He was so upset by what had happened and his inability to explain. Scenes filled his mind and he saw deals that had gone wrong, the stupidity of the boys, the nagging face of his wife, and at that moment saw himself as the victim, the misunderstood husband. Everything was hanging on by a thread that might snap at any moment. While it held there was still hope of coming through this with his marriage intact and the love of his family weak but surviving.

Marie could almost see the way his mind was working, and to emphasize their need for money she told him again about the farmer bringing back the jacket.

'What jacket?' he demanded. As she explained, she wondered whether he was thinking of that other jacket, the one he had burned and which she had thrown away with someone else's rubbish.

'Poaching?' he said with a laugh. 'The miserable old miser. Kids is all they are. It isn't as though they caught anything, is it?'

Irritated by his determination to make light of it, she said, 'The least we can hope for when the boys appear in court are heavy fines. Without the money for decorating these flats we face years of you—' She was about to say, 'your debts', but changed her mind. 'Years of debt. If we are penniless and then made homeless, there's even more likelihood of the twins being sent to prison. We need to show the court they have a secure home and to do that we need money. We need it desperately, now and not next year, Ivor. I can't do this without your help.'

'And it's my debt, eh?' He stared at her then and, knowing that this was one battle she simply had to win, she stared him out until his expression softened and he said, quietly, 'All right. Just this once, mind. For the boys. Just this once.'

Geoff was driving past as Ivor came out of his office the following day, and he called to offer him a lift. In the lane a short distance from his house he stopped the van and turned to face him.

Ivor reached for the door handle. 'Don't tell me you're going to have a go at me as well. It's none of your business.'

'You're right, it isn't. At least it wasn't, until I found out about your father.'

Ivor's face paled and Geoff began to think he would faint. 'You haven't told Maric?'

'Of course I haven't. I don't know much, only that an ex-schoolfriend was talking in the pub and mentioned something that I picked up on. No one else knew who he was talking about. Is that where the money's been going?'

It wasn't the whole truth. By sheer chance Geoff had seen Ivor on the night he had found his father, and, made curious by his furtive manner, he followed him as he left the road and walked through the woods. Some distance from the village he had watched as Ivor met an elderly man gathering firewood. He couldn't hear what was said but it was clear that the old man was pleased initially then upset as they began to argue. They walked off together along a path between the trees, anger increasing Ivor's speed and forcing him to stop and allow the old man to catch up with him.

The path twisted and turned, which made it easy for Geoff to follow unseen. The two men talked spasmodically, the younger angry and the older pleading for something that went unheard. They left the trees and jumped down on to a quiet lane and into the overgrown front garden of a rather large cottage tucked into the edge of the wood.

Geoff dared not go any closer but he saw them both inside, Ivor gesturing with his arms and the old man standing with bowed head as though being verbally chastised. Geoff was puzzled about who the old man was and by a coincidence found out the following day.

He had gone to the pub for a pint at lunchtime and had met Jinks Jenkins, who had regaled him with stories about how Ivor had been teased as a boy. Geoff had only half listened; he was thinking that the chance meeting would enable him to tell Ivor he knew about his father without mentioning that he had followed him.

'Don't tell Marie or the children. I couldn't bear it, Geoff, I really couldn't.'

'I found out, so there's always the possibility someone else might. I know Marie and she'll cope with anything as long as she knows the truth.'

'I can't tell her now. The boys' problems are enough for her to cope with.'

'That and you causing her to be kicked out of her home!' Geoff's voice was sharp.

'Yes, that too.' Ivor was shaking and Geoff knew he had to be less harsh with the man. He was on the edge of a precipice.

'I won't mention it again, I promise you that, but you have to. She has the right to know.'

'I can't.'

'You've handled things so badly. Mainly by not trusting your wife. You've betrayed her love, haven't you?'

'All right! Don't rub it in!' In his distress, Ivor was shouting.

'Do something, man, before someone else tells her. But believe me, Ivor, it won't be me.'

'Thanks.'

Geoff restarted the engine but Ivor opened the door. 'I'll walk from here.'

Geoff watched him go: a stooped figure with a stumbling walk that was taking him towards a family in trouble, who needed him to be strong. He wondered whether he had helped or made things worse.

Ivor went in and began sorting out brushes and all the other items they would need for the decoration of the flats and, for the first time for weeks, Marie felt hopeful of a way out of their difficulties.

They began at the weekend, going down on Saturday evening while the boys, obedient in their anxiety, looked after their sister. Ivor worked fast and with surprising efficiency. Stripping the walls of two rooms was accomplished that evening, the walls washed and the paintwork sanded for painting. Marie felt very hopeful, but when Geoff came to help the following morning, armed with paint for the kitchen, Ivor glared at him and walked out.

Four

Marie didn't know what to do. Should she run after Ivor and plead with him to come back? Or ignore his behaviour and accept the willing assistance of Geoff? With a hardening of her heart she realized that, of the two, Geoff was the most likely to really support her. If she told Geoff to leave she knew Ivor wouldn't see the job through. She faced weeks of hard long hours of work and couldn't do it on her own, with no thanks, only criticism. And, she reminded herself, causing her brow to crease in a deep frown of anger, it was Ivor's debt!

Geoff sensed her dilemma. 'Shall I go?' he asked. She didn't reply, her mind still filled with anger and frustration at this predicament that was not of her own making.

'Perhaps, if I walk away, let Ivor see me leave, pacify his resentment, I can come back later. I should be able to get the undercoat on these rooms this evening.'

Marie stared at him, his words slowly penetrating, only half heard. 'Please, Geoff, please don't leave. I really need help, and

Ivor was just looking for a reason not to give it. He's found his excuse and he's off! This is his mess and he won't even help me to sort it out.'

Geoff said nothing more. He had a picture in his mind of Ivor going to meet the frail, confused man in the wood. However Marie worried, he couldn't tell her what he knew. That was for Ivor to explain. By talking about it now, he would be setting himself against Ivor, and that might alienate Marie when she needed a friend.

Sanding done, he began to wipe the skirting boards with a damp cloth. They worked for three hours with hardly a word spoken. Marie knew that if a hint of sympathy were offered she would burst into tears. Geoff knew that unless the day ended with some sign of progress she would give up.

It was ten o'clock that night when they washed their brushes and put everything away for the following day. Marie began to thank him but he waved her words aside.

'No need for thanks, we're friends and friends help without question. Right?'

When she reached home, she hesitated to open the door. Music was playing, so the boys were still up but was Ivor with them?

She stepped into the kitchen and called, 'I'm home,' and there was a scuffle from the living room and the record that was playing was hurriedly changed for another. When she opened the door, the twins were listening, ironically, to 'My Heart Belongs to Daddy' and Violet was asleep, still dressed, on the couch.

'Royston, Roger, why didn't you send her to bed?' she demanded, throwing off her coat and bending over her sleeping daughter.

'Got fed up with arguing with her, didn't we?' Roger moaned. 'It's not fair leaving us to look after her.'

'She said you'd told her she could wait up for you,' Royston added, leaning pointedly closer to the gramophone to show his irritation at her interruption. The pile of records slid across the couch and Marie saw two that were indisputably new.

'Where did they come from?' she asked. She sifted through them and saw several more that looked new, the slip covers crisp and clean. She picked one up and waggled it in front of Roger's face. 'Where have these come from? Have you been stealing again? Tell me the truth!'

'Mam! Of course they aren't nicked. Borrowed they are, from Arthur Malin. Said we could borrow them till his father comes home on Sunday week.' Marie looked at his guileless face, big eyes with an air of offended innocence. Marie stared at him, but his gaze didn't waver. She was almost certain the records were stolen, but she was too weary to investigate. 'Wait till your father gets in. He'll get to the bottom of it.' Fortunately she failed to see the amused glance exchanged between the boys.

'Go to bed. Now, this minute,' she demanded, and lifting Violet from the couch without waking her she struggled up the stairs and put her in her bed.

When at last she fell into her own bed she felt as though all her bones had softened and her muscles had hardened in their stead. Every movement hurt. Despite her exhaustion anger kept her awake. Anger at her own stupidity for getting into this situation. She had taken on the role of family saviour when she should have done nothing at all except to wait for Ivor to get them out of the mess he had caused.

She switched on the bedside torch, which was in fact an old bicycle lamp, and saw that it was almost two a.m. Where on earth was Ivor? He couldn't be playing cards – the usual reason for a late return. So far as she knew he had no money and no one was likely to lend him any.

She tiptoed downstairs and made a cup of tea. With the inexplicable hope of encouraging his arrival, as people at a bus stop will when their bus is late, she walked to the corner and looked along the road. The night was still. No moon, yet her eyes accustomed themselves to the darkness until she could gradually make out the nearby houses and the ghostly shapes of trees and bushes that imagination could form into strange beasts. There was no sound of footsteps and she went back inside, as wide awake as ever, and tried to read for a while.

Instead she found herself thinking about the flats. It was something she would have to do. Martyr or not, overworked idiot or not, if she did not there was little hope of paying the arrears and there was only one outcome to that situation. They would be out on the street.

She didn't hear Ivor come home that night even though she sat up, dozing, listening for the sound of his footsteps, or the door opening. At half past six she lit the fire, and as she began preparing breakfast he came in, looking neat and tidy, except for needing a shave. It was another woman, it had to be. She sliced the loaf for toasting, unable to see clearly for the tears in her eyes.

Ivor helped himself to a cup of tea from the teapot and, carrying it in one hand and a kettle of hot water in the other, he went straight upstairs to wash and change into the suit he wore for work. He hated this filthy situation. Last night he had washed in a freezing cold brook in an attempt to rid himself of the smell. Even after that, and although he had changed clothes and hidden the others in a hollow tree, the smell

127

remained, seemingly trapped in the pores of his skin.

Another two evenings and the wall papering and painting of two rooms was finished and the floors sanded and varnished. Once the kitchen and bathroom were painted she'd be able to ask for part payment. In one hand and out with the other. There were three more flats to be done and she looked ahead to days in the shop and evenings and half the nights decorating, and wondered how long she could keep going. With Geoff it was possible. With only Ivor she would fail. Her over tense mind drifted through the possibilities – and probabilities – for the future. Even at best they would continue to live hand-to-mouth with a man who had become incapable of supporting them. At worst they would be homeless, separated from each other and treated like rubbish, worse than the tramps who wandered around the countryside in increased numbers since the end of the war.

She went to bed light-headed with tiredness, on the edge of tears, her mind jumbled with a dozen questions to which there were no answers. She finally slept and didn't hear Ivor creep in at five a.m., his pockets empty and a few more IOUs in other people's pockets.

★ ★ ★

128

The following lunchtime, Marie gathered the suspect gramophone records and handed them into the shop on the high street, explaining that she had found them on a park bench. The manager smiled stiffly as he thanked her and then apologetically told her that her sons were banned from entering the shop. 'Nothing to do with your kindness in returning these records you "found", Mrs Masters, indeed not. There was an – er – an incident here last week and, well, we think it's best they stay away. Sorry I am to tell you, and you on a mission of kindness, too.'

She thrust the records into his hands and walked swiftly away. A strong desire to hit the twins and their father, to hurt them, filled her heart. The boys for their foolishness and their father who thought their behaviour was a joke. She bumped into several people as she rushed blindly back to the shop.

Jennie and Lucy had found a flat, and, in her usual confident way, Jennie asked Mr James for his opinion before she and Lucy signed the agreement. The flat was in fact two rooms in a house near the park and consisted of a basement room and one room up a flight of stairs, part of the ground floor of the house which the owners had furnished as a bedroom. They would have use of a bathroom, and the kitchen was a corner of the

129

living room with a cooker and a sink and very little besides, hidden by a curtain.

'It isn't much, we know that, Mr James,' Jennie said. 'It's our first strike towards freedom though, and we love it. We just wondered whether you, with your experience, could see any problems we haven't noticed.' The flattery was blatant as she went on, 'You're a businessman and clever enough to look below the surface of things, if you know what I mean. We'd really appreciate you looking at it, wouldn't we, Lucy?'

'We'd be ever so grateful, Mr James,' Lucy said, nodding earnestly.

The house was owned by a nurse and her family and she left them to make up their minds while she went back upstairs. Mr James looked around, checked the walls and under the floor coverings for signs of damp, and declared it sound. 'You'll need to keep the place warm, mind. It could get damp being a basement, and that can bring health troubles. We don't want you ill, do we?' He was looking at Jennie when he spoke but turned to encompass Lucy, adding, 'I need to look after you both.'

'I don't expect a lot of noise,' the nurse told them. Deliberately misunderstanding, Jennie said brightly, 'Don't worry, we aren't the sort to complain.'

'I meant from you. I don't like noise.'

'We'll be able to play our gramophone,

130

won't we?' Jennie looked aghast. 'Mr James, we couldn't live without our music.'

A few moments of reassurance from Mr James that his employees would be exemplary tenants and the matter was settled. The girls would move in the following week. 'Bill will help you move your things,' Mr James promised. 'I'm sure he won't mind.'

Bill did mind, and, rather than disappoint the girls, Mr James came instead, using his car to transport their belongings, including their collections of records, to the flat.

Jennie's goodbye to her parents was tearful. Belle and Howard had come to the flat with gifts on the day they moved in, and left after much hesitation, waving to their daughter as if she were off on an Arctic expedition or to face dangerous animals in a distant jungle. She sobbed with them but as soon as they were out of sight she shrieked with delight and danced around to music, until Mrs Roberts upstairs banged on the floor and shouted. Their laughter was almost as loud as the record.

'What are we going to eat?' was Lucy's first question. 'I'm starving.' Belle had packed them some food 'to get them started', and they tucked into meatless pasties and fatless cakes with gusto. 'Tomorrow it's chips,' Jennie said, munching happily. 'Isn't this great?'

With help from Geoff and offended criticism

from Ivor, the flats were finally finished and Marie went to pay off the arrears. Filled with relief, she almost ran to the office to pay off the full amount.

The clerk was nervous and he kept glancing around as though hoping someone would come to his rescue. 'Too late, Mrs Masters, sorry I am, real sorry. But it's been allocated to an ex-soldier and his family. We have to do our best for the men who went to fight, you can see that I'm sure. You have to vacate the property on – er –' he glanced at a piece of paper on his desk as though he'd forgotten. 'on the twenty-fifth of September.' He went around the counter and guided her to a chair as she had begun to shake.

'Less than two weeks? but I thought we had until December.'

'We tried to tell you that had changed. We've sent you two letters, Mrs Masters, I wrote them myself. You must have received them. I put the second one through your letter box on my way home to make sure there was no delay. Worried I was, you not replying, like, and I wanted to make sure you got the warning.'

Ivor must have found the reminders and hidden them. What was he playing at?

The embarrassed clerk stood nervously beside her, then began to explain about re-paying her debt. 'You still owe the money, Mrs Masters,' he reminded her gently. She clutched her handbag as though suspecting him of trying to rob her. 'That won't be cleared by your vacating the premises,' he went on softly, as though talking to a child. 'But I can arrange for you to pay it off real slow, a few shillings a week. Best I can do. Will that be all right?'

She thanked him vaguely and, still gripping her handbag with fingers white with pressure, rose from the chair like an old woman.

Half a dozen times she stopped on the way home to rest on benches and garden walls. The money in her handbag seemed unreal, heavy, weighing her down. All that work and it wasn't enough. Instead of going home, she went to Geoff's shop and knocked on the side door. When he came out she handed him the money she had intended to use to pay off her debts. 'Look after this for me, will you? If Ivor knows I've got it he'll wreck the house trying to find it.'

He took it without a word.

She didn't go back to the shop that afternoon. Instead she went to the woodyard office and told Ivor what had happened.

'We can't talk about it here, Marie. Go home and wait for me there. I'll get things sorted, I promise.'

'Your promises aren't worth anything. How can you sort this when we owe months of rent and are being thrown out into the

133

street?'

'Hush, love, I don't want our business touted all round the town.'

'Too late to worry about that. Everyone will know when our furniture is piled up on the pavement.'

He calmed her down and walked her home after a hurried word with his boss, explaining that his wife was worried about the boys, and his sympathetic employer told him he could take the afternoon to sort it out.

After seeing Marie into the house and making her a cup of tea, he left, after repeating his promise that he would sort it out. But instead of going back to work he went to the bus stop and, dragging the suitcase from its hiding place, changed into the filthy clothes with a shudder of disgust.

Jennie and Lucy decided to have a party.

'So long as everyone brings some food,' Jennie stipulated. 'I don't want the worry or expense of feeding people.' Lucy agreed, and besides some of their dancing friends, they asked Bill James if he'd like to come.

'Sorry, but I don't feel very sociable,' Bill excused.

'You can't give up,' Jennie coaxed. 'Life goes on. You got over Gloria, remember, and you're still young enough to find someone else.'

'Don't talk like some women's magazine! I

134

loved Emily. It isn't easy to recover from losing her.'

'You loved Gloria too, and that funny little girl before her. The one that disappeared so suddenly, remember?'

'Don't try to make me sound shallow, unfeeling.'

'I don't think you're shallow,' Jennie said as though surprised. 'I'm reminding you that grief isn't for ever, that's all.'

He gave her a penetrating look which she matched and then allowed to dissolve into one of her special smiles. As she smiled she was thinking, pompous ass, he's worse than his father. Old before his time.

Bill came and the party was a success, with too many guests crowding into the small space and somehow managing to dance to the records of Glenn Miller, Tommy Dorsey and Ted Heath. The noise increased as more and more people arrived, and the records were played louder to be heard by the dancers. Bangs on the floor from Mrs Roberts above went unheeded. Jennie danced with Bill several times, opening the door to the garden – which Mrs Roberts had insisted was her private domain – and kissing in the darkness, an experience Jennie found far from unpleasant.

The following morning they had a visit from their landlady, who stood at the door, glaring at the trodden-in food on the floor and the slithering pile of records against the wall.

Unwilling to tell the boys or Violet about their dilemma, and with only a couple of weeks before they had to leave the house, Marie began packing surplus china. Begging boxes from the shops and using the piles of newspapers put out for the ashmen, she worked until she could hardly move a muscle. Then she gathered the boxes and piled them as well as she could in the corners of the living room. Pictures came off the walls, garden tools were tied together with string, the contents of cupboards were stacked into yet more boxes, and when the children asked what she was doing she told them she was spring cleaning. As she was scrubbing out each cupboard as it was emptied, they seemed to believe her. Ivor said very little and seemed unaware of the turmoil.

She tried to persuade him to face up to the fact they were homeless, but although he promised that they wouldn't be out on the streets, assuring her he was dealing with it, he didn't offer any concrete hope of anything other than the sky for a roof. He was out most evenings and several times he came home very late.

Every day, when he came home from work and changed into less formal clothes, she made him promise not to go out, but most evenings his presence at home ended by nine o'clock after he had put Violet to bed and told her a story.

'It has to be another woman. What other reason could there be?' she asked Geoff one evening as they worked on a house refurbishment, a job he had found and insisted on helping her complete.

'I doubt it, Marie. I've heard nothing and in the shop I pick up all kinds of gossip, which I try to forget. There's no rumour about your Ivor and another woman.'

'I'm so tired by the time ten o'clock comes I have to go to bed, but tonight, if he goes out, I'll wait up and make him tell the truth,' she said.

It was a clear night with the moon riding high, three quarters full and adding a glow that was like an enchantment. The air was still with not even the tiniest movement in the trees. It was a temporary balm to her weary spirits, until fears and imaginings beat against her brain and she wondered if she would ever find peace again. She would miss this house where so many happy memories resided. She couldn't think clearly. Not knowing where they would be in a few weeks time was a barrier to any attempt at making plans. She looked up at the sky and thought the emptiness was matched by her own situation. Miles of emptiness without a goal in sight.

Although it was chilly, she sat in the garden for a while, trying to stay awake after the three children were asleep and the house was quiet, trying to recapture that momentary peace of a few moments ago.

She didn't like being in the living room any more. It was no longer hers. All her possessions had been packed away apart from the bare minimum. Soon someone else would be there putting their mark on it, and in no time at all every trace of herself and Ivor and Roger and Royston and little Violet would disappear, floating in space like the moon and stars. It would be as though they no longer existed. Ghosts for a brief moment, just until every last trace of them had been overlaid by the newcomers, then gone.

Although she was cold, from time to time she dropped off to sleep, her neck at an awkward angle, then jerked awake to momentary confusion and further disappointment. A blanket she had brought out had fallen to the ground and she gathered it around her. In the distance a church clock chimed twelve. It was tempting to give up and get to bed; the thought of a couple of hot water bottles to warm it appealed to her, making her realize how cold she had become. She went inside and put the kettle on the gas to fill the stone hot water bottles, then took them and placed them in the bed. She was about to refill the kettle to make a hot drink when she heard footsteps. She switched off the gas under the kettle and went back outside. Someone was approaching, and momentarily she felt a spasm of fear. It could be a thief, looking for something to steal, but the footsteps were quick and, with no sign of secretiveness, undoubtedly Ivor.

'Marie? What are you doing outside? The children are all right, aren't they? Is something wrong?'

'Fine they are, and so am I, apart from wondering where we'll sleep next week. Where have you been?'

'Oh, talking to Jack Harris. He said our Roy's doing all right, working hard and he's pleased with him. That's a relief, eh?'

'Chatting with friends, there's nice for you. What have you done about us? Homeless we are and there's you having a nice chat with Jack Harris. "Fiddling while Rome burns"!'

'"Fiddling while Rome burns", that's good that is, but I haven't been doing nothing. I've been trying to work something out. I've a plan in mind but I don't want to talk about it until everything's certain sure.'

'Forgive me if I don't believe you!'

'Be patient a little while longer, Marie. We'll have a place to go, I promise.'

'You have to tell me what's happened, Ivor.' Aware that he was keeping his distance from her she stepped towards him, suspicion making her search for evidence of another woman. It was too dark, impossible to see his expression or any telltale marks on his clothes, but there might be a hint of perfume – something she couldn't afford for herself. Once inside she might see a mark on his clothes; lipstick is a stubborn stain and he could hardly come home without a shirt. His scarf was tight around his neck under his overcoat; what was it hiding? She would stay close until he took it off. She stepped towards him and he backed away.

'I'll go and have a wash,' he said.

She reached out and pulled him towards her and then the smell hit her, and it couldn't be described as perfume. It was a noxious odour of sourness, of rotting food, of fermenting fruit, and the deep, unwashed smell of the tramps she sometimes passed in the bus stop shelter, forcing her to wait outside.

'Where have you been?' she demanded, holding on to his coat as he struggled to get away. 'You stink! You haven't been talking to Jack Harris. His house doesn't smell like an ash bin. Tell me, Ivor! I want to know where you've been going. Who's keeping you out all hours and making you ignore what's happening to us?'

'Let me have a wash and change my clothes, please, Marie. I'll be sick if I don't

140

get out of these things soon.'

Her arms fell from him as though their strength had failed, and she watched as he hurried through the back door and up the stairs. Once before he had been in clothes that stank and he'd told her he'd been in the farmer's barn, but the smell wasn't of chickens, it was filthy rotting food and unwashed humanity.

He came out of the bedroom smelling clean and dressed in freshly laundered pyjamas, with his hair neatly combed, and shiny faced as though he'd scrubbed himself to get rid of the last vestige of that awful stink. Aware of the children sleeping nearby, she repeated her demand for an explanation in a hissing whisper.

'Get into bed, love, I'll make us a hot drink and come up in a minute or two. You must be frozen, sitting outside like that.'

'I want an explanation. And I want it now, this minute!' she whispered harshly, her voice louder than she intended, startling in the silence of the night.

'We both need a hot drink, Marie, love. Go to bed and wait for me to make it.'

'Then we'll talk?'

'Soon, I'll explain everything soon,' he promised, as he ran softly down the stairs, his head buzzing with possible reasons for his behaviour that didn't reveal the truth.

Marie slid into the bed that had been

141

warmed by the hot water bottles, and felt the comfort relax her, her body becoming limp, her eyes succumbing to drowsiness, and, in the welcoming warmth, anxiety eased away, and as the minutes passed she found it more and more difficult to stay awake. An hour later, Ivor looked at her, bent over and kissed her gently and went back downstairs.

Marie woke and, before she opened her eyes, stretched out a hand and felt across the bed for Ivor. He wasn't there and his pillow showed no sign of his ever having been. She rushed downstairs but his coat and umbrella were gone. On the table was a note. 'I'll be late tonight, but don't worry, Everything will be all right.' He had signed it 'Your loving Ivor.' She heard the twins rising and stuffed it into her dressing gown pocket.

As she began to get breakfast she felt the threat of tears as she realized how badly she needed someone to talk to, someone to whom she could open up and in whose sympathy and understanding she could wallow. Her parents wouldn't want to know. Theirs was a simple, uncomplicated life in which any problems had been spirited away before they became serious. There was only Geoff, and somehow she couldn't tell him about the filthy state in which Ivor had arrived home. She had to keep it to herself, like the bloodstained jacket, which Ivor had told her had been an accident caused by chopping wood.

Fastidious as he was, she had almost accepted his explanation that he couldn't bear to wear that jacket again after such staining, even after cleaning. Almost, but sometimes she wondered about the coincidence of it happening on the same evening that Emily Clarke had died in a road accident. The jacket incident, and last night's return covered in the disgusting smell, would remain a secret. Until she made sense of it herself she would have felt disloyal discussing it. Stupid as it might seem, she still felt loyalty and told herself there would be a logical explanation for his behaviour.

She wondered briefly whether he had been helping at one of the reception centres that had opened around the countryside to accommodate the vagrants, ex-soldiers many of them, men and a few women, whose lives had been disrupted by the war and who had lost touch with where they were from or who they were. But surely if that were the case he would have told her. Ivor was vain enough to want admiration for any such altruism. And surely such goodness didn't necessitate depriving your own family to help those less fortunate. That would have been replacing misfortune with misfortune, wouldn't it?

She fed the children and watched as the boys left for work. She forced a cheerfulness

143

into her voice as she walked with Violet as far as the school gates then left her and hurried to the shop. It opened at nine a.m. but the staff were expected to be there fifteen minutes before, to make sure everything was in readiness for their first customer. Again that forced cheerfulness as she helped a young woman to choose a dress for a birthday party. A birthday celebration far different from her own, she thought with a sigh. How wonderful to be spoiled as this woman appeared to be. She carefully pinned up the hem of the full-skirted dress and marked a few tucks in the bodice to ensure a perfect fit, then watched as the smiling customer swept out to buy the accessories, for which her doting parents had given her their clothing coupons.

'There are two pins on the floor, Mrs Masters!' The sharp tone of her boss brought Marie out of a daydream in which she was fêted and spoiled and made into a star for the day at an imaginary birthday party held in her honour. At that moment her sister came in and asked to speak to her.

'Can it wait until lunchtime, Miss – er –'

'If it must, Mr – er,' Jennie replied cheekily. 'I'll wait outside, shall I? How fortunate it's only raining and not the season for snow.' She smiled at Mr Harries and he succumbed to her gentle criticism and gestured towards a chair. She thanked him and sat, with her legs crossed, showing an inordinately generous amount of leg.

She clearly made the pompous Mr Harries nervous, as, fifteen minutes before her usual time, he told Marie she could leave early and come back at the usual time. Grabbing her coat she hurried out offering effusive thanks, and followed her sister along the dull, damp street.

'What got into him?' Marie said, laughing at the unexpected freedom. 'He's never done anything like that before.'

'Oh, just an inch or two above the knee, that's all it took to transform him to a jelly.'

In spite of trying to disapprove, Marie laughed, and when her sister suggested they went to a café for a coffee and a bun she agreed.

'I shouldn't really,' she said. 'I promised to pick up Mam's bacon ration. You know she always likes bacon and egg and chips for Tuesday's dinner.'

'Honestly, our Marie! D'you think I won you an extra fifteen minutes out of that miserable boss of yours so you can get Mam's bacon ration? Coffee and a bun and I'm paying. What more d'you want, woman?'

'How is life in the flat, enjoying it are you?' she asked.

'Wait till the waitress has brought our order then I'll tell you.'

Marie sensed trouble.

They were guided to a table near the window, and as the waitress delivered their order Marie was staring into space, lost in thoughts of Ivor, wondering what he was up to and whether it was legal. With the boys due to appear in court in a month's time, and the threat of eviction hovering over her, what was she doing sitting here drinking coffee as though she were a lady of leisure?

'Come on, sis, cheer up, or I'll wish I'd invited old Mr Harries instead of you! And he looks more boring than Mr James!'

'What did you want to see me about?' Marie forced her attention back to her sister.

'It's Mam and Dad.'

'Jennie, I can't do more than I'm doing at present. You know how I'm fixed. Thanks to Ivor, I don't know where we'll be in a month's time and I have to take work when it's offered, to pay off the debts we're leaving behind.'

'I've decided not to stay in the flat Lucy and I found. Her boyfriend is coming home, leaving the RAF, and I can't afford it on my own. They're getting married, see.'

'When?'

'Well, not for ages yet, but—'

'What's the real reason?' Marie demanded. 'Come on, Jennie, the truth.'

'All right, we've been told to leave. That Mrs Roberts is a real misery. Can't bear to think of us having fun. There was some trivial complaint about noise. I ask you, can anyone have a party without making some noise? Besides, I hate being away from Mam and Dad. I miss them.'

'Their spoiling more like.'

'All right, I miss their spoiling. And I want to go back home but I don't want Mam and Dad to think it's for selfish reasons. Can you tell them you persuaded me to go back for their sake?'

'Why make complications? Tell them you are moving back home and they'll kill the fatted calf.' She tried to hide the resentment she felt.

'Don't be like that, our Marie. I can't help it if I'm not as perfect as you!'

'I just wish you'd help me sometimes! We're in a real mess you know.'

'Most of it's your fault! Soft you are, Marie. A bit of backbone is what you need!'

'Would you like anything else, ladies?' the waitress enquired.

'Backbone and a kick up the—' Jennie hissed. The waitress straightened up, offended.

'Sorry,' Marie said. But catching sight of Jennie's unrepentant face, and hearing the whispered, 'I'm not sorry. Do her good it will, stuffy tart,' she felt a bubble of laughter working its way up her throat. Whatever Jennie's intentions had been, the result was a far more cheerful Marie returning to work that afternoon.

Someone else called to speak to her the following morning, and fortunately it was while Mr Harries was out of the shop. Geoff explained to the first sales lady that he needed to give her a message. She stood in the porch without giving him a chance to speak, assured him that everything was under control and Ivor was arranging for them to rent another house. He said nothing, just stared at her for a long time. Then, as the false smile left her lips and sadness filled her eyes, he said, 'I'll wait for you after work and we'll talk it through, right?'

'There's nothing to talk about, we'll be all right.'

'I'll be waiting and I'll drive you home. One o'clock, is it? Half day closing?'

For the rest of the morning she kept busy, finding tasks both useful and unnecessary, telling herself all the time that she wouldn't discuss the most recent events in the saga of the Masters household.

Geoff began the conversation by offering her some more decorating work, small jobs, painting a shed and a garage, but she refused. Her sister's comments, unkind though they were, about her lacking backbone, and other things she'd said in previous arguments, reminding her that she had taken responsibility from Ivor instead of making him deal with things, had made her change her mind about the importance of working to pay off Ivor's debts. Cleaning and decorating the flats had almost killed her. Jennie was right, or partly so, and although she didn't hold her sister up as an example on which to model her life, she decided not to do more than work at the shop. She would leave it to Ivor, see where it got them.

Geoff listened to her reasoning and nodded agreement. 'If you change your mind, I'll help you,' was all he said. She watched him as he drove carefully along the road. He gave her the impression he had more to say, much more.

When they reached the house, he held her arm as she prepared to alight. 'Now, Marie. I want you to tell me what happened when you waited up for Ivor to come home. I know I'm interfering and I make no apologies. If I know all the facts and you need help in the future, I'll be in a better position to give it. Nothing more than that. And what you tell me goes no further. You have my promise on that.'

'Nothing. He told me nothing. Just made useless promises, telling me I mustn't worry, that "everything will be all right".'

'Did he give any explanation for his absences?' He needed to know whether Ivor had told her about finding his father.

He listened in silence, still touching her arm as she told him everything that had happened, about the foul stench on Ivor's

149

clothes and his putting them into a bag for the dry cleaners, and his evasion when she demanded an explanation, He released her arm and said, 'Give me until tomorrow. I'll know something by then.'

'What are you going to do?'

'Find out what he's up to. Don't worry, if it's a police matter I'll talk to you before I do anything, but I doubt it's anything worse than poaching. He tried to cheer her up by adding, 'What a family. If Ivor's in trouble for poaching, he could be standing as a good character witness for your sons just before appearing in the same court accused of stealing the farmer's fish and fowl!' He was rewarded with an amused smile.

His mind was made up. He would have to threaten Ivor that he would tell Marie himself if he didn't explain. He had only seen the father's house from a distance. The outside was neglected and from Marie's description of the foul smell emanating from Ivor when he got home, presumably from visiting the place, the inside must be far worse.

Marie hurried into the house, anxious to make use of the afternoon off by clearing the bedroom drawers and packing the surplus items in tea chests borrowed for the move. Where they would be unpacked again she tried not to consider.

Geoff returned to his shop but he couldn't

concentrate on his work. It began to rain, darkening the office behind the shop. He didn't switch on the light, unaware of the gloom, his thoughts taking him far away, to a place where Ivor and Marie would be together, and the worries about her husband's dishonesty would vanish and he would become a reliable provider again. Ivor was lucky that Marie wasn't the sort to give up on a marriage. Her vows were immutable.

He sat looking through accounts, listing those overdue for payment, but the invoices didn't get written and after a while he gave up, pushed them into a drawer and closed the shop. It was earlier than planned but his intention of talking to Ivor until he persuaded him to take Marie into his confidence overrode everything else. He drove to the edge of the farmer's three-acre field, in which a small herd of cows stood staring at him with their soulful eyes. Leaning against the bonnet of the car he could just see the entrance to the wood yard and the sound of saws reached him from the work sheds. He seemed unaware of the rain as he stood, glancing at his watch from time to time, tilting his head to allow rain to spill from the brim of his trilby.

At five o'clock he moved away from the car and slipped through the hedge and across the field to a position from which he could see the office door. At five fifteen the sound of the hammering and sawing ceased. He heard doors being dragged shut and locks rattled as the place was made secure.

At twenty past five Ivor came out of the office, neatly dressed in a mackintosh, waterproof over-shoes covering his feet, and wearing a trilby. He stepped cautiously across the yard, avoiding the few puddles and the slush of wet sawdust and mud, carrying an umbrella high above his head. Geoff thought he looked a dandy, yet there was nothing about the man, with all his finicky attention to his appearance, that was effeminate. Moving with great caution, Geoff prepared to follow him. They left the area around the wood yard behind them in a procession of two, heading for the other side of the wood from where Geoff's car was parked.

At a bus shelter about a mile from the village, Ivor stopped. After looking around furtively Ivor changed his shoes for wellingtons he had previously hidden in the hedge. Geoff watched him take a battered suitcase from its hiding place deep in the trees and, removing his mackintosh and jacket, folding both with infinite care, he put them into the suitcase from which he took other clothes. He saw him put on an overall and a shabby overcoat, rather too large for him, tighten the belt to take up some of the slack and, after replacing the suitcase in the tree, walk on, head down, in a hurried, purposeful manner.

With relief, Geoff followed, thankful that the dull and wet evening discouraged the man from looking back. They left the country road, crossed fields, with Geoff holding back several times to avoid being seen. Once he thought he'd lost him, but the sound of cracking twigs helped him to relocate him easily. After about twenty minutes the path led them out and into a clearing in which a cottage stood, forlorn and apparently abandoned, as no light showed on this dark evening and no smoke issued from the chimney. Ivor went in without knocking.

Cautiously Geoff approached. He heard voices, one angry and loud, the other frail and quaking. Looking through a window he saw a scene such as he'd never imagined, even in nightmares.

The old man who sat on a chair near the empty grate was surrounded by filth. Papers of all description and what looked like stale food and empty bottles and tins were strewn around the room and the old man held his arms up as though to protect his face. He couldn't see Ivor but he could hear him shouting at the man, the words indistinct but clearly angry.

Forgetting the need for secrecy Geoff stared through the grimy window at the mess, and half imagined, half smelled the foulness of the place. The old man was saying something in reply to Ivor's tirade and, presuming he was still standing there, Geoff was startled into a shout as Ivor appeared silently behind him and shoved him angrily away from the window.

'What are you doing here? You've followed me!'

'I came to find out what was going on and to insist you tell your wife!' Shock and anger made Geoff shout as loudly as Ivor. 'What's going on?' Geoff recovered his balance and returned to stare through the window.

'Why did you follow me?' Ivor demanded. 'Did Marie ask you to?'

'She doesn't know I'm here. I had to find out what was happening that was making you change from a good husband and provider to a man who gambles to the extent that you're making your family homeless. How can rediscovering your father cause that?'

'You know?'

'Yes, but Marie doesn't and as your wife she should!'

'Are you sure she doesn't know?'

'She thinks it's another woman.'

Ivor relaxed his shoulders, his body drooping. 'Not another woman, just that dirty old man.'

'But I don't understand.'

'Look at him,' Ivor said in disgust. 'That filthy confused creature is my father. How

154

can I tell her?'

Geoff said nothing and they watched as the man inside gathered papers and a few sticks and lit the fire in the grate, the glow from the dancing flames making a mask of his lined old face. Seeing him close to, it was hard to believe in a connection between the meticulous Ivor and the dirty, pathetic old man. Then he said, 'Get help for him, Ivor. But you have to tell Marie.'

'I can't do that. The truth is, my marriage has been built on lies.'

'Now is a good time to rebuild it, this time on honesty. Marie deserves that, surely?'

Ivor shook his head. 'I can't.'

'That old man is suffering, desperately in need of help, and I don't have to tell you that your wife is suffering too. She's trying to hold everything together. How much longer are you going to wait? Is your pride worth all this misery? Will you wait until everything falls apart with no hope of rebuilding?'

There was no word from Ivor.

Geoff turned and grabbed him, glared into his face then shook him like a dog with a rat. 'You pathetic, cowardly excuse for a man.'

'I've lost her and nothing else matters.'

Geoff shook him some more and threw him against the wall of the house.

'Tell her!' he shouted.

Five

Ivor stared at Geoff, wanting to argue, searching his mind for a reason for not telling Marie, Geoff glared back defiantly. There was a lot more he could say but he didn't want to completely alienate the man and put himself in a position where he could no longer be available to help Marie. He looked at Ivor but it was Marie he was seeing.

He stared through the dirt-rimed window and saw the man was making a futile effort to gather the piles of old newspapers into some order. Resignation showed clearly in the bent shoulders and the droop of the man's head, as the untidy pile slithered slowly across the wooden floor, a waterfall of white and yellow.

'Can't we help him?' Geoff said at last, glancing at Ivor.

'I've cleared the room twice and the kitchen at least four times. But he goes out on the road, searching the ashbins, and within a day or so it's all back again. I've stayed through the night to stop him going

156

out but as soon as I leave out he goes and drags it all back in again.'

'He's sick, is he?'

'It's since my mother died. Although she wasn't much better,' Ivor added bitterly. 'Although there was no food left about, not when Mam was alive. Just papers and empty bottles and anything people put out for the ashman that she thought was worth saving, perhaps selling. Most of it didn't find a buyer and ended up in there.'

'What are you going to do? Something has to be done, he won't get better on his own. Can I do something?' There was no reply and he asked, 'Shall I go with you to the authorities?'

Ivor turned angrily then, and demanded, 'What are you doing? Sneaking around, following me.'

'Marie was worried. You should have told her.'

'What, that I was brought up in a home like this? That he's my father? I told her a load of lies. Everything I told her about my life before we met was an invention. She mustn't find out the truth.'

Geoff touched the man's shoulder and urged him to move. 'Come on, we can at least make the room safe by taking the papers away. We can get the fire going properly – there's plenty of wood around – then get him some food, find some clean

157

clothes for him.' Like a child, Ivor allowed himself to be led back into the noisome place.

'Wait,' Geoff said as they began to gather up some of the mess. 'Whether you seek help or not, I think we need a photograph of this. Come with me to get my camera.' Geoff was afraid to leave him there in case he locked the door and refused to let him in, or tidied up the worst of the filthy room. Ivor was in such a depressed state he didn't think to argue.

They were gone about an hour, Geoff driving them back in Ivor's van. The old man was exactly as they had left him, trying in vain to pick up the papers then watching as they slid back down again. Geoff took half a dozen snaps then handed the camera to Ivor. 'Is there anything you want to record?' Ivor shook his head, he seemed as unaware of what was going on as his father. Geoff hung the camera around his neck, afraid to put it down in all the filth surrounding him, and began the work of clearing up. He gathered some empty boxes, plenty of those thrown haphazardly around, and began filling them with the newspapers and books that were in untidy heaps around the floor. Ivor put a scarf around his hand and collected the half-empty food tins, and the wrappings from chips, and, with a shovel, scraped up potato peelings and other unrecognizable vegetation that had stuck to the slate floor. The man sat in the solitary armchair and watched, rocking rhythmically to a tune only he could hear.

'You have to get some help for him, Ivor,' Geoff said, when they had succeeded in creating some order, and had a fire of logs burning cheerfully in the grate. 'You can't manage this on your own.'

'Don't you understand? I can't allow people to know he's my father, that my background has been an invention.'

'I understand that you should have told Marie. She's your wife and you'll have to tell her sometime.'

Ivor took from his coat pocket a package of sandwiches, which he handed to his father. The old man stared at them as though he didn't recognize what they were. 'Eat them, damn you,' Ivor shouted, and with a jerk of alarm the man began to eat. Sometimes he spat a piece of crust into his hand and was about to drop it on to the floor, but each time he glanced at Ivor and put it back in his mouth.

Leaning against the window sill, from which they had removed several dozen milk bottles, their contents mildewed, Ivor looked at Geoff as though trying to come to a decision.

'I won't tell her, if that's what you're wondering. This has to come from you,'

Geoff said.

His mind made up, Ivor began to explain, his voice a low monotone. 'I ran away from my parents when I was twelve. I'd tried to get away several times before, but people knew me, they could smell me a mile off! I was always taken back home. I always knew I didn't belong with them. I wanted cleanliness. I wanted smart clothes and a decent place to live.

'I lied about my age and got a job in a garage, but I didn't like the dirt. I wanted clean hands, I wanted to work in a place where I could dress in smart clothes, not a pair of greasy, ill-fitting overalls that had been worn by God knows how many people before me.'

'Where did you live?' Geoff couldn't imagine how such a young boy could cope all alone.

'Rough for a while, then I shared a room with two others. I hated it. They were lazy and put up with any mess if the alternative meant doing some cleaning, but I put up with it knowing that I was managing to save a little and I wouldn't be there for ever. Then I found a position in an hotel and for the first time I found a place where my skills were valued. I was quickly promoted and was soon given the post of manager, and I found a woman who understood what I was trying to do to work as housekeeper and together we made the place shine. It became the cleanest, most smoothly run hotel you've ever seen. I made sure the staff polished and scrubbed, cleaned windows and made the brass fittings glow. I learned everything the business could teach me and left there a changed man.

'I married Marie after meeting her family and seeing how mannerly and particular they were. She gave me all I'd ever dreamed of, a clean, well-run home, and children to nurture as they should be. Time passed and although I had moments of conscience when I thought I should find out how my parents were, I never did. I tried to pretend the first twelve years of my life hadn't existed. They'd happened to someone else.'

Almost afraid to interrupt, Geoff asked quietly, 'So how did you meet up with your parents again?'

'That was the worst imaginable luck. I met someone from my school days.'

'Jenkin Jenkins?' Geoff said.

'He bullied me when we were at school, made those years a misery, and now he's turned up to ruin my life again. Do you believe that some people are bringers of bad luck? I do, and Jinks Jenkins is one of those for me. From a chance encounter with that cursed man, I learned that my mother was dead and my father was living only a few miles from me. I found him living like this.'

'So it was conscience that brought you here?'

'Morbid curiosity to begin with. A short walk intended only to allow me a peep through a window, but that moment destroyed everything I've achieved.'

'It needn't. I think Marie will be relieved. She believes you are seeing another woman.'

'She believes I'm a gambler who puts his needs before hers and the children's. She's right on both counts. I've gambled in the stupid belief that it would give me the money to see my father right and allow me to leave him again without having to tell Marie. Because of the guilt that old man revived, I've made us homeless. And in my desperation for the boys to love me, I've tried too hard to be their friend. I've covered up their foolishness. In an attempt to earn and keep their love I've made excuses for them when what they did was inexcusable. I was always on their side whatever they did, and even admired their worst behaviour, pretending it was normal for boys to behave in that foolhardy way. I've ruined everything by trying to be as unlike my parents as it's possible to be. I don't deserve Marie. She'd be better off without me.' He turned to look at Geoff and said, almost cheerfully, 'She said that once, you know, that they'd manage better without me.'

'Tell her,' Geoff urged. 'If you think there's

162

nothing to lose, tell her, take the one chance of surviving all this.'

'I can't.'

Marie was in her parents' house. The twins and Violet were with her and she was doing what her sister asked.

'Mam, why don't you ask Jennie to come home? I think she'd come if you explained how difficult it is for you with your arm weak and Dad not as fit as he was.'

'I can't ask her to give up the flat. She and Lucy are enjoying their freedom.'

'You don't stop her doing anything she wants to do. Ask her, tell her you really need her. I think she'll come.'

'You're finding it a bit much are you? Coming here at lunchtimes as well as in the evenings?'

The criticism was there as always. It didn't matter that she had a family to care for and worked at two jobs most of the time. Jennie was always the important one. Holding back a sigh, Marie said calmly, 'Mam, I'm not asking this to help me, I think you need her here.'

'But better for you, too, Marie.'

'All right, Mam, better for me too. Although, apart from the relief of knowing you and Dad have someone here at night, I don't quite see how. She's out practically every evening and at work all day, I'll still have to come, won't I? Or will you manage without me?'

'I'll leave it to your conscience, Marie,' her mother said.

Marie was watching the clock. Perhaps Ivor was home and perhaps Geoff had learned something about where he went when he returned so late. She felt a shiver of fear as she tried to imagine how she'd cope if her suspicions were true and Ivor had been meeting another woman.

'You'd better go,' her mother said. 'You've been watching the clock since you arrived.'

'I have a husband due home, wanting to be fed,' she said, forcing a smile. 'I'll just do these dishes before I go.'

Without being able to explain why, she dawdled on the way home. Darkness was throwing shadows into corners, and, apart from an occasional bicycle passing, the roads were empty. The twins played hide and seek as they strolled along, Violet hiding in alleyways and behind trees and the boys pretending not to find her so she could jump out and frighten them. They always allowed her to find them and, although she knew they were cheating, she loved it. Marie forced herself to laugh at their antics and prided herself on her acting skills as she joined in and hid in her turn, shrieking with laugher as she was found.

As they approached Hill Crescent she saw

164

that their house was in darkness. Ivor was not yet home, and there was no sign of Geoff's car. It was more than an hour after Ivor's usual time to return from work and she knew she was facing another evening of wondering.

The boys dealt with the fire as she began to prepare a meal. No meat today, just bubble and squeak: potatoes and a few vegetables boiled, mashed then fried until they were crispy. She had three eggs, so the children and she would have half each and Ivor – if he came home – would have a whole one.

They had just finished eating when she heard the kitchen door opening. Ivor appeared, neatly dressed, his hair combed and his skin glowing. She felt a yearning of love for him, startling in its intensity. His handsome face made her forget all their problems as she looked at him, and saw the real Ivor returned, come home to solve all their problems. She wanted to run to him, feel his arms around her, hear him saying he loved her and only her.

'Hello, Marie,' he said, and then as Geoff appeared behind him and echoed the words she felt her spirits drop and a painful disappointment overwhelm her. 'What's happened?' she asked in dread.

'Boys,' Ivor said, 'take Violet in the living room and play a game of Ludo, will you? Your Mam and I have something private

165

to discuss.'

Marie sank into a chair as Ivor began. Behind the door, the boys listened.

'I've been lying to you, from the moment we first met,' Ivor began. 'I wasn't brought up in a children's home and I'm not an orphan.'

'I don't understand—'

'Let him tell it his way,' Geoff said, touching her arm, gripping it to show her she had his support.

'I ran away from a disgusting home and made my own way, and I'd almost convinced myself the life I'd invented was the true one.'

With a few encouraging words from Geoff he told her everything.

'So the gambling was to try and help your father? Why didn't you tell me?' Marie couldn't take in all he was telling her, the strongest reaction was his being unable to confide in her.

'There's nothing to be done about this house, but I wondered whether we could move in with my father,' he said.

Geoff gasped. 'You're crazy to imagine living there!'

'I have to get help, I know that. I should have done something sooner. But I kept hoping I'd be able to get him straight then walk away. That isn't going to happen.'

'I want to see him,' Marie said.

'I don't want you to,' he said quickly.

166

'That's why I couldn't tell you any of this. Why I've been trying to sort it without you knowing.'

Breaking off to get the children to bed, they then continued to talk until the early hours of the morning. Marie was frustrated by her lack of knowledge. Until she had met Ivor's father and saw for herself how he was living, she couldn't marshal any plan, form any ideas of how to proceed.

'Tomorrow I'll phone the shop and tell them I'm sick. I'm going to visit your father and if you won't come with me I'll go alone,' was Marie's final word as Geoff stood to leave.

'Geoff, wait for me,' Ivor called and, grabbing his overcoat and hastily discarding slippers in favour of slip-on shoes, he hurried after him. If he heard Marie pleading for him not to go, he ignored her.

An hour later he still hadn't returned and Marie sat at the kitchen table, wide awake, convinced that the fault lay with her. She must be unapproachable, too difficult for Ivor to talk to when he met trouble. Had her sister been right when she said a man didn't want a capable woman, but someone who made him feel needed? Would she have been better to leave it to him and hope that he would miraculously find a solution? Even with her new knowledge she found that hard to believe.

★ ★ ★

Geoff and Ivor returned to the house, and while the old man slept they carried away as much as the van would hold and took it to the council tip. They threw the rubbish out and went back for more. As dawn broke they were returning from their fifth load, and a solitary figure was already walking across the chaotic wasteland to see what they had left, perhaps hoping for some wood to mend a fence and maybe a half-full tin of paint to decorate it.

At the lonely house, Ivor's father still slept. Geoff left Ivor there washing the slate floor with water and a brush he kept in the van and went to find some food. They wanted the place to look as clean as possible before Marie saw it. The saddest thing was that once the rubbish had gone and the floor washed with water, bucket after bucket swishing away the dirt and smells, there was nothing there apart from the mattress on which the old man was sleeping, and one greasy, food-stained armchair.

'At least there's plenty of room for your furniture,' Geoff said. It was seven o'clock when he came back holding a paper carrier filled with food.

The kitchen was empty apart from an oven range that was red with rust and a large sink. Making do with the carrier bag as a tray, they set out the vacuum flask of hot tea and bread rolls, still warm, from the bakers. Geoff had brought his cheese ration and a scraping of margarine and when the old man woke they set it before him.

Looking at Geoff, he rolled his eyes and shook his head, pushing away the food. 'Eat it!' Ivor snapped, and, giving that jerk of fear, the man began to eat.

Now it was light enough to see clearly, Geoff went upstairs to bring down the first of the rubbish from the bedroom, while Ivor stood over his father in a threatening pose as the food disappeared.

The wide blue eyes, so like his own, watched him, and then he seemed to notice the empty room for the first time and the eyes showed dismay, tears filling them. 'Where's it gone, boy? Now I'll have to start all over again. I can't stand it empty, see. I can't stand the loneliness of an empty room.'

'Where did the furniture go?' Ivor asked.

'Sold it.'

'You shouldn't have done that.'

'Had to, didn't I? How else was I to pay for medicine for your Mam, eh? Tell me that.'

At seven thirty Ivor left his father, after threatening him with 'trouble', unspecified, if he so much as moved, and went in the van with Geoff to fetch Marie.

Geoff dropped them off then left them, promising to come at lunchtime with some chips and another flask. They needed time

169

together to deal with this and he needed to open the shop.

Marie, having heard such a disjointed explanation of Ivor's behaviour, expected to be afraid when she entered the house, but she wasn't.

It had a smell reminiscent of the stink Ivor had brought home with him when things had gone wrong, but there was also a smell of dampness, clean water and fresh air. All the doors and windows were open and the empty kitchen and living room contained nothing sinister.

There was no sign of his father, and Ivor told Marie to wait there while he ran upstairs to find him. Most of the rubbish had now been moved from the bedrooms, and he found his father sitting on his mattress in the back room.

He knew from his limited experience that the only way to persuade his father to do what he asked was to shout. 'Downstairs. Now,' he said, and he pulled at both of his hands, heaved him up off the mattress and guided him down the stairs, alarmed at how little weight there was in that frail body.

'Marie,' he called, softly. 'Come and meet your father-in-law.'

Marie stood frozen with shock at the sight of the old man. Emaciated and shivering with fear as he was, she couldn't face touching him, even though her heart went out to

170

him. 'How do you do' seemed a ridiculous thing to say and 'pleased to meet you' was even worse. Compassion for the frightened old man went hand in hand with curiosity, and the knowledge that this dirty creature had all but ruined their lives. She acknowledged the introduction with a slight nod, and went to stand closer to Ivor.

'I'll go back and get some cleaning things, shall I?' she said finally, when the silence became oppressive.

'No, that's my job,' Ivor said.

She touched his arm and said softly, 'The responsibility is for us both.'

'You should get to work. They'll be wondering.'

'Not today. Today is for you and your father.'

'Where's our Marie?' Jennie called as she ran into her parents' house. 'She's not at the shop and old Harries said she's ill. I went to the house but she isn't there. What on earth has happened, our Mam?'

'I don't know,' Belle complained. 'I managed to make a sandwich for our lunch, but I don't know what to do about dinner if she doesn't come this evening.' She touched her injured arm. 'I can't even peel a potato, this is still so painful, and your father's worse than useless. Where is she? She knows I need help.'

'Could something have happened to her?' Jennie asked. 'She's always here at lunchtime.'

'What are you doing home?' her mother asked. 'You usually eat at the flat, don't you?'

'We've run out of everything. There's no time to shop, working all day like we do, and the shops closed at the same times as ours.'

'Make yourself a piece of toast. I've saved a bit of butter in case you called, and there's some jam after that if you're still hungry.' With only two ounces of butter to last a person for a week, it was unheard of to waste it by smothering it with jam. Belle looked at her daughter and wondered whether Marie had been right and she would be willing to come home. The house was so quiet without her. She made a pot of tea and carried the china and the teapot in separately, her arm still causing a little discomfort. As she poured, she watched as Jennie finished the second slice of buttered toast and begin to spread jam on a third.

'That was good,' Jennie mumbled as she finished the crust.

'I don't think you're getting enough to eat, dear.'

'Of course I am, we manage all right. Neither of us is as good a cook as you are, mind. We fill up on bread and scrape. Stale bread toasted mostly. It's the rationing, it's so miserable, a couple of ounces of this, that

172

and the other, not enough of anything to make a meal. I don't know how you've managed all these years, I really don't.'

'Why don't you come home?'

'I couldn't let Lucy down, Mam.'

'Isn't she getting married soon?'

'Well, yes. But I'll cope until I can find someone else to share with.'

'Of course you will, dear, but you don't have to. And we miss you, Dad and I. We'd love it if you came home. Think about it, will you?'

Hiding her relief, Jennie agreed that she would.

Hurrying from the house, Jennie was heading back to the hairdresser's shop but she met Bill at the corner and he asked why she was rushing.

'It's almost a quarter past two, we have an appointment for a perm. We have to get those started early or we don't leave on time.'

'Going somewhere special?'

'I might be.' She couldn't resist mentioning his father. 'Mr James has taken an interest in dancing and we sometimes go together. I'll let him know that there's a dance on at the church hall and he might come.'

'The church hall? That's a bit lowly for the old man.'

'Don't call him that.'

'Isn't that how you think of him?'

'No, it isn't. He's kind and very interesting and I enjoy his company very much.'

'You wouldn't prefer someone your own age?' He was walking beside her and he caught hold of her arm and pulled her round to face him. 'Like me for instance?'

'I doubt whether you can give me a better time.'

'Try me. Forget the twopenny hop in the church hall and come out with me.'

'Where?'

'I don't know. Meet me at seven and we'll decide. Better still, I'll meet you at your place. You've got a flat haven't you? Sophisticated woman, with a place of her own.'

She didn't say no. But she didn't say yes, either, as she explained to Lucy when they had a chance to talk. 'I can choose to be there when he calls or you and I can be "not at home". What d'you think I should do?'

'He's rather nice looking, but I don't think he'll be as gentlemanly as his father.'

'You think he'll try it on? Rubbish. I can look after myself.'

'Don't ask him into the flat, then. He might take that as an invitation. The doorstep is as far as he should go.'

Jennie laughed at her. 'Really, Lucy, sophisticated women of the world we are, with a flat of our own. We can't act like scared kids.'

'Kids is what we are in spite of being twenty-eight. A few weeks of independence and we're running back to Mam.' Lucy smiled to take the edge of disappointment from her words.

After talking to her father-in-law for a few hours, Marie said she thought he wasn't suffering from a serious mental illness, he was just grieving. 'Grief shows itself in many ways,' she told Ivor, 'and with care, the right kind of help, he'll recover, I'm sure of it.'

She wasn't sure. In fact, she had no experience of such distraught behaviour, but this wasn't the time to admit that. Both Ivor and his father needed reassurance, strength, the belief that all would be well.

Ivor nodded agreement but knew her opinion was far from the truth. His childhood had taught him this wasn't evidence of grief. The obsession with filling the house with other people's rubbish was only a part of it. Barricading himself in was another of his father's delightful habits. The reason they had lost their home on several occasions, though, was far more worrying. At least the other – far more devastating – problems had been with his mother, and she was dead. He felt no shame at his lack of grief. With his father it was possible for there to be a happy outcome, with his mother there would have been no chance at all.

Within two days the old man, who insisted Geoff and Marie call him Rhodri, was in hospital, and after a few examinations the hospital decided to keep him there for a few weeks, to feed him up and allow him to get to know his son and daughter-in-law. They had been told an edited version of the truth. Ivor had made the excuse of the war separating them. His story was easily believed as the bombing and moving from one place to another had caused many hundreds of families to lose touch with one another.

Marie and Ivor went every day to see his father and the doctors told them that Rhodri was confused, his mind sometimes going back to a situation about which he refused to talk. 'Can you think of any traumatic event that might account for it? Did he serve in the first war?' Ivor shook his head. How could he admit that since he'd been old enough to think his only interest in his father was how soon he could get away from him? 'Until we can persuade him to talk, we must presume his mental state, his confusion, has been exacerbated by malnutrition, grief, loneliness and an understandable inability to cope. He's a sad old man and he needs loving care.'

Marie promised he would have all the care and love he needed. Glancing at Ivor expecting agreement she saw disappointment. Realizing how the embarrassment at his lies must have affected him, she squeezed his hand and whispered, 'We'll cope.' There was no returning pressure and when she let go of his hand it fell into his lap like a dead thing.

When the doctor suggested that a home might be the answer Marie and Ivor spoke at the same time, but Marie shook her head in protest, Ivor nodded agreement. The doctor noted the difference of opinion but Marie said, 'I could never allow my parents to be cared for by strangers and I feel the same about Ivor's father.' Aware of the silence from Ivor, who had hoped this would be the end of a miserable time, she couldn't condone him abandoning the poor sick old man.

The house that had been so filthy surprisingly needed very little to make it liveable. It had been Marie's idea, and Ivor and a willing Geoff painted the walls and scrubbed and varnished the floorboards upstairs, papered the walls and scoured the slate floors downstairs. They refused to allow Marie to help, insisting that her job was packing in preparation for the move. From time to time she went to check on their progress, taking measurements to ensure that the curtains they had would fit.

When Geoff cleaned the small back bedroom, he noticed signs of burning on the floorboards. He said nothing; it was possible the confused old man had brought something burning up there in the hope of keeping warm. When the floor was painted, the stain was hardly visible and there was only a shallow depression in the floorboards to show where it had been.

A second-hand shop provided a few rugs and some thick curtains for the living room, their only expenditure apart from fuel. The coal man delivered their allotment of coal into the coal house outside and they bought two loads of logs from a farmer. Unhappily, but with no alternative, Marie paid for them with the money she had earned decorating the flats to pay off their arrears and handed to Geoff for safe keeping. Their debts would have to wait.

She handed the papers relating to the arrears to Ivor.

'I will pay this,' he promised.

'*We* will,' she emphasized.

He just looked at her with huge, sad blue eyes and said, 'Thank you.'

His thanks gave her an uneasy feeling. Spoken like a stranger. All their conversations were like that now, formal, polite, with no indication of the love they had shared.

On the day of their move, Roger and Royston, with a willing and very excited Violet as their assistant, shovelled the coal left at the old house and wheelbarrowed it to the new. They got dirtier and dirtier and even Ivor made no comment. They would be cleaned up at bed time and there was no way to get this day over without getting in a mess.

Neighbours stood in doorways and watched as load after load of their possessions was taken to the new address, Ivor and Marie turning away in embarrassment when something fell from the hastily packed vehicles. At the new address there were other people doing the same outside the few cottages dotted along the lane, watching with undisguised curiosity.

Marie hated that more than anything else, the disapproval and the gossip, people whom she had thought of as friends staring at the items that made up her home as they were dragged out of the house to which they no longer had any right. As Violet rode on top of the last load on the fruit and veg seller's pony and cart, singing happily, Marie, unpacking as the goods arrived, met her first problem.

There was no bathroom – which she had expected – and there was cold water from the solitary tap in the kitchen, but apart from the fire there was no facility for heating it. So far they had used cold, with a kettle boiled on the fire being sufficient for their needs. How was she going to keep them all clean?

Geoff solved the problem by finding a neglected but usable boiler in an outhouse that had not been cleared of the seemingly endless rubbish collected by Rhodri Masters. Marie had brought the long galvanized bath, so, with the boys organized into gathering wood for the fire underneath the boiler, the hot water supply was another difficulty sorted. Geoff also managed to find them a gas cooker, which he had fitted into the large kitchen.

Their belongings looked pathetic, boxed and packed or thrown into untidy piles. The removal had shown up the tattiness of many of their possessions. The six years of war and the years of austerity that followed had meant never replacing things that had worn out. Carpets with a hole worn in the middle had been given extra life by an oval of linoleum placed over the weak spot. Curtains had pieces added to the bottom to disguise the frayed ends. Chair and settee cushions had been covered with oddments of material to hide their worn state. Taking it out and putting it on to the removal van and the farmer's cart had revealed everything in all its shabbiness. Only the few decent items of furniture she had bought when she had married Kenneth stood out. And these she had carefully wrapped with blankets to protect them, so the best pieces weren't on view.

Jennie seemed unaware of her sister's situation, or at least the thought of offering help had not occurred to her. When seven o'clock

Saturday evening came, she was in the flat waiting for Bill to call. Since that first date, when he had taken her to a dance in a rather grand hotel in a nearby town, they had met twice more, each time going far away from Cwm Derw. Nothing was said to Mr James, and if he was aware of his son's friendship with Jennie he chose to ignore it. With Bill's flattering attentions and his generosity regarding small gifts and endless treats, Jennie began to feel confident in the relationship developing into something more exciting.

'Why is it a secret?' Lucy wanted to know. 'If he really likes you then why does he hide you away?'

'It's not like that. He comes to the flat to pick me up and once I'm living back home it'll be different. He'll hardly expect me to wait for him out on a street corner, will he? He'll have to come in then, won't he? Meet Mam and Dad, and it will all be out in the open.'

Lucy had her doubts but Jennie put them down to jealousy. Lucy's boyfriend was due to leave the RAF soon and so far he hadn't mentioned a thing about their getting married. 'I might be walking up the aisle before you,' she said, unaware of Lucy's hurt reaction. 'Or we could have a double wedding. Wouldn't that be fun?'

'Don't count your chickens before they're hatched!'

This Saturday evening she had dressed with care. Perhaps Lucy was right and she ought to make their courtship public. His kisses were becoming more demanding, and although she had never given in to a man she knew that it wouldn't be easy to resist him for much longer, especially if he was offering a ring. Perhaps a few gentle hints might do the trick. Lucy was right, it wasn't usual to be wary about meeting friends.

To her surprise, instead of calling with his father's car, tooting the horn and waiting for her to run out, he knocked the door and at once caught hold of her and kissed her, pushing her back into the living room. Flattered at first, Jennie began to be a little nervous. Lucy was out visiting her future parents-in-law and wouldn't be back for hours. Bill was strong and she knew that if he tried to force himself on her she stood no chance.

She wriggled out of his embrace and headed for the door but he grabbed her and began kissing her again. This time the kisses were not pleasant, they didn't do delicious things to her body, they created panic. Afraid now, she pushed him away and shouted loudly for him to leave. At least Mrs Roberts upstairs might come down and complain, giving her the chance to get away.

He was persistent and she felt herself weakening, she couldn't fight him off much longer She felt increasingly vulnerable, so when an opportunity offered she bit him, her teeth pressing into his chin until he shouted with pain and pushed her away. She ran to the door and fled into the night.

Tearfully she ran to the bus stop. She had to get home to Mam and Dad. She wouldn't be able to tell them what had happened, but explaining that she wasn't well would be enough to have them fussing over her.

Before the bus came, she heard Bill shouting after her.

'There are names for women like you. Flirting, teasing, giving the come-on then backing away like an innocent. I don't know why I wasted my time on you.'

What had she done that he could treat her like this? A bit of flirting, that's all, a bit of fun. It crossed her mind that he might be dangerous. One fiancée had vanished without a word and two others had ended up dead. She began to imagine him pushing her in front of the bus when it came, and she began to scream. When the bus hoved into view and he moved away from her she cried out in relief. He disappeared into the shadows and she climbed on to the platform like a woman saved from drowning.

Over the weeks since the discovery of his father living in such poverty, Marie was increasingly aware of another change in Ivor.

The man she had married, the confident, loving and caring family man, had disappeared a few months before. He had changed into an inconsiderate stranger. Now he had changed again.

He spoke to the children lovingly, but to her he addressed hardly a word. He answered politely when a reply was necessary but added nothing to reveal his thoughts or opinions. He went to work and came home, did what was needed without complaint, but seemed lost in his own thoughts. He seemed unwilling to participate in family life or the rebuilding of their home. Nothing she said could persuade him back.

Once they were in and they had all settled into the routine of coming and going from their new address, and life seemed to show hope of a return to normal, Geoff no longer came. He was aware of the difficulties Ivor faced now his secret life had been discovered and understood they needed time together to adjust.

News of the discovery of the old man living in the filthy house got out, as the deepest secrets always will. It spread from previous neighbours only too willing to talk about their shameful exodus from their home and the re-emergence of the forgotten old man.

Gossip about Marie and Ivor hummed in every tea shop in the town, the children at Violet's school jeered at her for having a potty grandfather, as children will, and the twins faced both humorous and unkind remarks as they served customers in the chip shop and the wholesale fruit and vegetable store. The pain of it ate at Ivor and he seemed to shrink from the shame.

Meanwhile, helped by a caring nursing staff, visited regularly by his son and daughter-in-law, Rhodri Masters made spasmodic progress. Often he seemed unaware of where he was and who the people visiting him were, but other days he was lucid and pleased to see them. Marie hoped that once he had fully recovered, then Ivor, too, would be able to hold up his head and, instead of being tortured by guilt, would accept praise for rescuing the old man whom everyone else had forgotten.

The weather became a serious problem as Christmas approached. Snow settled in great drifts and ice caused accidents and held up deliveries. Fuel was scarce and in many places factories closed for the lack of it.

The snow showed no signs of stopping. Every morning people were woken by the sound of scraping shovels as workmen and householders struggled to clear the overnight falls. Marie found it impossible to get home at lunchtime, so they took sandwiches and hoped for a quick thaw.

The court case was held in January and the

185

twins were given a fine and time to pay. The light sentence was down to two reasons. Firstly a plea by the record shop owner from whom they had stolen, who insisted that with their family trouble, they had been temporarily distraught but had learned their lesson and were unlikely to re-offend. Everyone in the town had heard various versions of the neglect of the old man and his subsequent rescue, and the murmurs of both approval and derision echoed around the court. The second point in their favour that day was the contentment of the magistrate, whose wife had recently returned from a long visit to her mother and who was therefore in a mood to be lenient.

As they left the court, with the forms signed and promises made, Marie was relieved. She turned to Ivor to tell him that this was their fresh start, a new and happy beginning, but he wasn't there. He was hurrying towards the railway station heading for Swansea in South Wales, where they had once spent a happy holiday.

The realization that he had left them there came slowly to Marie. Seeing the children on to a bus to take them home, she waited until the small crowd around the court had dispersed and, when there was no sign of him, walked around the area, rushing as she came to each corner, convinced she would see him there. After an hour she went home.

All evening she waited, opening the door from time to time and standing in the cold darkness, listening, hoping for the sound of his quick footsteps. Frost glistened on the trees cementing the remnants of the most recent snow fall to their branches. Violet slept, grasping a book she had hoped Ivor would read to her; the twins went to bed, disappointed not to be able to talk to him about the events of the day. Still Marie waited, determined to be there when he came in, to offer food and a loving welcome. With all their worries behind them, surely it was time for each other they needed now?

It wasn't until she went upstairs to turn down the bedcovers that she found a note, telling her he was going away for a while, to think things out. He assured her that he loved her and the children, but at the moment couldn't face what he had put them through.

'Ivor,' she said aloud, 'why can't you talk to me?'

She told her parents what had happened, and they offered sympathy tempered with the usual hint of criticism. 'Are you sure some of the fault isn't with you, Marie? Ivor's always seemed such a decent man and he did what he could for his father when he found him. A less honourable man would have walked away.'

Jennie was upset and wouldn't explain

187

why. Safely ensconced in her parents' care she seemed unwilling to go out apart from to work and even then she called for Lucy to walk with her. She went into the hairdresser's shop with her friend, afraid of coming face to face with Bill when she was alone.

'Whatever her problem was, it can't be as desperate as mine,' Marie said to her father one day.

'I know that, Marie, and so does your mother, but Jennie is such a butterfly. She can't cope like you.'

Not for the first time, Marie wished she had been the helpless kind, it got you out of doing a great many things you didn't want to do.

Jennie went to Mr James a few days after her last date with Bill. Having refused his most recent invitations she had to make up an excuse. She needed to know he was still a friend. 'It's Mam, Mr James,' she began. 'Since she broke her arm she's afraid for me to go out at night. It's why I've decided to leave the flat,' she lied. 'I know Dad's there, but he can't look after her like I can. And our Marie's got a lot on her plate. That's why I refused your kind invitations. I didn't want you to think I didn't enjoy our little outings because I did, very much.' She gave him her practised 'shy' look. 'You're very good company, Mr James, really you are.'

'All right,' Mr James said, 'we'll go out on Wednesday afternoon. Alter any appointments that will make you late and we'll go for a drive and have dinner somewhere.'

She looked prettily hesitant. 'But Mam—'

'We'll be back before evening so your mother won't be worried,' he promised, patting her hand.

The afternoon was a success. He drove her to Swansea and to the small village of Mumbles where they walked along the cliff path and visited a castle that she learned was called Oystermouth. They ate in Swansea and she told Ernie about the mysterious events in the life of her sister.

'Any man fortunate enough to marry you would never want to leave,' he said, and there was a seriousness about the way the words were spoken that made her wonder whether a life with Bill's father might not be a good way of paying Bill back for humiliating her. Besides insisting that she call him Ernest, he kissed her gently when they parted. She managed to look coy and even felt a faint blush rise in her cheeks. She hoped Bill would be upset when his father told him where they had been. He had hurt her badly but it wouldn't happen again and she might have the last laugh.

One morning Marie received some money

with a brief note from Ivor promising to send more when he could. She examined the envelope, with a South Wales postmark across the stamp. What was he playing at? Why didn't he just come home?

She discussed it with Geoff, wondering where he was and who he was with, and Marie asked herself time and again why he didn't come home. She blamed herself for his inability to talk to her, she believed she had failed him and it was eating her up with guilt.

Through the wintry weeks that followed, the one-sided contact continued, other gifts of money arrived without a regular pattern, without an address and no clue apart from the South Wales postmark. Marie put the money into a bank account and determined that one day she would go to Swansea and find him, bring him back to where he belonged.

The harsh weather dragged on and people were unrecognizable even to their best friends as they wrapped themselves up in extra clothing, wore wellingtons or put old socks over their shoes to stop them from slipping. Marie still couldn't get home to get lunch for the twins and Violet and instead they met in the basement of the dress shop – a concession by Mr Harries that he sternly reminded them wouldn't continue once the weather eased, and ate sandwiches and drank metallic-tasting tea from a flask.

The children didn't mind the snow. Eating a sort of picnic in the basement of the dress shop was a novelty, something to boast about to their friends, and the walk home, all together, made a pleasant ending to the day.

Rhodri's health continued to improve and he was allowed home to the now neat and comfortable house for several days each week. With plenty of kindling in the woods close by he had a fire roaring a welcome for them each evening and the house was cosy and warm. He enjoyed the fun provided by the snow, cheering as other children began to include the twins in their games.

He mimed throwing from inside the house as one or other of the boys pelted snowballs, laughing when they reached their target, booing soundlessly from behind the window pane when they did not.

During these raw days when it was agony to be out in the cold for long, the house was a welcoming refuge.

They moved the couch and chairs close to the fire and ate their meal from trays, the rest of the house being so cold. Going to bed was a mad dash from the embers of the fire up the icy staircase and a jump into bed to hug a hot water bottle, feet snug in bed-socks. Coats were thrown over the top of the beds for extra warmth, and Violet learned to put her clean underclothes under the covers with her so they would be warm to put on. Every morning ice decorated the inside of the bedroom windows with frond-like patterns that were beautiful but which few paused to admire.

In March the hospital decided that Rhodri was well enough to leave permanently, and Marie made a room ready for him. He was pale but otherwise he looked well for his sixty-six years. Conversations were sometimes vague but as he grew stronger he began to take an interest in the garden and took great pleasure, when the weather allowed, in untangling the muddle of old, dead bushes, trying to turn soil too ice-bound to succumb to the fork and murmuring about his plans for the spring.

It was as he worked near the front fence, now fallen and overgrown, that he found the house sign. He called for Marie, who went running, thinking he might be hurt, and showed her the name. 'It's called Badgers Brook. I'd forgotten, but that's its name. We live in Badgers Brook!'

Marie helped Rhodri to drag the sign into the shed and found paint to restore it. Finding the name opened a door in Rhodri's mind and he took her and the children into the wood and showed them the huge mound of earth that was a badger sett. He followed a narrow path and pointed out the coarse hairs caught in the barbed wire that revealed the presence of the shy animals and told them of times when he and Ivor's mother used to sit watching a family of them leaving on their evening search for food. Marie felt a contentment that seemed to spring from the walls of the house, enveloping them. If she could have word to tell her where Ivor was, life would be perfect.

Rhodri was still odd at times, lost in a world of his own. Twice she had found him throwing so much wood on the fire that it was falling out and on the verge of setting fire to the rug. On another occasion she found him struggling to haul large branches through the garden to pile up on the lawn.

'Thank you, Rhodri. If we can saw and chop that lot, we'll have fuel for the rest of the winter.' It was piled very high and much of it was useless, thin and brittle, and would not give more than a short bright blaze. 'What about finding some good thick pieces? I'm sure Roger and Royston would saw it into logs for us.'

Thinking that by suggesting wood gathering she had given him something to do during the hours they were all out of the house, she was startled to come home to find the whole lot burned, and neighbours throwing water on to the wooden shed that housed the boiler.

'Don't blame Roger and Royston, Marie,' he said anxiously. 'They love a bit of a blaze.

193

We must remember they're no more than boys still.' He pointed a blackened finger towards Violet. 'And she loved it, just look at her face.'

'Why would I blame the boys?' Marie asked. 'They've just come home, with me and Violet. We've been out all day. How could I think they did this?'

'I'm not saying,' Rhodri said, touching his nose as though holding back a secret.

'This mustn't happen again,' she warned. 'If you have a bonfire it has to be when we're all here so we can make sure it's safe. If the doctor found out he might not let you stay with us.'

Again Rhodri put a finger to his nose, implying it was their secret.

As spring approached the house and garden were slowly being cleared of neglect. With her skill at decorating, Marie painted walls and woodwork and Geoff repaired a couple of windows that were worn where the paint had fallen away. Neighbours called with small gifts, sometimes a few offerings from their winter gardens, or a few eggs. Some called just for a chat and a cup of tea, friends visited to see the children.

'The house is friendly and seemed to want to be filled with people,' Marie told Geoff one day. 'I know that sounds foolish, but that's how I feel. There's a pleasant atmosphere there. People love to call and sit for a while. Old and young find it peaceful.'

Geoff thought the peaceful atmosphere came from her but declined to say so. She was a natural homemaker and wherever she had settled the home she built would have been welcoming and warm with love. He was tempted to wish he could share it but knew the time was not right, perhaps it never would be.

'And Rhodri?'

'He's a bit odd at times but he's very happy. And he loves the children.' She didn't mention the dangerous fire he had created.

'I see you've made a start on the garden,' he said one day, when he called with some chopped firewood for them. The worst of the neglected plants had been cut down and around the windows, rich earth was showing in semicircles that Marie planned to fill with geraniums with a border of lobelia and alyssum.

'Like the parks,' she said disparagingly. 'I can't think of how else to fill the beds and give a display all summer. I wish I knew more.'

'It will be perfect,' he said, thinking of starting to grow a collection of annuals for her to assure her of a good display. He wasn't a gardener, but he could see that an interest in growing things would be beneficial to Marie, helping to take her mind away from wondering where Ivor had gone.

She had lost weight, and although she no longer filled her evenings with painting and decorating she was still under a lot of pressure. Taking responsibility for Rhodri was not an easy task. Beside the constant worry about Ivor, there was her job as well as running the home and looking after four other people. It was all taking its toll.

'Do you fancy coming out one evening?' Geoff asked at the end of March. 'There are a few good films on and we could have tea first, or supper afterwards if you like. The boys and Violet will be there to look after Rhodri.'

'Rhodri can look after himself,' a voice called, and her father-in-law came into the kitchen smiling. 'You go, Marie. It's time you had a little treat. We'll be fine here.'

Straight from the shop at five thirty Geoff met her and took her to a café for tea. It was as he was helping her on with her coat when they stood up to leave that his fingers touched her neck as he eased her hair from her collar, and she felt a moment of guilty pleasure that ruined the evening.

She sat as far away from him as possible, stretching once or twice to accept one of the sweets he had brought, and when the film ended she stood up quickly and pushed her way out, putting several people between them, creating a distance as though imagining Ivor standing there watching her.

'Did you enjoy it?' Geoff asked anxiously. 'I hope so. I thought we might do it again some time.'

'Sorry, Geoff, but I feel like a traitor enjoying myself, not knowing how Ivor is living. Does that make any sense?'

'Of course it does. Next time we'll take Violet as well, shall we?'

He was so kind and understanding and she wanted to hug him and tell him so, but that would have been worse than sitting close to share his sweets and enjoying the experience. She knew that given different circumstances she would have enjoyed the evening, cuddling up to Geoff, glorying in his devotion and strength. The tantalizing promise of his love was there, but she was bound to Ivor, who had left her to cope alone. Why was her life such a mess, while Jennie sailed through smiling, enjoying herself, being forgiven for any stupidity or unkindness?

Jennie had confided in her and described the distressing date with Bill, although she didn't tell her sister of his accusations. She had told her about the revival of her friendship with his father, which seemed to offer Jennie a life of wealth, comfort, position and even more pampering. We must have been born under different stars, Marie thought as she climbed the stairs to her lonely bed.

Six

Jennie and Lucy went back to their parents. Lucy was rather disappointed – having been treating the flat-sharing as a practice for when she ran a home for her husband – but eventually she gave in to Jennie's persuasions not to look for somewhere else to practice their independence.

'What worries me, Luce,' Jennie confessed, as they gathered the last of their possessions into boxes, watched by a suspicious landlady, 'is I often think of getting married one day and having a home of my own, but after a few weeks here I can't see me managing to look after it. I'd hate all that routine of boring jobs Mam has to do. I'll have to find someone very rich.'

'I wouldn't worry, most people start in two rooms, like Gerald and I will, or sometimes sharing the house with your parents. There won't be much to do, not until you move into something bigger, when you have a child.'

'A child?' Jennie gave a shuddering sigh, the prospect clearly horrifying. 'Oh, I don't think I could cope with a child. Our Marie's three are enough to put me off motherhood.'

'You'll be lucky to find someone who's rich *and* doesn't want to start building a family.'

'A family? You mean more than one?' She exaggerated the look of horror on her face. 'That's it, I'll stay fancy free for ever.'

'We're heading for the dreaded thirty now, mind,' Lucy warned, trying to hide a smile. 'And the fancy-free bit doesn't last much longer than this. I'll be glad to marry Gerald.'

'And have children?' Jennie was still pulling faces to make her friend laugh but Lucy remained serious.

'Oh yes, if it isn't too late. One or two. There's no point in anything unless there are children.'

'Who told you that yarn?' Jennie shook her finger. 'Blackmail, that's what that is. Or a great big confidence trick, like someone bathing in the sea, blue all over, shivering fit to fall to pieces and saying "It's lovely, you must come in!"'

Jennie rarely mentioned the prospect of Lucy marrying her Gerald. Apart from Lucy's visits to his parents and an occasional letter, there was no evidence he was ever going to name the day. Lucy had been waiting for him to decide for six years. She saw the unhappiness in her friend's eyes and regretted her remarks. A mention of children

199

was something to avoid in future, even in jest.

A taxi came to take them to their separate homes and they both looked back with dismay at the failure of their brief flight to freedom. Lucy was dropped off first and she paid her share of the taxi, then Jennie began to work up sobs and a tearful countenance, ready to be greeted by her mother's open arms. The taxi driver saw her and turned slightly to ask, 'Is there something wrong, miss?'

'No, there isn't!' she snapped, with no sign of the tearful performance she was preparing. 'Mind your business and keep your eyes on the road, why don't you!'

It was seven o'clock on a Friday evening, and to her dismay she saw her sister standing beside her mother when the door opened. Disapproval was a constant feature of Marie's face these days, she thought. Behind them her father waved a welcome. She grabbed her shoulder bag and ran past them indoors, tears in her eyes and distress on her face, her mother following, leaving Marie and her father to bring in the rest of the boxes and pay the driver.

'Jennie, love?' her father called, as he walked into the hallway, where a sad Belle was staring up the stairs.

'Leave her a minute or two,' Belle said. 'Upset she is, anyone can see that. She was

200

so enjoying having a place of her own.'

Marie said nothing.

When Jennie had calmed down from her self-imposed tearful state, she sat warming her hands on the cup of tea Marie had made and said sadly, 'I feel so let down by Lucy, Mam. We were doing fine but she wanted to go back where she could save a bit more money ready for her wedding to boring old Gerald.'

'It wasn't that looking after yourself was too much for you?' Marie said innocently, unable to resist some gentle teasing. 'I thought it was you who'd had enough.'

'Hush, Marie,' Belle scolded. 'Lucy would say that.' She patted Jennie's arm, glared at Marie and went out to attend to the meal.

''Specially if it were true!' Marie muttered, grinning at Jennie. Their parents came back having dealt with the meal and stored the boxes of Jennie's belongings in her room, and Marie said soothingly, 'Mam and Dad are so pleased to have you back and I'm sure it's for the best, Jennie.' Playing Jennie's game was a way of life. She caught her sister's eye and saw laughter there. Marie was smiling as she went home to her family.

Although it was a relief to settle back into the comfort of home, Jennie knew she had to do something to get away, before she was trapped into the situation she had always dreaded, that of being the dutiful daughter staying home and looking after Mam and Dad for the rest of their life and most of her own.

Bill James would have been no great catch, working on the railway and with no ambition to rise higher than a ticket clerk. Who did he think he was, treating her so badly? She had convinced herself she'd had a lucky escape, although she was still hurt at the way he had humiliated her. Being Jennie, she tried to plan a revenge in which humour was stronger than resentment. She needed to do something to give herself and Lucy a good laugh.

If she could find someone both good looking and rich she'd make him jealous and it would be she having the last laugh if he recognized what he'd missed. He'd regret reducing her to a terrified wreck with his demands and accusations.

'Who do we know who's handsome and rich, Lucy?' she asked her friend the following morning as they left two clients under the dryers and had a few moments to drink a cup of tea. Lucy's eyes twinkled as she nodded towards the street door, which, on cue, opened to allow their boss to enter.

'Is everything all right?' he asked as Jennie spluttered over her tea, trying to subdue her laughter. 'Not upset about anything, are you?'

Calming herself she said, 'No, we're trying to cheer ourselves up after leaving the flat.

202

As I told you, I'm worried about Mam and Dad. They're getting on a bit, see, and Mam hurting her arm and, well, I felt it was my duty to stay. Just till they're feeling better. I let Lucy down but she understands that I have to think of my parents, don't you, Luce?'

'Very commendable,' he said and when he had disappeared into the house, Jennie mimicked him. '"Very commendable!" There's a way to talk! Not "There's kind," but, "Very commendable." What a stuffed shirt.'

They hissed a warning as the door to the house reopened and Mr James came back. 'Jennie, when you have a moment, I'd like a word.'

'Yes, Mr James.' Then in a whisper, 'See? There he goes again. He'd like a word, not, "Will you pop in for a moment," like a normal person would say.'

'I wonder what he wants?' Lucy said. 'I hope he isn't closing the business.'

'It'll be nothing exciting, that's for sure.' She posed dramatically, and said, 'My life is devoid of excitement, Miss Jones. What do you recommend I do to change it?' She giggled. 'There, did I sound like him?'

Behind the door, Ernie James listened, and chuckled with them. She was a real livewire, that Jennie.

Jennie waited until the shop closed at half past five before she knocked on the dividing door and went to see Mr James. He was sitting in shirtsleeves, working on some papers, and he closed his fountain pen and placed it carefully on his desk as she approached.

'You wanted to see me?' she said.

'Yes, that's right, I wanted you to "pop in".' He was smiling and she guessed that he had overheard some of their conversation. She sat on an armchair and waited for him to explain what he wanted. If he thought she was going to apologize he was very mistaken.

He reached into a drawer of his desk and brought out two tickets. 'I was given these. It's a variety concert in Cardiff. I wondered whether you fancied going.' She looked at him wide eyed. Surely he didn't mean with him? If only he'd mentioned the date so she could offer a genuine-sounding excuse to decline 'There are two,' Mr James added, 'and I thought you and Lucy might like to go. Perhaps your sister would stay with your parents.'

Relieved, she stood up, thanked him and was about to take the tickets when Bill came in.

'What's this, secret assignations with the workers? The shop is closed, isn't it?' His father looked angry and Jennie felt a need to hurt his son. She turned back to Mr James. 'I'd love to go with you. I'm really looking forward to it. Thank you for inviting me.' Without giving the surprised man or his son

204

a moment to recover, she left.

They hadn't been anywhere together since their visit to Swansea. He had invited her but she had refused. He had obviously taken her refusals to heart and now she had invited herself.

She regretted her stupidity immediately but felt there was no way of getting out of it. Surely Mr James would find a way. Invent some previous engagement that made him unable to go with her. The evening was less than a week away and, as the days passed and nothing was said she began to consider various illnesses as an excuse to get out of going.

'What can I do?' she wailed. 'What if Bill gets nasty and tells his father stories about us?'

'Something contagious is best, spots on your face, or a runny nose, put rouge on it to make it look sore,' Lucy advised unsympathetically, making fun of her friend's dilemma.

Jennie made no further reference to the plan but found herself making cheeky remarks to customers when she knew Mr James was listening. Watching him smile gave her enjoyment and made her feel smart and worldly. She said little to Lucy; the expected derisory comments would have spoilt her growing anticipation of a pleasant evening.

On Saturdays they worked until one o'clock but they stayed on so they could set each other's hair. Lucy took even more care than usual over Jennie's bleached curls. 'There's no escape,' she teased. 'You're going to the theatre with your boss. An old, old man.'

As an added treat, making matters worse, Mr James invited her to have a meal with him first. She hoped it would be at the smart café where they sold her favourite spicy buns, but this wasn't to be a simple tea; he was taking her out to 'dine'. He showed her the menu for the evening meals and rather nervously she copied his choice and ordered a dish of lasagne, wondering what it would be as it was something she'd never heard of.

The dish of vegetables and a small amount of minced meat in pasta was tasty and, to her relief, something easy to eat. She had dreaded bones, or gristle, knowing she'd embarrass herself. She was used to eating out, but after the brief flirtation with his son, sitting with this man who was her boss, and just about old enough to be her father, made her nervous and she wondered how she would get through the evening. Swansea had been different, relaxed and comfortable. She wondered what had changed.

The variety show was the usual mixture of song and dance acts, conjurers and illusionists. Although she initially felt some unease sitting next to Mr James, and trying to ignore the double entendre from some of the sauciest comedians, the evening was enjoyable. They were soon sharing glances, both glad to share the laughter or the admiration for a performer's skill. The mutual pleasure added to the entertainment in a way it hadn't with anyone else. The stage worked its magic and by the first interval she was relaxed and talking to Mr James as easily as to any of her friends.

He drove her home talking about the various acts, laughing at the remembered jokes, and as they reached Rock Terrace he went quiet, then embarrassed her by telling her in his pompous manner that he couldn't remember enjoying an evening more. If he had been one of her usual boyfriends she'd have been able to think of a cheeky retort and lighten the sudden formality into laughter, but she couldn't think of anything to say except a muttered and ungrammatical 'me too'.

He unnerved her further by jumping out and opening the car door for her. She pushed open the gate and ran up the path without looking back.

'Did you enjoy your evening, dear?' her mother asked.

'It was all right,' she replied casually, but she knew it had been more than just all right; she had enjoyed his gentlemanly attentions far more than she'd expected. Everything had changed. She had developed a warmth, an affection for him.

There was flattery in his concern for her comfort and pleasure, and she felt a flush of embarrassment for her earlier self and knew that in some inexplicable way the evening had changed her life. From now on she would be looking for something very different from her usual companions. Sadness enveloped her as she wondered whether she would be able to find it.

Ivor had remembered to collect his identity card and ration book when he left the home he had shared with Marie for so short a time. He presented the ration book when he had found a place to stay, dealing with the change of address at the local office. He found a room in a lodging house where the landlady provided a breakfast and what she called supper at nine thirty. Three other lodgers appeared at these mealtimes, two young men who worked on the council ash carts, who slipped in through the back entrance and went in turns straight to the bathroom, from where they would emerge shining clean and neatly dressed. Ivor was amused to notice that they took it in turns to be first, the other sitting patiently on a wooden stool outside the bathroom door.

The fourth guest was a rather quiet young

woman who dealt with the office work in a local grocery shop. She was pale, with a mass of auburn hair that fell in natural waves and curls around her rather pinched face, emphasizing her plainness. Her eyes were small and her mouth was almost lipless, so tightly did she hold them in, tense and unforthcoming. It was only when she smiled that she showed friendliness and animation.

Apart from the brief social moments when they ate together, Ivor was on his own. He didn't encourage conversation and he knew that his serious expression, his apparent lack of interest in the other guests made him appear unapproachable. He didn't want to be sociable, he deserved to be friendless and alone.

He had started work as an insurance agent, walking around an area of the town where most of the payments were pennies on fifteen-year endowment policies. Boring work as the occupants were often not at home and he found the books and payments left for him in a way that reminded of him of what he had done to Marie and the children, robbing the books she had left out with payment. New business was hard to come by, but as he became known his politeness and smart appearance persuaded a few to add to their policies, and his income gradually improved.

The loneliness was heartbreaking and he

bitterly regretted leaving. Surely they could have worked through it? What a fool he'd been, to lie for all those years, and even after that, when Marie had found out about his father living in that filth and had given him the chance to put everything right, he'd walked away to nurse his shame and guilt instead of facing it.

A bad start in life never leaves you, he thought sadly. Isolated by his parents' inadequacies he'd accepted none of the squalor but had been unable to shake off the humiliation and lack of social skills their behaviour had caused. Only with Marie had he felt true to himself, but all the time he'd been with her, happiness beginning to be an accepted right, his past had been hovering like a threatening shadow waiting for the opportunity to engulf him.

He'd been a fool to expect to cheat the past, to try to live up to Marie's standards and forget his disastrous beginnings. His father was weak, his mother was dirty and lazy – and worse – and he must be the same. If not now, then later. When life became harder, or when old age wore down his determination, he would succumb to those traits and go under.

A child of such parents, how could he escape the inevitable? His dearest hope was that he hadn't passed on those tendencies to his darling Violet. By running away, not giving her the chance to see his deterioration into the blackness of such illness, he hoped he had lessened that chance. He knew nothing about such illnesses and could only do what he thought best. Staying away was the worst and the best thing he could do. He loved them so much. Marie was better off without him. But he missed them all, Marie, their children, his comfortable home that his fears of the past had managed to destroy.

One thing he had not brought with him was clothing coupons. He had managed to bring most of his clothing by taking a taxi to the railway station, but he was seriously short of socks. Somehow, in the careful plan to move, he had brought only one pair and they were in need of darning, as he had worn them every day, washing them out each evening and putting them back on – sometimes still damp – the following morning. Without clothing coupons he couldn't buy more.

He asked his landlady how and where he applied for replacement coupons but she couldn't help, and in desperation he spoke to the quiet young woman who shared his table at meal times, and whose name he had learned was Euphemia. 'But everyone calls me Effie,' she had explained.

During their supper, he broached the subject and Effie immediately offered him sufficient coupons to buy a few pairs of socks.

'I couldn't take yours,' he protested, Effie was always smartly dressed – her clothes neatly cared for, her shoes immaculately polished. 'There can't be any to spare from someone who cares about their appearance as you obviously do.'

She fumbled in her handbag and offered him the book of coupons. 'I don't need them, my mother makes my clothes from second-hand garments and I have only to buy shoes and stockings and things.' She pressed them into his hand. 'We'll make it a loan if you prefer, but I'm not short, honestly.'

'The problem is, I don't know when I'll get more.' Almost without thought he began explaining his circumstances. Shame making him look away as they finished the watery custard and two small tinned plums.

'I've left home, you see. I've left my wife and children. I can't tell you why but I had no choice. I didn't pack very well, not wanting to take anything more than I needed, and, well, I forgot a few things, socks and handkerchiefs, and even if I had remembered clothing coupons I wouldn't have taken them. My wife will need them more than me.'

Effie was curious but she refrained from asking questions. She knew he was from

Cwm Derw, a place she had once known, having seen him address a letter there. She thought that this man, who was so distressed, would perhaps tell her one day, and she didn't want to put him off by trying to persuade him. She guessed he would need someone to talk to.

'First thing tomorrow you must go to the town hall and explain that you've lost your coupons,' she said. She smiled then, a wide smile that lit up her eyes, brightening her rather dull expression. 'They might not believe you, mind. I think a lot of people try it on. You know, tell lies in the hope of getting extra coupons.'

He had to tell the girl in the office more than he wanted to, but left there with the promise of ten coupons to tide him over until the new issue. With the coupons borrowed from Effie, he bought socks and a couple of handkerchiefs. He wondered sadly how long they would last and where he would be when they needed replacing.

Effie sat next to him at supper and asked how he had got on.

'Spendidly, thanks to you.' He handed her the remaining coupons. 'I'll be issued with ten coupons tomorrow and I'll be able to repay those I've used.'

'Keep them, in case there's something else you've forgotten,' she said, pushing them back at him. 'If I need some I'll ask my

213

mother.'

The ice broken, they talked easily during meal times over the following days, and sometimes, when he went to bed, Ivor felt an overwhelming guilt. He'd enjoyed the evening, sitting talking to Effie, and he shouldn't be enjoying life, not for a single minute. For two nights he didn't appear for supper, easing his conscience by eating in a café. His money was sufficient for his needs. He'd brought a small nest egg with him saved from the last horse race he'd gambled on, and which he'd intended to give to Marie for some extra furniture from the second-hand shop in town. Now, as he was earning a small wage and not risking any of it by gambling, he managed to send a few pounds occasionally to Marie.

To Jennie's surprise Mr James offered a second invitation. 'There's a concert on at the church hall and I've been asked to make an introductory speech. Would you like to come with me?'

'I wouldn't be on stage or anything, would I?' she asked doubtfully.

'You'll sit in the front row and clap enthusiastically when I've finished' he said. 'Just promise not to boo or jeer when I start telling them how wonderful everyone is.'

'I can manage the front row. Yes, I'd love to go with you.'

'Good. I call for you at seven.'

Oh, er, Ernie, what should I wear?'

'Long, I think, as we're guests of honour.'

'Long dress? Guests of honour? God 'elp, you're going up in the world, aren't you?' Lucy teased, later. 'I'll do your hair up in a swirl on top with curls in the centre, and you can borrow my pearl necklace if you like. I'll want a blow by blow report of what happens, mind. Every little detail. I've never met a "Guest of Honour" before!'

Laughing at the unexpected excitement, they went to Jennie's house and searched through her wardrobe to decide on the most suitable outfit.

Marie heard of the invitation from her parents. 'She's so excited,' Belle told her. 'Your father and I have begged and borrowed coupons so she can buy a new dress but she's convinced that her pink dress made over from your bridesmaid dress will do. I ask you! Pink! It isn't elegant enough for a guest of honour. Try and talk to her, Marie, I know she'll be more confident wearing something new and special.'

'I'll spare her a few coupons too,' Marie replied. 'Ivor sent us some a couple of days ago.'

'So you know where he is? And why he doesn't come home?'

'No idea, he won't say.'

'That's disgraceful. You really don't know where he is?'

'I think he's in Swansea. We once had a wonderful holiday there, exploring Gower, but it's a big town and if I went there, not knowing his address or where he's working, I'd never find him. He'll be found when he wants to be found and not before.'

'And his father, is he intending to stay with you?'

'He's got nowhere else to go. I said he can stay until Ivor comes back and they can talk. The thing is, I don't think Ivor will come back while Rhodri's there.'

'Does he know he's with you? When Ivor left his father was ill and in hospital. He might think he's still there.'

'I don't know what Ivor thinks and I'm beginning not to care.'

'You aren't thinking of divorce, I hope!' She hesitated, then added, 'Geoff is a good friend to you I hear.'

'No, Mam, I'm not anxious to end my marriage. I want to restart it, but how I do that is a mystery to me when I can't find Ivor, let alone talk him into coming back to us.'

'You'd have him back?'

'Of course, Mam. I just want to talk to him, find out why he left us. I know I'll be able to persuade him to come back.'

Marie went home with her thoughts

216

jangled. It was so frustrating to be unable to find Ivor. Waiting until he felt able to come home was hard. It was easier for him; he had chosen this separation and he knew where to find her if he wanted to.

'Any post?' she called to her father-in-law as she closed the door behind her.

'Only the rates bill,' he called back. 'I opened it and threw the envelope on the fire. No point in littering the place with unnecessary rubbish is there?'

She was not completely at ease with this man who was her father-in-law, grandfather to Violet and step-grandfather to the boys. He was often vague and lost in his thoughts and sometimes did unlikely things She had made Violet promise never to go out with him 'Except when I'm with you.' She had spoken lightly and had added, 'I like to be with you every moment I can. And share everything you do. I love you very much, you see. Roger and Royston, too.' She didn't want to frighten the child with what were only unsubstantiated fears that Rhodri would return to being the sick man they had so recently known.

She threw off her coat and went into the kitchen to start preparing their evening meal. The boys would be in soon and Violet was already settled with her drawing book in the corner of the living room, close to the bright log fire. She went to the kitchen to find that saucepans were simmering ready for the vegetables and a few sausages spluttered in the frying pan under a low heat.

'Rhodri? This is a nice surprise.' She glanced at his hands and hoped fervently that he had washed them before touching the food. Cleanliness was still low on his list of priorities The vegetables were chopped and the table in the small room off the kitchen was set for five. She stared at the table. Underneath each plate was a pile of not very clean newspaper.

'I know you wish it was set for six, but not today,' he said, misunderstanding her stare. 'Perhaps tomorrow.'

'Perhaps,' she said doubtfully. She wished she didn't have to work. Her uneasiness was growing and having the children home before she finished work was something she couldn't change. Or could she? She began to work out the possibility of managing on fewer hours. Perhaps, if Mr Harries would allow her to finish at four instead of five thirty, the time Violet had to spend alone with Rhodri would be too short for anything to happen. What could happen? He saw the doctor regularly and if there had been any possibility of danger to her or the children she would have been told.

By being careful and adding the money sent by Ivor, Marie had almost paid off the arrears owed on the house in Hill Crescent.

When the debt was finally cleared she intended to start looking for Ivor. If he were to see them settled into this comfortable house at the edge of the wood, and no longer in debt, she thought she might persuade him to return to his family. First she had to find him. As usual when she faced a problem, she went to see Geoff.

He was attending to a small queue of customers on that Saturday afternoon and she began to anticipate his needs, collecting tins of paint or other small items from the shelves or stores as soon as the customer requested them. Having so frequently bought the materials, she knew where everything was kept. When there was a lull in the stream of customers planning a weekend of work, she interrupted his thanks by saying, 'Geoff, once more I need your help.'

'It's yours, you know that,' he said, encouraging her to talk by sitting on the counter beside her and smiling his willingness to listen. The counter was littered with unwanted items that needed to be replaced on the shelves but he held her hand as she began to move them. 'Leave that, I can deal with tidying up later.'

She slowly pulled her hand away, and said briefly, 'I want to find Ivor. Why would he want to hide from me?' she asked sorrowfully. 'I've let him down. If he'd been able to talk to me he'd still be here.'

'He's hiding from his own mistakes, not from you, Marie. He was stupid, pretending to be someone different from who he really is, and when he was found out he couldn't cope. That's the truth of it.'

'I want to find him,' she repeated.

'And I want to help. Shall we go to Swansea and just drive around, ask a few people, show his photograph and see where that takes us? It's unlikely we'll find him, but it's better than doing nothing.'

'Thanks, Geoff.'

Leaving the boys and Rhodri, they planned to take Violet the following day. At ten, as she was about to set off, a small boy came with a message for her. She took the note and read it, alarm showing on her face.

'It's Dad,' she said. 'He's fallen and Jennie's gone out for the day. I'll have to go.'

Leaving Violet in the care of the twins, Geoff drove her and they found Howard sitting at the bottom of the stairs nursing his arm.

'I don't believe this!' Marie gasped. 'First Mam and now you.'

They took him to hospital and were reassured that the arm wasn't broken, just badly bruised. By then it was after one o'clock. 'Too late to go now,' Marie said.

'Next week we'll try again,' he said to comfort her.

They went back to Badgers Brook where

the boys were clearing a corner of the garden of some overgrown and straggly bushes. 'Where's Violet?' Marie called, and they shrugged their shoulders and carried on with their task. 'What d'you mean? Where is she?'

'She went for a walk in the wood with Grandad Rhodri.'

Roger said. 'It isn't fair, I wanted to go but Royston said we had to finish this.'

A cold panic overwhelmed her and she leaned against the side of the van. 'How long have they been gone?'

'I don't know. I know we're starving and he promised to make us some sandwiches,' Royston said, clutching his stomach theatrically.

Sensing Marie's alarm without her saying a word, Geoff slammed the van door and took charge. 'I'll go through the trees towards the stream and you go across to the village,' he said, and the boys, catching the urgency of his words, dropped their tools and asked where they should look.

It was almost five o'clock before they found her. She came through the trees singing and carrying a clump of wild daisies, which she insisted on planting in the garden the boys had recently dug.

They had walked further than they intended, looking for birds' nests, Rhodri had explained apologetically. 'Then we sat near

221

the badger sett. I've half promised that we'll go out one night and watch for them, all of us. So long as we sit to windward and we're very quiet, they'll go about their business undisturbed.'

When Geoff left, after a simple meal of soup and crusty bread, Marie followed him to the van.

'I know she was unharmed, but I don't like leaving her with him. He's so erratic and unreliable, and I can't forget how confused and ill he was not so long ago.'

'She can come to the shop after school if you like. She'll be safe enough with me and I can bring her home when the shop closes and arrive at the same time as you. How will that be?'

To avoid hurting Rhodri's feelings and perhaps bringing back thoughts of his recent illness, they told Violet that she was being offered a job and would be paid every week on Friday night. She was delighted and asked Marie to make her a special apron so she looked smart.

'Clothes your first thought, just like your father,' Marie said sadly.

It was Jennie who first saw Ivor. She and Ernie James had gone to Swansea for a day out one Saturday, leaving Lucy to deal with the Saturday morning clients. Ernie had suggested a walk on the sandy bay that curved south-westward the six miles to Mumbles. The centre of Swansea was a short walk from the sea but the shops were too tempting for Jennie and at three o'clock they were still wandering around the market, buying the odd item and admiring many others.

It was as she was looking at some inexpensive jewellery that Ernie presented his bombshell. 'Don't look at cheap rubbish. You deserve better than that.'

She laughed. 'Me deserve better? Better has to be paid for, Ernie, and besides, I like cheap jewellery. Wear it, enjoy it, then throw it away. No worries about it being stolen if it's worthless.' She turned and smiled at him and saw that there was no echoing smile on his face. 'What is it? Have I said something utterly stupid? I'm sorry but I've never had the money to even consider the best and the only way to deal with that is to pretend you don't care.'

'I want to buy you the best. I want you to have everything you want.'

Jennie didn't know how to react. Was he offering to buy her a gift? And if so, what should she accept, something valuable or only moderately so? Certainly nothing from this stall! If he took her to a decent jewellers would it be better to play down his words and insist on the least expensive thing she could see?

'I want to buy you a ring.'

Her heart leaped painfully. Surely he didn't mean...? 'I can see a pretty little imitation pearl over there,' she said, afraid to look at him. 'That's nice.'

'A diamond ring is more suitable for an engagement ring.' His voice had a trembling quality, revealing his nervousness. 'Don't you agree?'

She had to force herself to turn around and face him. How should she react? It might be a joke, or he might be buying it for someone else, she didn't know his friends. Afraid she had misunderstood him, she asked, 'Ernie, what are you saying?'

'Marry me. I know that Swansea market isn't the most romantic place for a proposal, but it just came out. I had to ask when I felt brave enough. If I'd waited for the right moment I'd have lost my nerve.'

'But we haven't known each other very long, not really known each other.'

'I knew how I felt about you when we went out together for the first time. I hadn't enjoyed myself like that for a very long time. You create happiness around you, Jennie. And if you're thinking of Thelma, well, she was very fond of you and I'm sure she'd be happy for me. Well?' he coaxed as she didn't say anything.

In stories the heroine always asked for time to think about it and Jennie had always thought that stupid, and hurtful, to the handsome hero, but now it seemed the right thing to do.

'Can I give you an answer tomorrow?' she asked. 'There's a lot to think about and if I slept on it...'

'Of course.' His jaw tightened, the primness was back in his voice, disappointment in his eyes, but Jennie saw only a wonderful future, with no shortage of money, and a loving, considerate husband. There would be no need to worry about his wanting children – he was too old to cope with babies – and she would have someone to do the boring things she'd hate. She clasped his hands in hers, looked up at him and said, 'My only consideration is whether I can make you happy, dear Ernie, that's what I want more than anything.'

'My concern is the same, for you, my dear little Jennie.'

'Then it's yes, Ernie, I'll be proud to become your wife.'

They went to one of the finest jewellers in the town and chose a ring. After they made sure it was a perfect fit, it was placed in a box lined with rich blue velvet.

'Before you wear it, I must talk to your parents, assure them of my determination to make you happy,' he said, placing the precious symbol of love in his pocket.

'Let me try it on just once more,' Jennie pleaded, and, smiling happily, he took it out for her to admire. 'It's perfect. The day's perfect and so are you,' she breathed.

It was after they had been to the Mack-worth Hotel for a celebratory tea that Jennie saw Ivor. He was in a bookshop and when she called his name he took a step as if to run away. 'Ivor! When are you coming home?' she demanded in her forthright way. Ernie was behind her and he stood back politely to allow her to greet the man, unaware of who he was.

'I – hello, Jennie. How is Marie?' He was so shocked he didn't know what he was saying and he glanced around as though searching for an escape route. Sounding like a distant stranger he added, 'I hope she's well?'

'Oh, she's fine. Very happy. Everyone's happy.' In her present euphoric state of mind, happiness was all she could think of. Giving Ivor the impression he wasn't needed or even missed didn't occur to her. As she turned to beckon Ernie forward to introduce him, she saw a young woman approach carrying a book. She came up to a pale and shocked Ivor and handed it to him. 'Here you are, Ivor, a little gift. It's the book on aeroplanes you wanted.'

Jennie backed away as the woman pushed the book into Ivor's hands. Ivor called after her, 'This is a lady who stayed in the same hotel as me,' he called, unable to resist exaggerating, even at such a time.

Jennie didn't wait for explanations, she pulled on Ernie's arm and they hurried from the shop.

Finding a place to sit in the small park in the middle of the town she explained about the disappearance of Ivor. 'My sister mustn't know he's with someone else,' she said, sobbing a little. 'It would break her heart. Oh, I wish we hadn't seen him, it's almost spoiled our perfect day.' She wiped tears from her beautiful eyes, took a deep breath and added, 'but I won't let it. Nothing can make me unhappy today, not even my sister's deceitful husband.'

Ernie told her how much he admired her for being so brave, and she hugged him.

'Ernie dear, you're so understanding.'

They drove home and she relaxed into dreams about the wonderful future that was spread out before her. She allowed him to open the car door for her, and after kissing him with a passion that startled them both, Jennie waved him out of sight then ran in to tell her parents the unbelievably good news, feeling so excited she began shouting the news before she opened the door.

The following day she was surprised to find Bill waiting when she and Lucy opened up the hairdresser's shop.

'Don't think you'll get away with this,' he said almost conversationally as Lucy pushed past him and went inside. 'My father might be a fool for a pretty pair of lips and saucy blue eyes, but I'm not. I know the sort of woman you are, and what you hope to get from my father. If you don't tell him you've changed your mind and won't marry him, you'll have me to answer to.' He stood and leaned towards her the expression on his face a clear warning that he meant what he said. 'Tell him today.'

Jennie had nowhere to go. She couldn't tell her parents, or even talk to Lucy about Bill's threats. She would feel belittled by the situation. Marie, who would normally be her confidante, was best avoided, in case she let slip that she had seen Ivor the previous day. And she could hardly tell Ernie that his son had threatened her.

What could she do except carry on as though Bill hadn't spoken and hope his threats were nothing more than hot air? And jealousy, of course! That idea cheered her. Yes, she had succeeded more than she had intended in her attempts to make him regret his treatment of her. Bill wanted her himself and regretted the cavalier way he had dismissed her. This was the version she told Lucy, and later, when she no longer feared letting the cat out of the bag regarding Ivor, it was the version she repeated to Marie.

Seven

The snows and frosts of the winter had caused chaos and now, as the thaw began, other disasters were revealed. Expanded pipes burst, and once the ice melted water gushed out and plumbers were racing around the town dealing with flooded houses. There had been no hint of a problem at Badgers Brook until Marie awoke one morning to see an ominous damp patch on the ceiling, which seemed to grow as she watched.

Slipping on a dressing gown she went outside to see that a large piece of guttering had become detached; the barge board behind it had rotted and most of it had fallen. The ageing wood could no longer support the metal gutters and as she walked around the building she could see that in other places, too, it was in need of replacement. Several slates had shifted and it was this that had caused the water to creep in.

Warning the others not to venture around the house, she wrote to their landlord and explained the need for workmen to come at once, before there was a serious accident. The piece hanging was outside her bedroom window and she pushed at it until it fell. She didn't want it crashing down on someone's head.

Effie was curious about where Ivor had lived before coming to the lodging house, but, determined not to discourage him from talking to her, she tried not to ask any questions, allowing him to talk when he wanted or needed to and not intruding between confidences. She noticed that he avoided using the names of the people he told her about, and she accepted that he wanted to keep away from the subject of his marriage. Excited by the coincidence of him coming from Cwm Derw, she knew it was an omen and she was very careful. A wrong word here or there could have a devastating effect on their burgeoning friendship.

He was a very private person and sometimes, when temptation was too strong and a few questions were asked during a meal, he would avoid the dining room for a few days, presumably eating at one of the cafés in the town. She was the only person he spoke to about anything except the weather, which continued to be a serious problem in many areas, with floods blocking roads and isolating villages.

She knew he wrote a letter to Cwm Derw

once in a while and knew that occasionally coincidences came for a purpose.

If Ivor lived in Cwm Derw, Valley of Oaks, he would know the man who had ruined her life. But would any good come of raking up the past? It was over, the episode was left behind now, reviving it once again would bring only pain and misery. Yet fate had a way of making you face things.

Having read the address on Ivor's letter, she decided to be honest and tell him she'd seen it and knew the town and a few of the people who lived there. Telling him might encourage him to talk, but she knew there was a risk of it having the opposite effect.

When they were sitting at the supper table and the other boarders had gone, she decided to broach the subject.

'I couldn't help seeing that one of your letters was addressed to someone in Cwm Derw,' she said. She watched his face for signs of alarm or disapproval.

'You know the place?' he asked and his voice was calm.

'I once knew someone who lived there.' From his expression and lack of curiosity she knew there was no point in elaborating. He knew, and if he wanted to talk he would, and if not no harm was done. She smiled at him, thankful that he had not taken offence, and with nothing more said they finished the toast and marmite with a few cubes of cheese that was their supper.

Ivor might have shown no curiosity about her connection with Cwm Derw but she was unable to let the matter drop in her own mind. She wanted to go there and just see how the family she had known was getting on and whether they had all forgotten her.

'Do you remember hearing of a family called Masters?' Ivor surprised her by asking the following day.

'Your family d'you mean? No, I have no recollection of anyone called Masters, except the woman—' she stopped, regretting speaking without thinking. 'No, I don't know that name from Cwm Derw.'

'You were about to say the woman who set fire to the school, weren't you?'

'Well, yes, I do remember being told something about that. A long time ago, mind.'

'She was my mother. The school criticized something I did and she "repaid" them by burning the building down.'

'That was your mother? I'm sorry. I should not have read the address on your private letter and I regret mentioning Cwm Derw.'

'She also tried to burn down a neighbour's house when they'd had a quarrel.' It was as though he hadn't heard her speak. 'That's something else I haven't told my wife.'

'I'm sorry. But it isn't too late, is it?' Ivor shook his head. 'If she loves you, she'll understand why you couldn't tell her before.

After all, it isn't as though you're like your mother.'

'She's better off without me.' He spoke emphatically, the subject was clearly closed.

Why had he mentioned his family? Those few words spoken by Effie had reminded him painfully of why he was here and not at home with the people he loved. He couldn't sleep and slipped out to walk along the sands, where the edge of the waves and a misty moon gave some light, and passed the night hours listing his regrets and dreaming of what might have been.

In Cwm Derw, everyone was surprised at the speed with which Ernie James was replacing his wife. It was less than a year since her death. There was disapproval, too, that he was marrying someone more than twenty years his junior. Particularly after the even more recent death of Bill's fiancée. Congratulations were offered, but behind every smile was a query, an unspoken question.

'Marie, they all think I'm expecting!' Jennie told her sister one evening when they were spreading out the skirt of a second-hand wedding dress to cut it into a style to fit Jennie's slim figure. 'Make sure that dress fits as tight as tight, mind, so there's no room for gossip – or a baby!' she said. 'Gossip about the age difference, and remarks like Thelma not being cold in her grave I can

233

take, because they're true, but to hint that I've done – you know – before we're church-ed, well it isn't true and I don't want anyone to think so. It's funny,' she mused, 'Mam and Dad don't seem worried about the age difference, or the fact of my having a stepson I went out on dates with. Or even the brief time that's passed since Mrs James's death. But they'd think it would prove that I wasn't properly brought up if I was expecting. They'd be shamed by that. Daft, isn't it?'

'And you're not?'

'No, our Marie, I'm *not*!' She pushed a cushion under her skirt and paraded around the room humming the bridal march until Belle came in. Her shocked expression made them collapse into laughter.

Belle and Howard Jones had been dismay-ed when Jennie had told them about her engagement to Ernie James. Hiding their disappointment they had smiled and congra-tulated her but later they had discussed it long into the night. They both agreed that Jennie needed someone to look after her, that was what they wanted for her, she wasn't capable like Marie. Marrying a 'sugar daddy' was in many ways degrading, but at least it would ensure she was cared for and spoiled. Ernie, being older and reasonably wealthy, would be able to do that.

Marie wondered how her lively sister would cope with the dullness of living with an older man. Jennie had always liked the company of men a lot younger than herself, and not dancing, and flirting and having fun might subdue her until she lost the vitality and *joie de vivre* that made her who she was. Her personal fear was that after a few months Jennie would break out, look for some excitement that didn't include her staid husband. She said nothing to her mother, who would only accuse her of lacking understanding, or of jealousy, or some other negative emotion, when in fact her concerns for her sister were genuine.

During the weeks before the wedding Jennie didn't work. She spent her time preparing, leaving Lucy and a new assistant to cope in the shop, going each evening to cash up and hand the appointments book and takings to her betrothed, as she jokingly called him.

An hotel was booked for the wedding breakfast and arrangements made to cater for thirty guests. The plans to marry in St Mary's Church were in hand. Having decided to marry on April 12th it was a rush to get everything organized. The hasty arrangements adding to speculation about a baby.

Lucy's doubts remained unspoken. She hoped that either Jennie would come to her senses or Ernie would admit to making a mistake. Bill repeated his warnings to Jennie, threatening to tell his father about her reputation.

'But what people say about me isn't true. I've had fun but it never went further than a kiss and cuddle,' she protested. He made her feel nervous even though she told herself he was simply warning her off marrying his father for reasons of his own,

'My inheriting money that should be his must surely be his main concern,' she told Lucy. Lucy agreed and crossed her fingers, hoping that the wedding would go off without any trouble.

Although she wanted to arrange for the redecoration of a couple of the rooms before moving into the house where Ernie had lived with Thelma, Jennie stayed away except when Ernie was with her.

Marie helped her sister to decide on colours and wallpaper patterns, but she was adamant about not taking on the whole job, even though Ernie had promised to pay her. 'I can't take money for helping my sister,' she told them both with an edge of anger in her voice. 'I really can't find the time.' It was insulting for Ernie to ask her to work for him when he was marrying her sister, but for Jennie's sake she agreed to oversee. She found them a decorator willing to do the job quickly, and one afternoon, when she had called in to see how he was getting on, she found the man struggling on top of a ladder, trying to paper the ceiling. She stayed to help him, putting a plank between two ladders, and showing him how to fold the paper and unfold it as he worked across the room. When she rushed guiltily into the gown shop ten minutes late Mr Harries was waiting for her. He handed her her cards and told her she was no longer needed.

'But I'm never late,' she gasped in disbelief. 'You know I work more than my hours and I don't watch the clock and leave the moment we close. I apologize, I'll work my half-day to make up.' He waggled her cards as though impatient for her to take them. To lose her regular wages would be an absolute disaster. 'I'm responsible for three children and a sick old man,' she reminded him in a voice that shook with emotion.

'Your mind hasn't been on your work for weeks, Mrs Masters. In fact, I think we are boring you.' He stretched out his arm and forced her to take the envelope containing her wages and the stamped insurance card and employment details.

In utter disbelief she found a letter waiting for her from the owner of the house, telling her to vacate. It explained that when they received her letter asking for repairs to be made, it had become clear she wasn't entitled to the tenancy. It was not transferable and the agreement had been with Ivor's mother, who was dead. The letter went on to say he intended to sell, and vacant possession would be a condition of the sale. The difficulty of removing tenants from rented properties was the subject of much discussion at that time, but she knew that as she wasn't officially the tenant, she had no rights.

She went to see him to plead her case, pointing out the improvements they had made, and threatened court action knowing she hadn't a chance of winning.

'Mrs Masters might be dead but Mr Masters isn't, and surely it was he who signed the agreement?'

'I thought that he too was— I'm sorry, Mrs Masters, I had no idea he was still there.'

'So?' she demanded, glaring at him, hands on his desk, leaning towards him like an angry terrier. 'He's a sick man and as such can no longer be acceptable as a tenant?'

'All right, Mrs Masters, I'll continue to rent the property to you.' Relief made her legs weaken but she knew there was something more from the tight smile on his face. Anxiety rising to a pitch, she stared at him, waiting for the blow to fall. 'But with the improvements,' he went on, 'I'll have to increase the rental by another three shillings and sixpence a week. And only until I can find a buyer, then you will have to leave. The law is on my side, Mrs Masters.'

It was an effective way of getting her out, as there was no way she could afford to buy the place. No home, no job and she could hardly blame Ivor this time. She should have checked, made sure the house had been transferred to herself and Ivor. She was responsible for five of them and the future looked bleak. How could she keep them together?

Jennie left most of the wedding plans to Ernie and her sister. The guests at the top table would include Lucy, and an invitation was sent to Gerald, who replied immediately explaining he couldn't get leave. Bill said he'd be there in the hope of something going wrong. The sister of Thelma, Ernie's first wife, would be there, and when she and her husband came to meet the bride their disapproval was in no doubt. Jennie was unfazed by the whole thing; concentrated on looking her best, trying various hairstyles and make-up with Lucy, amidst much hilarity.

Effie had not yet visited Cwm Derw, and she heard about the wedding by chance. She was on a bus heading towards Cardiff one afternoon, going to collect some forms from the printers, when she overheard a conversation between two women sitting in front of her. 'Fancy that James fellow getting married. Next week it is, and the girl is half his age.' She listened intently but apart from learning that the church was St Mary's and the date

239

was April 12th, she couldn't find out more before the two women, still criticizing Mr James for his inappropriate choice of bride, left the bus.

It was him. It had to be. She arranged for the day off and on April 12th set off for Cwm Derw very early, not waiting for breakfast. Food would make her sick on a day like this.

She went to St Mary's Church and after trying and failing to find someone to tell her the time of the wedding, she sat on a cold slab, leaning against a tombstone, and waited. There was still snow hanging about, although its beauty had long gone. Earth and dead leaves had gathered on its surface, which was pitted with raindrops, and it hid its dirty self in hollows and shady corners.

She wrapped the swagger coat she had worn tightly around her and sat on the extra woollen scarf she had brought but the chill crept through her until she thought she would have to give up and find a café to warm herself. It was only the thought of why she was there that forced her to stay.

She would wait for the right time in the solemn service then wake them all up. She'd shout an objection, she'd scream and tell the congregation what he had done to her. No one had believed her before, but this time she'd make sure he didn't marry and live happily ever after. He hadn't the right, not after what he'd done to her.

Revealing her hatred of the man had its risks, she knew that, but once she had heard about his wedding she had been unable to deny herself this pleasurable moment.

People began to arrive and she didn't know any of them. But perhaps she did. She didn't know them well and might not recognize them in their smart clothes, they all looked so different, particularly the women, who usually spent their days wearing crossover aprons and slippers. Even their figures were altered, improved by the well-fitted and carefully chosen outfits. She rose to her feet stiffly, rubbed her cold bottom and stamped her feet a few times. She had to find someone she knew, a member of his family, to assure herself she was at the right place and time. She spread the second scarf, now damp and unpleasant, around her shoulders, lifting the edge a little to conceal her face and wandered around looking under the smart but ancient hats. But she still failed to see anyone she recognized. Had she got it wrong?

At ten thirty on April 12th 1947, Jennie walked up the aisle and became Mrs Ernest James. Lucy was the solitary bridesmaid in a dress made of muslin washed and tinted a pale green, decorated with a belt of white ribbon. She wore wild flowers in her hair and carried a sheaf of dog daisies picked in the fields that morning.

Marie had been there to help Jennie get ready. 'All right?' she had asked when her sister was dressed and ready to leave.

Jennie said, 'No, sis, I'm all of a doodah thinking about what's to happen tonight.'

'If you love him and he loves you everything will be wonderful,' Marie said.

'What if we don't – love each other – what then?'

'It will still be fine. Be happy, Jennie,' she said hugging her, trying to ignore the implication of her sister's words.

Belle and Howard Jones were tearful, belatedly regretting they had done nothing to stop their beautiful daughter from giving herself to an older man. To stop their anxiety transferring itself to Jennie, Marie packed her mother off to wait for the car with friends and told their tearful father to go upstairs out of the way while the beautifying processes were completed.

Ernie was dressed formally and he looked older than usual, his face pale, straight grey hair sticking out in a small fringe from beneath his top hat. He was a colourless contrast to the heavily made-up Jennie with her flowing dress and veil. Her blond hair fell in loose waves around her shoulders. She carried a huge bouquet of spring flowers, which showered down in a display that descended almost to the ground, especially made by the local florists to Jennie's own design. Hopeful young women in the congregation wondered how she would manage to throw it and whether they'd be lucky enough to catch it without being knocked to the ground unconscious.

The church was well attended; more than thirty relatives and friends had been invited and few had declined. They all wanted to see the wedding that had been the source of gossip ever since news of it had first been whispered just weeks ago. The churchyard was scattered with groups of onlookers come to see for themselves the 'spring and autumn' wedding of two well-known families.

Watching everyone walking into the church and hearing the organ music swell, Effie realized to her chagrin that due to her wanderings she had missed the arrival of the groom. As the last of the guests found their seats and the doors were being guarded by attendants watching for the bridal car, Effie made her way into the dimly lit building.

The pews were full and the back of the church was crowded but she moved forward to have a view of the place where he and his bride would stand. She waited for her eyes to become accustomed to the dull light and looked for the man she had come to see. He was seated and out her of sight but would stand when his bride arrived.

As long as she was in time to stop the wedding, it didn't matter where she stood. All she had to do was shout. There was no chance of not being heard at the moment that everyone superstitiously dreaded.

She didn't have much room to move, squashed against the back of the last pew in the church with those who had not been invited but had pushed in as soon as the guests had been seated by the attendants. Like so many of the crowd, she was wearing a large hat that shadowed her face and acted as disguise, although she attracted little attention. Everyone's eyes were watching the door for the arrival of the bride. A few of the congregation gave her mildly curious glances, wondering about her connection with the families, a question half formed then quickly forgotten.

The organist stopped the melody and struck up 'Here Comes The Bride'. Effie didn't look towards the back of the church; she waited for the groom to stand so she would get her first sight of the man she had come to see. She stared in disbelief when the man on the right-hand side of the front pew rose to greet his bride. It wasn't Bill James. The groom was his father and his bride, coming down the aisle with a demure smile, was a girl no older than herself.

Behind the bride and her still tearful father

walked someone she did know. Bill had been sitting beside his father and was standing to take his part in the ceremony.

In stunned disbelief, she left the church before the bride and groom left the service to sign the register, and hurried to the bus stop. As she waited for it to arrive she tried to think of other things to hide her disappointment at failing to embarrass and hurt Bill James.

She concentrated on Ivor and wondered if she should stay and learn something that would enable her to help him. She forced herself to think through everything Ivor had told her, but she had learned nothing that would help her recognize his family. She had no idea what his wife looked like and no names had been mentioned in the whispered conversations going on around her.

She wondered whether to tell him about her visit and the wedding she had witnessed, but as she would be unable to tell him who was there it seemed pointless. He'd hardly be interested in Ernie James and his stupid bride. Perhaps she would buy a newspaper in which the wedding was reported and leave it out for him, just in case he wanted news of his home.

A few days later she placed the newspaper report on the wedding in front of him. 'I don't know whether you know anyone there, but as it's an apparently important occasion in a town you know, I though you might like to see it,' she said. 'I was looking at some of the churches in the area and happened to see this wedding,' she added as she walked away.

He looked at the grainy photograph then ran after her and wanted to know everything she had witnessed.

'I can't tell you anything because I didn't know any of the guests, I'm sorry,' she said, avoiding mention of Bill James and his father, the reason for her going there.

He pointed to a group at the side of the photograph. 'That man is my father. What was he doing there?'

'Why shouldn't he be there? It seems half the town was out that day.'

'I thought he was in hospital,' he said, half to himself. Effie waited for him to tell her more.

'I wanted the house for them. I spent days cleaning it up, for *them*. I wanted him to stay in hospital. He's unwell, you see, unwell and I didn't want him near the boys and little Violet. She mustn't be near him.' He stared at her as though she might answer his question and asked, 'What shall I do?'

'You'll have to go there. You won't find any answers standing here staring at a photograph.'

Marie had to find a way to pay the extra

rent. She didn't want to uproot the family again, and, besides, she had to stay in case Ivor came to find them. They'd been told they had to vacate the house temporarily, to allow more work to be done, and an un-believable few weeks since moving in they packed what they needed and left.

Geoff had insisted on them staying with him.

They squashed into three rooms, with Rhodri confused and shaking uncontrol-lably. Marie took him to the doctor, but whatever happened in the privacy of the doctor's room, there was no suggestion of him going back to hospital. He had to sleep on a bed-chair in a small room cleared of brushes and mops and buckets and bowls, next to the store where Geoff kept paint, white spirit, paraffin and candles.

When Jennie returned from honeymoon she was smiling and telling everyone who asked that it had been wonderful, but a glance at her face told Marie that she was far from happy.

'What happened?' she asked when they managed to find a few moments alone.

Jennie blustered for a while, insisting everything was perfect, but as her sister wait-ed patiently for her to stop repeating the automatic responses, she admitted that it was 'Hell.'

'In what way?' Marie coaxed, handing her a cup of tea she had made in Geoff's kitchen.

'He treated me like a child, and apart from a chaste kiss before turning over and going to sleep, he might have been my brother.'

Marie didn't want to listen to details of the private side of the marriage but her sister was in such a state that she encouraged her to talk. 'Better to tell me and be sure it won't go any further,' she said, taking Jennie in her arms. The story was a simple one. There had been no loving embraces, and the days were spent sightseeing, the nights in lonely isolation, Jennie on one side of the bed and Ernest on the other.

'He seemed perfectly happy.'

'It may be that he wanted to wait until you were home. I've heard of some men who are afraid to show their love in someone else's bed,' she went on, inventing the story but convinced that nothing was impossible.

'We've been home two nights and nothing has changed,' Jennie sobbed. 'He must think I'm ugly.'

Marie laughed. 'Come on, Jennie, leave the dramatics to film stars, it will only make you feel worse.' She tried to comfort her sister but in her heart she wondered whether Ernest had intended the marriage to be unconsummated. He might have thought the relationship, which had not involved sexual desire before the wedding, would be all Jennie needed. Jennie had behaved in an exaggeratedly coy manner towards him, avoiding declarations of passion, of a longing for his loving, afraid that he would readily believe any story of her previous behaviour that Bill might tell him.

Marie sadly thought that this was one time when things hadn't turned out for the best for her lively sister and regretted the brief moments of jealousy she had felt towards her. Neither of them had been blessed with happiness, or at least it had been short-lived, she mused. Was there a plan all mapped out for life that was immutable? Did parents sow the seeds of their children's future? Was there no such thing as self-will? She shook defeatist musings aside and went back to Geoff's shop determined not to surrender to such cowardly thoughts. Opportunities were there, they cropped up in every life she was sure of that, and it was only the weak who ignored them.

She went to the Labour Exchange determined to take any job she was offered, no matter what. Her parents would look after Violet if she worked beyond the school day so there was no excuse for turning anything down. 'Apart from decorating,' she said to Geoff. 'I don't think I want to do any more of that, not since working on those flats.'

A small dress shop was opening on a

corner of the main street opposite Geoff's hardware store and the owner needed a manageress. Nerys Bowen seemed seriously lacking in interest when she went for an interview, saying she had others to see, but the following day Marie received a letter offering her the job. The wage was less than she had earned at the gown shop, but it would be sufficient to get them back on their feet.

'I am grateful to you, Geoff,' she said when she told him the news. 'We'll be out of your way next week.'

'Stay here as long as you wish,' Geoff said after congratulating her. 'I'll be sorry to see you all go but when you're ready to move out I'll help you to get settled in, even though I'll miss you.' He leaned forward and kissed her gently on the cheek.

'Geoff, I'll never be able to thank you for what you've done for me. For us.'

'Be happy, that's all the thanks I need.'

With Ivor far away and having lost the home they had loved and thought was theirs for ever; taking on the responsibility for his father; finding Badgers Brook and losing Ivor...she wondered how happiness could ever be achieved. 'I'll try,' she said.

Ivor was increasingly afraid. He visualized Rhodri sitting in that rubbish-filled room and feared for Marie and the children living

250

with the crazy old man who was his father. In his confused state he was capable of anything. The only consolation was that he was not a fire-raiser. That had been his mother's entertainment. He covered his face with his hands. He'd had to lie. How could he have told Marie about the bad blood he had inherited and maybe passed on to his darling child?

After what the wedding photograph had revealed he had to go to Cwm Derw, at least to reassure himself. Perhaps Rhodri had been allowed out just for the day. Or had run away and been taken in by Marie until he could be returned to the hospital. He couldn't be free, he told himself. He was seriously sick. He borrowed a car from one of the other insurance agents and drove to a spot some distance away from the house where he had left all his happiness.

Badgers Brook looked different. The garden had been neatly dug, the grass mown and flowerbeds carefully cut out in an orderly arrangement that pleased his eye. The windows shone in the sun that had finally melted the last of the snow, and everything glistened with the freshness of spring. Trees wore mantles of new leaves and birdsong filled woodland. Hawthorn blossom perfumed the air with its sweet scent.

He was surprised to see the name on the gate. Badgers Brook. He wondered whether

251

Marie or the boys had found it or had made it. On closer inspection it looked shabby compared to the rest of the place now the mess had all been cleared.

Taking a deep breath, wondering whether Marie would greet him with relief he didn't deserve or whether he would be sent away, an unwelcome and unwanted intrusion, he walked towards the door with a racing heart and shaking legs. The path had been cleared of the overgrown grasses and wild flowers that had infiltrated around the paving. They had worked hard and he felt shame like a shower of icy water slide down his back. If he had been honest he might be still here, working alongside Marie, surrounded by a loving family. Why had fate led Jenkin Jenkins to him that day? Why of all the people had he been the one man who could tell him where his father was living; as soon as he and his father met his life had been ruined.

He reached the front door and knocked, tentatively at first, then louder, but there was no response. A man walking along the lane called to him, 'If you want Mrs Masters she's gone,' he called.

Ivor looked through the window and saw that the place was clean and orderly, the fire set ready in the grate, the old pine table scrubbed and put where they had found it covered in filth. He was too late. He called to

252

ask the man where he could find them but the man shrugged. 'Couldn't pay their rent was what I heard. The landlord increased it, see, and it was too much, with her husband running off like he did. The swine.'

They were gone and he had no idea where to find them.

Ivor turned away, afraid that the man would recognize him as 'the swine' who had abandoned his family. He drove back to the town and went to see Marie's parents. Surely they would know where he could find them? But once again he was denied.

He found Howard to be a very angry man. 'My daughters deserve better than they're getting,' he ranted. 'Jennie married to an old man and YOU, walking out and leaving our Marie and the children without a home. Get out, go on, clear off! Useless you are, promising to look after her and the children, and what did you do? Steal from them, lose them their home then run away. Get from my sight, you useless apology for a man.'

Stricken with shock and shame, Ivor heard Belle call from in the house, 'Who is it, Howard?'

'No one, dear. Only some beggar who should be ashamed to look an honest man in the eye.'

'Please, tell me where I can find them. I need to see her.' As Howard was closing the door, he asked, 'At least tell me where my father is.'

'Wherever they are they're best without you,' he shouted. 'Get away from here, you don't belong here any more.'

He went next to find Geoff, although he knew the man was hardly likely to be on his side. He went into the shop, which was dark after the bright sun outside, and for a moment he couldn't make out who was standing behind the counter. Geoff had seen him before he had opened the door and had called to Marie to stay out of sight, unless she wanted to see him. That decision was hers and something with which he would not interfere.

'Ivor?' he said questioningly.

'Where are they?'

'It isn't for me to tell. But if you want to see them leave me your address and I'll pass it on.' As Ivor hesitated as though to argue, he went on, 'I think the decision must be hers, don't you?'

There was a note pad on the counter, and on it Ivor wrote the address of the lodging house where he lived.

'Is there any message?' Geoff asked coldly, offering the pad and pencil once again.

'I'm afraid that my father might be bothering them. He's – well, you saw how he was living and I don't want them upset. Was he the reason they had to leave the house?'

Geoff shook his head. 'None of your

father's doing.'

'He is still in hospital, then, isn't he?'

'Under their care, yes,' was Geoff's evasive answer.

'I gather Jennie is married. Strange her marrying a man of that age,' Ivor said, trying to delay his departure.

Geoff came around the counter and opened the door. It was clearly a dismissal and without another word Ivor left.

A tearful Marie took the piece of paper on which Ivor had written his address and tore it up, dropping the pieces into the waste paper bin. 'Why should I want to find him? He has to find *me*,' she sobbed. 'Search with determination and face me, talk to me, not leave addresses and wait for me to find him!'

Ivor drove around for a while, passing the school and the shop where he presumed Marie still worked, but there was no sign of her or the children. Unable to take more disappointment, dissatisfied with his attempt to find them, feeling hated and despised by everyone, he drove back to the lodgings to find Effie waiting in the dining room.

It was only five o'clock and supper wasn't until nine thirty so she suggested a walk. She went with him to return the car to its owner and pay for its use, then they caught a bus to the seaside village of Mumbles and walked along the front, following the road and paths to Langland Bay and then Caswell, while he talked.

He told her about his miserable childhood. About the bullying at school, where, as a badly dressed only child with a mother who had been in prison for setting fire to a school and attempting to burn a house, he was a gift to those who teased. A mother who had also burned a barn and a stack of hay, although neither had been proved, when the man had accused Ivor of poaching. As if his crazy mother weren't enough there was his father, who wandered around, staring at people, often unaware of his surroundings. He was a farm labourer, who had been unable to work since his return from the great war in 1918, but with no wound about which a son could boast to explain his confused state.

Effie listened and swore to comfort him and help him to forget the woman who had cared so little for him she had allowed him to walk away once she found out about his family. She didn't deserve him.

It was again Jennie who was the next to see Ivor. Ernie had invited her to visit the town, promising her a walk along the beach and tea in a smart hotel. Jennie wanted to scream. What she needed was a night out with Lucy. A dance with wild music in a hot, overcrowded hall, with plenty of make-up, her hair loosened from Ernie's favourite tightly controlled style, with lots of young men admiring her and telling her how wonderful she was, not a sedate walk and tea in a nice hotel!

They parked the car beside the railway line, following the route of the famous, overcrowded Mumbles train to ride around the wide sandy bay towards the village of the same name. It was later, as they were driving past the Swansea shops as they closed for the evening, that Jennie again recognized her brother-in-law. He was going into the picture house with a young woman on his arm. Ernie slowed the car and stopped outside and they watched as Ivor put an arm around his companion to guide her through the entrance, where a small queue was already forming. The girl stood aside, opening her coat and easing off her gloves as he bought their tickets.

'It's the girl he was with before. What shall we do? We can't tell Marie he's seeing another woman, it would break her heart.'

'I think she'd prefer to know,' Ernie said, shaking his head as he held his hand out of the window to signal before easing the car back into the line of traffic. 'I would.'

'Perhaps later, but not now, her unhappiness is still raw.'

'I think we should go straight to Geoff's hardware shop and tell him what we saw.'

'Good news about her new job. I might like

257

to go back to work myself one day, Ernie.'

'No need for you to think of doing that, my dear. We're perfectly happy as we are, pleasing ourselves, going out for nice afternoons whenever the fancy takes us.'

Hoping she had successfully distracted him from what he saw as his duty, she said, 'You're right. Why don't we eat out this evening, instead of my struggling to make a meal from some corned beef and a few potatoes?'

He agreed. 'And we could call on Geoff to tell Marie about seeing Ivor.'

The following morning she went to see Geoff and, finding him alone, told him what they had seen. It was up to him whether or not to tell Marie.

Geoff thought about the information for a long time. He came to the conclusion that he needed to find out more before telling Marie anything. It could be perfectly innocent; they might have met by accident. They could have been part of a group of people out for the evening.

He thought of the many people he knew who went out regularly, the same evening every week, and, hoping this was true of Ivor, on the same day the following week Geoff went to the cinema where he had been seen, and watched. There were several other cinemas in the town but he pinned his hopes on them being persuaded back by the previous week's trailer. He was lucky and, sitting in a café and then a public house until the programme finished, he was there waiting as they came out, and he followed them back to the lodging house.

She was holding his arm, and laughter rang out occasionally as they discussed their evening. Geoff felt anger rising with every step he took. Ivor shouldn't be laughing. He had no right to be happy. He went back to where he'd parked the car and drove home, trying to work out what he should say to Marie. Was this woman the cause of it all? Had Ivor tried to see Marie to tell her he'd found someone else? Marie was in bed when he went in and he sighed with relief. At least he had a reprieve; he needn't make up his mind what to say to her until tomorrow.

Eight

Jennie was confused by Ernie's neglect of her. Confused, hurt and deeply unhappy. She couldn't tell anyone, as she believed the fault lay with her. Yet what had she done that was so wrong?

She had bathed and applied light make-up, arranged her hair around her shoulders as attractively as she could, and worn the most beautiful nightgown and matching negligée. It had been made by a professional dress-maker from delicate material and trimmed with lace and swansdown, which had taken a lot of finding and cost a lot of money. He hadn't even looked at her wearing it.

On that first night when anticipation had heightened her desire, he had slipped into bed after undressing in the bathroom of their hotel and, turning his back to her, gone immediately to sleep.

Every night of their honeymoon had been the same. On one occasion he had kissed her lightly, briefly, almost apologetically, pulling away before she could sink into his arms as a wife should. Since then there had been nothing. Every morning he ate breakfast then immersed himself in the morning papers.

She watched him now, eating his breakfast toast, one and a half slices, never more never less. She could predict what would happen every hour from now till bedtime

After breakfast and having perused the papers they would go for a walk and occasionally eat lunch in a restaurant. In the afternoon he dozed a little and the evening was spent listening to the wireless. At ten forty-five it was cocoa and bed. For a man of fifty it was a very dull life. Twice a week he went to his club and she went to see either Marie or her parents. For a lively minded young woman longing for romance it was utter misery.

A lady came to clean but Jennie was expected to cook their meals and do the shopping, wandering around like the other women of the town, looking for something with which to feed them. Domesticity, even with the help provided, did not make Jennie feel like a fulfilled woman.

Every night in her dreams she lived a very different life, with someone who roused her body from its torpor with love and attention. Every morning when she woke, the misery of her existence was revived.

There was no one she could tell. How could she admit such failure? Lucy would probably laugh, convinced that as usual she was exaggerating. Marie found it difficult to discuss such private concerns. Since the few revelations on returning from her honeymoon, Marie quickly changed the subject when anything private was mentioned. No, this was something she would have to cope with alone.

Early one evening, she was sitting outside the back door in the small boring garden, looking at the boring houses nearby, wondering how she had got herself into this boring situation, dreaming of a way out of it, when she became aware of someone watching her. She turned to see Bill leaning on the doorframe staring at her, his face stony and his eyes cold.

'What time will you be getting supper?' he asked.

'Nine thirty on the dot, as always.'

'As my father insists.'

'Yes,' she agreed, turning away. 'He likes the house to run to a timetable.'

'Like the local railway station.'

She turned again to look at him; it was the closest they had got to a conversation for a long time.

'How do you cope with it?' he asked.

'I'm very content.' Her reply was spoken primly, and his response was to laugh. She stood up and tried to push past him. 'It's time for me to see Lucy and collect the appointments book and money,' she said. His hand on her arm held her back. 'Exactly twenty past five, on the dot,' he said, his lips close to her ear. 'Tea-time at six, supper at nine thirty. What time is fun?'

'Get out of the way, Bill.' She struggled but his arm came around and held her.

'Be honest, you're hating it. Marriage to my father isn't the soft life you expected it to be, is it?'

'I'm fine, leave me alone.'

'Not quite yet. It's almost half past five, so he'll be in the bathroom, getting ready for the evening. Taking off his second best suit and changing into an older pair of trousers – still neatly pressed of course – and a sports jacket.' Then he kissed her.

The effect on her was startling, then she was enveloped in a rush of hot desire. He released her and stared into her eyes, his breath fast. A need for him swelled and tearfully she pushed him away and ran towards the door to the shop. She didn't go in, but stood there trying to compose herself, shame and an almost desperate need fighting within her. This was something else she couldn't tell Lucy.

Geoff said nothing to Marie about seeing Ivor going into the lodging house with the young woman. He had watched them on two other occasions, always on the same night, always going to the pictures. Whatever was going on, it seemed Ivor wasn't suffering loneliness.

Had it all been planned? The chance of him finding a woman friend so soon after leaving his family was remote. More and more he believed that Ivor's departure had little or nothing to do with the revelations about his father, and instead had been to do with this other woman. Had he moved them from their home deliberately, avoiding the embarrassment of walking away while living among people he knew well?

If this were the case then his infatuation for this rather plain woman must be very strong. So how could he tell Marie?

Rhodri had found it easy to go out at night. He slept on the ground floor of Geoff's shop so there were no creaking stairs to worry him. He simply unlocked the back door and walked down the path and out into the lane. The lock was well oiled, the doors a good fit, so he left without a sound. It had been raining but now the air was clean and fresh and he paused a moment to savour it.

There was a street lamp at both ends of the lane behind Steeple Street but the lane was shadowed by high walls and there was never anyone about. Stepping cautiously out on to the street, he straightened up and with a purposeful stride set off for Badgers Brook.

264

He knew he would look less suspicious if he appeared to have some destination in mind rather than wandering around aimlessly.

The first night he went out he saw a For Sale notice propped carelessly against the gate and immediately picked it up. This couldn't be right. Nearby was the house name sign. It had been broken, presumably by workmen as they pushed wheelbarrows and tools through the gate. Nearby was a scattering of oddments: paint tins, left over putty, pieces of wood. He carefully removed the wood and built it into a pile ready to burn. Struggling and having to stop repeatedly for a rest, he managed to transport both signs into the wood and hide them behind some straggly bushes.

For a long time he stood staring up at the house, and then he looked through the window. Devoid of people, the place was bare, unwanted, deprived of a purpose, and it bothered him. Houses should be filled with things, and alive with the sound of voices. For a moment he heard names called, the names of old friends, long gone, and the loved voice of his wife, which in its turn was overlaid by the calls and the laughter of Ivor, Marie and the children.

He rubbed the glass with his sleeve to see more clearly and choked back laughter when he heard someone approaching, whistling merrily the George Formby hit, 'When I'm

Cleaning Windows'.

He leaned close to the glass, which was cold against his face, and he could hear the hiss of bicycle tyres on the damp ground. Backing into the shadows as the early morning traveller came nearer, he leaned on the door, hiding his face against the freshly painted wood. The lock gave way, sending him sprawling on to the cold slate kitchen floor. He jumped up quickly and pushed the door closed. He could still hear the whistler, the sound fading away, the melody uninterrupted.

Dawn was breaking and he didn't have time for anything more than a brief look around. Then, smiling happily, he hurried home and was in bed deeply asleep when Marie came in to the storeroom where he slept, with a cup of tea to wake him. For a moment or two he wondered whether he had dreamed his escapade.

The following night he went out again. This time when he passed the front of the shop he saw a face staring out of an upstairs window, ghostlike in the darkness. He stopped and stared and a hand waved before the face disappeared. A moment later, an excited Violet emerged from the house and ran towards him.

'Can't you sleep either, Grandfather?'

'I was going for a walk. Would you like to come?'

'Please.'

'Then could you bring some matches? I forgot to bring them. And get your coat,' he whispered.

He led her to Badgers Brook and into the wood beside it, where he had hidden the For Sale notice and the house sign.

'This is a mistake, you see,' he explained, 'and I think it's best if we burn it. The house name, too, as it's broken. I bet Geoff will make us a new one.'

They built a fire from paper taken from an ashbin of a nearby house and dry grasses found in the lee of a hedge, and added thin branches and the oddments he had gathered. Once it was blazing he added the two wooden notice boards. Once it was ablaze Rhodri touched Violet's arm and pulled her away to hide behind a thick oak tree. 'Remnants,' he told her, 'of a forest after which Cwm Derw was named.'

'If they see us they'll tell us off, won't they?' Violet said.

'Badgers Brook isn't for sale you know,' he replied with a frown.

No one came and the fire slowly died out. Rhodri darted forward and moved the unburned wood so it was caught in the flames, then went back to Violet. 'My wife was the one for fires. Marvellous she was. She could burn anything.'

Violet's eyes glowed in the flickering light

from the final burst of flames. 'She was my grandmother, wasn't she?' He seemed surprised, and smiling widely, agreed that she was. 'Can I come with you again, Grandfather?'

'I'll throw something up at your window if I'm going anywhere interesting,' he promised.

'Gravel, or a piece of stick.'

Like conspirators they parted at the house with whispered goodbyes, and Rhodri waited until the face reappeared in the window and the thin arm rose in a final wave before going inside for a few hours of sleep. He was whistling softly, the tune the early morning cyclist had been whistling: 'When I'm Cleaning Windows'.

He and Violet went out several more times, one night spending hours watching as the badgers from the sett in the wood foraged for their nightly feed. Time was forgotten as they saw the animals play, chasing each other between the rows of crops in the farmer's field, eating noisily and with obvious enjoyment the grubs and small creatures they found. The crunch of peas in their powerful jaws wouldn't please the farmer, although he objected to their snacking on his crops far less than he did to poachers. After all, the land had been theirs for many years, long before the ancient oaks had been cut down.

After watching the badgers depart, back to their sett, they had sat in the kitchen of Badgers Brook for a long time, talking about the magical scene they had witnessed. When they suddenly realized that it was light they hurriedly ran out of the front door and towards the town.

Police were everywhere. Roger called to let the others know she was found and ran to her, his relief showing in the anger he displayed. 'Where have you been, you stupid girl?'

Marie was sobbing as she ran and hugged her. 'Are you all right? Did he hurt you? Did he make you go with him?'

Tearfully, trying to hold on to Rhodri's hand, Violet protested they'd had a lovely walk, but Rhodri was grabbed and taken away in a police car.

Marie and Geoff were confused. They had no idea he'd been out. The following day the doctor made it clear she had failed her father-in-law, given him insufficient care, especially when he saw the room where Rhodri had been sleeping. 'It won't do, Mrs Masters. It really won't do.' The hospital took him back and insisted that it might be a long time before he was again released into her care.

The shop Marie had been employed to manage was depressing. The outside was painted

269

brown but much of the paint had worn away, the weather having taken its toll through many winters and summers. The window was dressed to attract the older woman and had very little appeal even to the limited custom it hoped to coax through its door. Heavy vests, huge knickers, lisle stockings and corsets had been given valuable window space, and these Marie hid away in a drawer hoping she would never be asked for them. It was no longer going to be that kind of shop. Clothes were rationed but, after all, the coupons *were* used, and she was determined that, once she had taken over, more ladies of the town would be spending their precious allocation with her.

Living behind Geoff's shop, it was easy to spend time browsing through the tins of paint, choosing suitable colours. The changes would be dramatic rather than tentative, she decided, and she chose a buttercup yellow for the paintwork outside and a paler primrose yellow for the shop itself.

'I swore I'd never touch another paint brush,' she said to Geoff with a wry smile, 'but it seems that if I want the work done I'll have to do it myself or accept the state of the place as it is. I'm determined to make a success of this, so out come the tools and on come the old clothes again.'

'I'll help,' Geoff promised.

Cleaning the place was hard, but compared to the awful mess they had dealt with in Badgers Brook the job was a small one. She found some curtaining in a second-hand shop which she draped across the space – little more than a cupboard – that had been allocated as a fitting room, and in a week the place was transformed. Mrs Nerys Bowen was delighted.

Buying was a complicated business and something Marie had never done. Nerys, a lady of sixty-two, dealt with officialdom with a confident manner and a very loud voice, leaving Marie to select the clothes she wanted to stock. It was June, and with the early arrival of hot summer days, the holiday season was well into its stride. Even so, Marie was careful not to over-stock on summer things. Autumn was when she planned to start her advertising campaign.

The arrival of the New Look, with designs showing an hourglass figure courtesy of Christian Dior, aroused great interest, but Marie only bought a few moderate examples. The best were so smart they would be remembered, and the fashion-conscious wouldn't like wearing them too many times. With fourteen clothing coupons needed to buy a suit, it was an extravagance many would avoid.

As usual with a new business, people came out of curiosity but many were tempted by the bright new dresses and jackets that

271

Marie had chosen as a speciality for the season's outfits.

The shop was in Steeple Street, on a corner opposite Geoff's hardware store, and Violet was content to go there after school, watching her mother's skilful sales technique and occasionally helping in the fashion shop by tidying the small space. She began taking a sketch book, drawing the outfits and some of the customers.

One day as Marie was serving their supper she showed her book to Geoff.

'Who's this?' he asked, pointing to the round-faced woman with short, tightly curled hair and small rather piercing eyes, drawn cartoon-like standing beside the shop's counter.

'Oh, she's called a couple of times but she never buys,' Violet said airily. 'A nosy parker, Mam says, wanting nothing more than a snoop around. Why, d'you think my drawing's good?'

'Very good,' Geoff said seriously. The drawing, although in the exaggerated style of a cartoon, looked remarkably like the woman who had been arm in arm with Ivor.

Was she snooping, as Violet had remarked? Not to examine the clothes on sale, but to report back to Ivor? To assure him that his wife was managing well without him and he needn't worry? He watched as Marie, smiling at her daughter and sons, served the stew

272

she had prepared using bacon bones begged from the grocer for flavour.

She seemed to be coping so well after the shock of Ivor's departure. He couldn't tell her what he'd learned about Ivor's own situation. If she found out from someone else, then it would be him to whom she turned for comfort, and he wanted that more and more every day.

Effie went back to Ivor and assured him that she had seen Marie and the shop where she now worked and all seemed to be well with her.

'And you're sure my father isn't with them?' Ivor asked anxiously.

'Quite sure. They have rooms in Geoff Tanner's house, but don't worry. I gathered from talking to a few people that Marie and Violet share a room, so you don't have to worry about Marie being disloyal.'

'Her loyalty's certain. And more than I deserve.'

'I did see your father there earlier, but I gather he's been taken away by ambulance, wandering around at night and taking a young girl with him.' She omitted to tell him the young girl had been his daughter.

'And they're all safe?'

'Safe and apparently very happy,' she said, hoping his dream of going back to them would slowly fade. 'I think they are happier,

273

from what you told me about them, more settled. Marie is relaxed and she smiles a lot. The boys are working hard. I suppose they've begun to pull together, that always brings families closer, doesn't it?'

'We were all very happy until I found my father and tried to help him.'

'Maybe you were, maybe you weren't,' she said. 'but if you'd been really together, you and Marie, wouldn't you have told her the truth before you married her?' He looked stricken but didn't reply. She went on softly, 'Now you can tell me anything, anything at all, can't you?'

'Yes, but with Marie there was so much more at risk than with you. I loved her. I always will.'

It was Effie's turn to look stricken. 'Of course, I can understand I'm not so important, Ivor, dear. But your reluctance still shows a lack of trust in Marie, doesn't it?'

Ivor was too unhappy to realize he had hurt her feelings. A few days later he told her he was considering a change of occupation. 'Instead of going from house to house collecting the weekly insurance payments, I've been offered a position in the office. My employers know I'm studying for an accountancy qualification and they encourage me. They've promised me time to study and even offer financial assistance to pay for books and other needs.'

274

'I do give some good advice then? Suggesting you tried your accountancy exams?'

'I'll always be grateful to you for that, and for listening to my tale of woe.'

'Wait a moment, this is beginning to sound like goodbye.'

He still dreamed of one day returning to Marie and the children, but apart from missing them dreadfully, he had no complaints about his new life. 'No, I'm not going anywhere. For one thing I can't afford anything better, can I? I have to continue sending money to Marie.'

Effie was a good friend, Ivor mused. She was supportive of his ambitions and, when they went out once a week as a break from the routine of study, she was excellent company, light-hearted and easy to talk to. She boosted his confidence when he felt low and by encouraging him to achieve his qualification she unknowingly reinforced his belief that one day he and Marie would be reunited.

Borrowing a car one day he took her out for a drive. He felt she deserved it after all the help she had given him. They went to Pembroke and found a secluded beach, where they sat for a while and talked. It was then that she began to talk about her own background and admitted that when she was only sixteen she'd had a child.

'You poor girl! What happened to it?' Ivor

asked, at once concerned.

'I was sent away and the little girl was taken from me straight after the birth. I wasn't allowed to see her.'

'Didn't the father intervene?'

'No. He denied it and walked away leaving me to the shame and humiliation. My parents have had little to do with me since. I worked in hotels where the accommodation was part of the wage, and it wasn't until a few months ago that I found a job that paid well enough for me to afford this boarding house.'

'Where is the father now? Do you see him or at least know where he lives?'

'Oh yes. I know where he lives.'

Jennie began to look out for Bill's return whenever he went out. Working shifts at the railway station he was at home at irregular times. Despite her determination to avoid him, his comings and goings were the pattern of her pleasure. After trying to ignore him, keep out of his way, he had worn her resistance down and now she was waiting for the small gifts of his attention like a lovesick schoolgirl.

When he was in the house, darting glances at her, looking at her with longing, she was alive. When he was away from her it was as though all the warmth and love she yearned for had been taken from her. Occasionally they would find themselves alone in the house and he would hold her in his arms as though she were the most precious thing. Then he would ease away from her with an expression of such regret that her need of him increased to a pitch where she was prepared to take a chance on their being discovered.

There were times when she wondered if he was playing with her affection, teasing her for his own amusement. He had never wanted her to marry his father, believed her to be a cheap tart, and this could be his revenge. But then she would see him, recognize the hurt in his eyes and know that although theirs was an impossible love, it was real.

The inevitable happened one evening in late June, when Ernie had gone to his club to meet friends. Believing she was alone in the house, Jennie had bathed and was sitting listening to the wireless, dressed in a silky kimono, a shawl around her shoulders, drinking a cup of tea before going to bed.

The door opened and closed and, although it was early, she called, believing it to be Ernie.

'I'm in here, Ernie, dear. Would you like a hot drink before bed?'

'Dad won't be home for more than an hour. He's at his club.' His breathless voice startled her and she stood up. As she turned he came towards her so they collided, and neither had the strength to move away.

There was a celebration at the shop in Steeple Street. Geoff had told them that Badgers Brook was ready for their return. He also told them he had bought it and the tenancy was safely in Marie's name. 'Only until Ivor comes back,' he added, 'then the rent book will be transferred to him.' He wanted to be sure she didn't turn the offer down for fear of proprietary interest on his part.

'It was meant to be,' he told Marie and an excited Violet and the twins. 'Apparently a couple of prospective purchasers went to see it but couldn't find it. Someone had taken down the For Sale notice and burned it in the wood.'

'It was us!' Violet shouted. 'Grandfather and I did it! He said it was wrong, that the house was ours, and said the notice had to be burned. So he took it into the wood and I gave him some matches and we had a wonderful bonfire.'

'Violet, love, I think it's best you keep it as our secret. Can you do that?' Geoff asked. 'If you tell anyone we might have to give the house back.'

'We can tell grandfather though, can't we?'

'I'll take you with me when I go to see him,' Marie said, hugging the excited child, 'and you can tell him yourself.'

Violet clapped her hands and danced around. 'He said his wife – my grandmother – was very good at fires, but I think he's very good too, don't you?'

Anxious looks passed between Marie and Geoff, who said, 'I think that's part of our secret too.'

Violet nodded agreement.

Rhodri came out of hospital after three weeks, and soon began going out at night again. Sometimes, when she was woken by gravel chattering against her window, Violet went with him. She would appear at the door with whispered greetings and offer her hand before walking with him to watch the badgers until dawn began to lighten the summer skies.

Effie told Ivor the news she had learned from a visit to the local shops not far from Steeple Street. 'Your Marie is moving back to the house near the wood now the repairs are done.' Putting the strongest slant on it she said, 'Geoff has bought it for her. That's a surprise, isn't it? People are beginning to suspect they're getting close. What do you think? She touched his arm affectionately. 'No one has suggested that he's moving in with them, mind, but it's possible.'

'Of course it isn't. Marie wouldn't do anything to embarrass the children, for one thing.'

'I just wanted to prepare you, so you won't have such a shock. After all, everyone knows *you* left *her*, so there'll be some sympathy for her.'

'I don't want to think about it,' Ivor said angrily.

'Pity, because I've had an idea that you might like to consider. If we shared a room, it would be much cheaper. You could put a bit of money by for the future.'

'We couldn't do that!'

'Don't worry, I'm not suggesting anything improper. We could arrange for the room to be partitioned at night, so we have a private sleeping area each.' She put a newspaper in front of him and pointed to an advertisement in the rooms to let column, tapping it with her stubby fingers.

He pushed it away, and after a pause she said sadly, 'All right then, I might as well tell you. There *are* rumours about your wife and Geoff, and it seems highly possible that they are more than friends.' She was lying, but doubted whether he would go and investigate. He couldn't face his wife, and unless he heard a denial from her lips he would never be sure. Working on his sense of failure would be easy. He was so ready to believe that Geoff was a better man than he.

She concentrated on making herself indispensable to him. She anticipated many of his needs, bought his newspaper on mornings

280

he was a bit late, ran errands in her lunch-time, returned his library books and chose others; she took his shirts to the laundry and collected them. She wanted him to know he could rely on her, believe that she cared.

One morning a letter came for him and she stared at the envelope as though X-ray vision would reveal the contents. It was hand-written but didn't look official and she was tempted to open it. Could it be from his wife? If so she didn't want him to see it. After a glance around to make sure she was un-observed she slipped it behind the hall mirror. He didn't need any contact with Cwm Derw; she would fill his life from now on.

He was more relaxed with her, accepting her friendly overtures, and flattered her with praise for her thoughtfulness. Sharing a room with him would be a big step forward in her plan to make him forget Marie and the children. She would make him think of his earlier life as a boring overture to the big performance, herself and Ivor in the love of the century.

Over the next few weeks as June drifted lazily out in a heat haze to make way for July, they went to see several rooms, many of which he discarded as being impossible to segregate into his and hers sleeping quarters. In the first week of a hot, steamy July, they found one that suited and moved in.

The letter from Geoff, telling Ivor of his father's release from hospital, remained hidden behind the mirror in the lodging house from where Ivor and Effie had just moved.

Nine

'I can't believe we're moving again!' Marie stared at the chaos of boxes around her then looked at Geoff. He stood with one hand on a hip, waiting for her to tell him which of the mysterious symbols indicated the first box to be loaded on to his van.

'At least we won't have to clear out all the rubbish, like last time. Which reminds me, where is Rhodri?' Geoff asked.

'He's been missing since early morning. He's probably waiting until we've moved back in before showing himself; he gets very agitated by upheavals. He'll probably wander in and inspect his bedroom and handle his few possessions without a word.'

Rhodri was happy to be once more out of hospital, and he had been given a list of jobs to do to help with the move. Before dawn, however, he had left the room where he'd slept since they had left Badgers Brook and, having taken a couple of slices of bread and an apple, was in the wood not far from the house, waiting for the van to arrive with the

283

first load. He was hiding behind a hawthorn bush, peering through the close tangle of branches, a dejected expression on his face, like a child expecting punishment and delaying it for as long as he could. His limbs shook with fear.

The van came along the lane and he darted further into the protection of the prickly branches. He heard the van doors open and the shouts as Geoff and the twins began to remove the load. Light footsteps ran down the path he had helped to clear of weeds. When they stopped he only imagined hearing the door of the house opening, but the gasp of annoyance from Marie, the shout for Geoff to come, was heard as clearly as though he were standing next to her, staring in at the mess he had once again created.

'No food or filth this time, be thankful for that,' Geoff said as he looked at the piles and scattered spread of newspapers that almost filled the kitchen and living room.

'We haven't looked upstairs yet!' Marie said.

They explored the house and found that apart from some rather neatly arranged newspapers in the bedroom that had been used by Rhodri the place was clear.

'So this is why he disappeared so early this morning,' Geoff said and he began to laugh.

Ruefully, Marie shared his amusement. 'At least I can't complain of life being dull.'

Emptying the van of their personal belongings then refilling it with the newspapers to take to the rubbish tip was hard work, and to Marie's surprise her sister turned up mid-morning and began to help. She had never known Jennie volunteer for anything, certainly not anything that could be described as work, but she helped Roger and Royston place the rugs and carpets then began emptying boxes and filling the kitchen cupboards while they moved the furniture back into place.

It was Jennie who made tea once Geoff had got the fire burning well. She also made toast with bread and margarine, which Belle had provided and which she had remembered to bring with her. Marie was grateful, but wondered what had happened for her sister to change so much. With a cynicism that shamed her, she wondered whether her sister wanted to ask a big favour.

When everything had finally been put back in place and every box unpacked, and Badgers Brook looked once more like a home, Geoff walked around the garden. He spotted a lone figure darting through the trees.

'Rhodri is out there,' he said when he came back inside. 'He's watching us but when I try to approach he runs away.'

'I'll go and talk to him, he must be hungry as well as upset,' Marie said.

'Better if I go, Mam,' Violet said. 'He'll talk to me.'

Jennie had gone home and it was almost time for bed and Rhodri still hadn't been coaxed into the house. It was again Jennie who came to the rescue. 'Rhodri's very fond of Jennie,' Marie said. 'Perhaps he'll come inside if she asks?' Marie looked at her daughter. 'It's very late, but will you come with me and ask her, Violet?'

She had guessed from her sister's appearance and her lack of joy that Jennie and Ernie had had a quarrel. Marie was dreading the meeting, convinced that she was walking into a row, but Ernie seemed pleased to see them. He kissed Violet lightly on the cheek and offered a hand to Marie. 'So you've finished for today, have you?'

'Jennie's been a wonderful help,' Marie said. 'I don't think we'd have done half as much if she hadn't been there. Now we'd like to borrow her again. I know it's late but we're worried about Rhodri. He's upset and won't come into the house. We think he'd come if Jennie asked him.' She declined to explain further, waffling about the move upsetting him rather than tell him about Rhodri filling the house with rubbish. Ernie wasn't too keen on Jennie befriending the confused old man and he mightn't allow her to go with them if he thought the man was even the slightest threat.

Jennie agreed at once and, carrying a cushion that she had bought as a house-warming gift for her sister, and a box of Cadbury's Milk Tray, she said, 'These will coax him back. He won't be able to resist a couple of gifts.' She climbed into the back of the van and sat with her feet curled sideways, and Ernie handed in a couple of cushions so she could be comfortable. Violet sat beside her and they set off, the little girl very excited, treating the whole thing as an adventure.

When they reached Badgers Brook Violet jumped down and went straight into the wood, Jennie following.

'Grandfather?' Violet called. 'Come on, silly. I'm allowed to stay up for supper if you come in now.'

'We're all starving and if you come home now I can have some too,' Jennie called. 'Come and see how cosy it looks.'

'And we've got presents for you,' Violet added.

Jennie held up the carrier bag containing the cushion and held out the box of chocolates. Then she offered her hand and he came slowly out. 'Here you are, a new cushion for your chair,' Jennie said, 'and some chocolates just for you.'

No criticism was spoken. They greeted him as though his absence had been something he couldn't have avoided, and they all went in for supper: their first meal back in their home.

It was eleven thirty when Jennie was once more dropped off at home, Ernie and Bill were there to welcome her. Jennie kept away from Bill, making sure that Ernie was between them. What they had done must not happen again.

When they weren't at work, the twins spent time clearing the garden of weeds that had flourished in their absence. They invited friends to help, which resulted in a party atmosphere that delighted Marie. The twins had changed a great deal, becoming more thoughtful and willing to help. They were protective of Violet, no longer considering her a nuisance. They were now fifteen and the troubles of the past months had sobered them, driven out the stupidity and rebelliousness of their age. Marie watched them with pride, and sadness too. Ivor should be here to share it.

Effie didn't tell Ivor that his family had moved back to the house he had found for them, or that his father had left the hospital and been given into Marie's care. She wanted him to forget his family. He belonged to her now and nothing would ever come between them.

Although they now shared a single room, it

had been a disappointment to realize that her suggestion to divide the room, partitioning off an area with curtains and bookshelves, would be more than a temporary arrangement. She had believed it would last just long enough to save embarrassment and ease those first few moments, after which the barriers would fall and they would share a bed.

When he continued to sleep on a couch that was too short to accommodate him comfortably she offered her bed, and when he'd looked startled she had hastily added that she meant to change with him and sleep on the couch. Although she had been able to cover her error, it confirmed her fears that he had no intention of moving into her bed. Somehow she had to make him forget Marie and his children. But how? She didn't harbour enough hatred for Marie and the children to really harm them. Not like that other girl who had come between her and the man she had loved. No, she had to convince Ivor that they no longer needed him and he was free.

Ivor's promotion and the reduced rent resulting from the shared room meant he could send money regularly to Marie at Geoff's, and he wondered how soon they would find themselves a home away from the cramped situation behind Geoff's shop.

Surely they could manage to rent a small house now, with Marie managing the gown shop and both boys in regular employment. And no one to steal the rent money, he added silently. What a fool he had been, basing his happiness on lies. Marie would have accepted his true story as easily as she had accepted the plight of the poor confused man who was his father.

He occasionally had to use the manager's car to go to out of town meetings, and late one afternoon when he was returning from an appointment he was passing near Cwm Derw, and on impulse turned the car and drove to Steeple Street. He had no intention of going into the hardware store, or asking about Marie and the children. He didn't want to ruin everything for them again.

He knew the car was not one Geoff would recognize, and he sat there for a long time, within sight of both the hardware store on one corner and Nerys's smartly painted gown shop on another. He didn't move, just watched customers come and go and wondered what time Marie closed her shop. He only wanted to see her, assure himself that she was well and looked happy.

Five o'clock came and went, and there was no sign of her. Geoff put the closed sign on his door and dropped the shutters on the windows. Ivor watched Marie's shop through the driving mirror but didn't see her leave. Then at twenty to six she came out and pulled the door closed and leaned on it to make sure it was firmly shut. She set off, high heels clacking, but not, as he had expected, towards Geoff's shop.

Puzzled, he wondered whether she was going to put takings into the night safe. But no, she went past the bank and stood at the bus stop. She was dressed in a smart sky-blue two-piece suit and white high-heeled strappy summer shoes and she carried a white handbag and wore a cardigan loosely over her shoulders.

An aching longing and an anguished regret swelled within him, love for her making tears threaten. He loved her so much and he'd destroyed their marriage by his lack of confidence in *her* love for *him*. His hand reached for the door handle and he was about to leap out and run to her, hold her and beg her forgiveness. As his fingers grasped the cold metal a bus turned into the road and lumbered to a stop. She jumped on and he started the engine prepared to follow.

It was unlikely she was going out for the evening; she would go home and attend to the family first. Yet the bus was taking her out of the town in the direction of Badgers Brook. What could she want there? At every bus stop he slowed the car and waited until the bus had deposited passengers and moved off again, making sure she was still on board.

At the stop closest to Badgers Brook she stepped off, waved to someone she knew and set off along the lane. He parked the car and, careful to avoid being seen, he followed.

Violet opened the door and hugged Marie and again he was almost overwhelmed with love and sadness. The door closed and he crept closer. Few people passed the house and neighbours were too far away to observe as he stood near the gate, hidden by the tall privet hedge. Although he watched for a long time, no one came out and he dared to step forward and look inside. The place was furnished with things he recognized. They were living there and it was as though they had never been away. So she was using the money he'd sent.

He was pleased about that. It was at least some compensation for what he had done to them. The owner had presumably changed his mind about selling. He hurried back to the car, telling himself he should be content to know they were safe, but his heart was heavy and he didn't think that would ever change.

It was after returning the car and beginning to walk to the room he shared that he wondered why Effie hadn't told him. Only days ago she had reported seeing them and assured him that they were with Geoff and apparently settled. From the little he had seen of Badgers Brook they had been there

292

for a while. The garden was orderly and obviously regularly tended. Perhaps they hadn't moved out after all. But Effie told him they had been living with Geoff Tanner above the hardware store. Effie was a friend and she wouldn't lie, there had to be another explanation. But he couldn't think of one.

'Sorry, but I didn't want to upset you by telling you they were happily settled back in the house you'd found for them, which they'd then lost,' Effie said, helping him off with his jacket.

'But you know I'd have been pleased to see them safely back in a home of their own. They must have been very uncomfortable in the rooms behind Geoff's shop. It was no way for a family to live.'

Seeing her chance, she said, 'How many rooms were there? Enough to give Marie one, and Violet, and the twins? And still find a room for Geoff? It didn't look big enough for there to be more than three bedrooms. Five they'd have needed.'

'Why would they need five?'

'Your father was there too.'

'I didn't know that.'

'I was trying not to worry you. Although he seemed perfectly well when I saw him.' She put an arm around his shoulder and bent her head towards him. 'Don't worry, Ivor dear. Let it all go, they don't need you now, you're free.'

'If you love someone you're never free, nor want to be.'

'Love has to be reciprocated.' Then she turned to set out knives and forks on the folding table set for supper. 'Three bedrooms? I wonder who shared with who?' She spoke the words almost silently, but he heard, she was certain he had heard. She took a salad from the meat safe and added two small slices of corned beef to the plates. Best she say nothing more, just allow the idea to germinate in its own time.

She could see that he was upset. The relief of knowing Marie and the children were safely settled again was gone. A depression emanated from him that filled the room like a fog. He looked at the food, shook his head and went into the small area that was partitioned off during the night. To her dismay he moved the bookcase and pulled the curtains across.

She left him for a while then offered an alternative meal or a cup of tea, then tried to coax him with the suggestion that they might go to the pub for an hour before it closed. To everything she tried he simply shook his head without a word.

At nine o'clock she went to bed but she didn't sleep. She was alert to the possibility that he would get up at least to undress. It was unimaginable that someone as fastidious as Ivor could sleep in his clothes.

She heard the church clock chime midnight and crept over to see that Ivor was still dressed, and hadn't moved from when he'd collapsed on the bed. She undid the buttons on his jacket and then removed his belt. The buttons on his trousers were a little stiff but she managed, and she gently eased them down, planning to remove them and cover him with a blanket from her own bed.

He sighed, hardly more than the expelling of air, and she stopped and waited until he was relaxed once more. With only a faint light from the street lamp outside, she didn't see him open his eyes or realize he was watching her until he sat up and pushed her roughly away.

'What are you doing?' he demanded, whispering out of respect for the hour.

'I was only trying to make you comfortable, Ivor. Here, see? I have one of my blankets to put over you.'

She was wearing a nightgown that was open at the neck, and seeing her generous figure so close made desire wash over him, quickly followed by anger. 'Go away.' His voice was threatening.

'I was only making you more comfortable so you'd sleep,' she sobbed, wrapping herself in the blanket she had meant for him.

It was five o'clock when she was again roused from light sleep by the sound of him moving. 'Ivor?' she whispered. 'Do you need anything?'

'I'm going for a walk.' Reaching in the recess for his coat, he left the house, giving her no time to follow.

At five o'clock that morning, Jennie was also unable to sleep. The afternoon before, while Ernie took his usual afternoon nap, Bill had opened the door of the room where she sat beside her gently snoring husband and beckoned to her. She turned away, but he came slowly into the room, his eyes watching her, his smile trying to share the amusement of his father's unconscious form beside her. He kissed her cheek, her throat, her neck, his breath like a tempting breeze, hardly there at all, but the gentle touch made resistance impossible. He offered his hand and she rose, guilt and desire in equal parts making her tremble. Ernie moved slightly, reacting to the loss of her weight beside him, then settled back peacefully into his slumbers.

'How can it hurt him?' Bill asked when they were alone in his room. 'He'll never know.'

'But I know, and he's been so kind to me.'

'Kind!' Bill snorted derisively. 'He's an old man and he's stealing your youth.'

It was easy to be persuaded. Jennie suffered loneliness and also the humiliation of Ernie's indifference. She desperately longed for evidence that she was desirable. She was in a marriage that was outwardly perfect but which was, in truth, a sham. It was taking its toll and she felt her attractiveness shrinking away. She would soon be middle-aged, yet a few short months ago she and Lucy were living like twenty-year-olds, with a constant stream of admirers, sure of fun and laughter every time they went out.

She was no longer encouraged to wear clothes that added to her attraction; instead Ernie constantly reminded her that she was now a respectable married woman, whatever he meant by that. Married? Hardly a marriage when he turned from her every night. Respectable? Then why was she in Bill's room allowing him to undress her, while Ernie slept the afternoon away?

So at five the following morning she lay awake, wondering how she could escape from the stupid deal she had entered and return to how things were. Even with the increase in the number of divorces since the end of the war, and the comparative case with which they could be obtained, there was still a stigma when a woman was the guilty party, and she didn't think she could persuade Ernie to allow her to divorce him.

At five o'clock that morning, as Ivor was hurrying from the room he shared with Effie, Jennie crept out of bed, being careful not to disturb Ernie, and taking the bicycle that had years ago taken Bill on long rides

297

into the country she pushed it into the back lane. She struggled for a while, cycling had never been a favourite mode of transport, it ruined her hair style and she'd always felt silly when she was dressed to go dancing. When balance was mastered she headed for Badgers Brook. She had to talk to someone and knew Marie would listen even though there was no advice she, or anyone else, could offer.

It was still early and she had to knock on the door a few times then throw gravel up at her sister's window before she had any response. A sleepy Marie opened the door and invited her in.

'What's happened? Have you left him?' she asked, seeing from the lack of make-up and the untidy dress that her sister was seriously depressed. 'I'll just make a cup of tea, and if I can revive the fire sufficiently we'll have some toast.'

'No, I haven't left Ernie, but I wish I'd never married him.' Jennie slumped down beside the scrubbed table and lowered her head on to her arms. 'Why didn't anyone stop me?'

'If you're asking whether I approved, well, no, I didn't. But to be honest, Jen, I thought you knew how it would be and had decided that a meal-ticket for life made the sacrifice worth while.'

'Sacrifice? Is that what I did?'

'You must have known that Ernie wouldn't be the most exciting husband.'

'At least he wouldn't run off without a word, leave me to fend for myself!' Having said the spiteful words, remorse made her cry. 'Sorry, Marie, sorry, sorry, sorry.'

Marie hugged her. 'It's all right, I understand how angry you are. We both made a wrong choice it seems. Although I'd welcome Ivor back with open arms if he turned up one day.'

'What am I to do?'

'Cope, I suppose, like the rest of us do.' She attended to the tea tray and cut bread for toast. 'I often stand and watch people busily rushing around about their business, all appearing to be content, smiling as they pass, cheerfully commenting on the weather or the shortages, and I wonder what they go home to. Is everything perfect for them? Am I the only one to exist in a state of constant anxiety, wondering why Ivor couldn't trust me, or talk to me, and asking myself whether things will ever change? Perhaps the calm countenance of those we see, and their ready smiles, change to misery and despair once the door closes behind them and they disappear into their private lives. Perhaps I seem trouble-free to those who watch me.'

'I believe I am ridiculed by those who watch me about my daily routine. Smiles change to jeers as they look away, politeness wiped from their faces, laughing at my stupidity in marrying a man almost as old as our dad.'

Marie placed a cup of tea in front of Jennie. She didn't know what to say. Too much and it would be returned as fuel for argument. Too little and she'd be accused of not caring.

'Perhaps it's better to do nothing, wait a while, then, after a year or so discuss separation. Mam and Dad won't like it, but it's your life after all.'

'I couldn't live like this for that long.'

'What's the alternative? It isn't as though there's someone else.' She was aware of a sudden jerky movement of Jennie's arm and she stared at her in alarm. 'Jennie? You aren't telling me the full story, are you?'

'I can't tell you everything, I'm too ashamed.'

'This is me, your sister who opened the bedroom window for you to climb back in after several of your escapades so you wouldn't get caught. Who lent you money. Covered up for you on a hundred occasions. Told lies to boyfriends you wanted to discourage. Tell me.'

'It's Bill.'

'Bill James? Your — what is he, your stepson? Oh, Jennie, what have you done?'

'Made an impossible situation a hundred times worse.' The frown left her face and for

300

a moment she was a schoolgirl again as she said, with a trembly smile, 'Our Mam'll kill me, won't she?'

'If she doesn't, someone else will!'

Ivor was standing in the wood with a distant view of Badgers Brook. He saw Jennie leaving and glanced at his watch. It was time he left. He had never been late for work and although he didn't want to spend the day dealing with finance when he could remain standing here, close to Marie and the children, he knew he must.

On occasions he felt a strong belief that one day he would return to the family he loved, and, as he stood at the edge of the trees, hope was strong. He had to wait until he felt brave enough to tell Marie everything. Not only Marie, but the boys and Violet. They must understand why he lied.

The trees around him were filled with birdsong. Blackbirds sang their mellow hymn to the glories of the morning. A thrush competed, repeating each phrase, 'Lest you should think he never could recapture the first fine careless rapture,' as the poet Browning had described it.

He had been standing so still that the birds had accepted him as a fixture and a robin searched for grubs around his feet where he had disturbed the earth a little. He stayed longer than he should, unwilling to disturb them. When he moved it was the blackbird who protested the most, its clacking alarm echoing through the trees, a warning to the rest. The house called to him, yet he felt as homesick for the woodland as he did for his home and family: it was all a part of the same loss.

Jennie walked back to Ernie and found he was still asleep. There was no sign of Bill; presumably he had gone to work. She felt the teapot and found it warm. Too miserable to make a fresh pot she poured a cup and drank it, cold and unappetizing, as though it were a punishment and she deserved no better.

Geoff watched the lodging house where he had last seen Ivor for two Tuesdays without there being a sign of him, or the young woman he had been with at the cinema. Taking a chance he knocked on the door on the pretext of having a message for Ivor.

'He's gone and that woman's gone with him.' It was clear the landlady had no great opinion of either of them.

'What woman?' Geoff asked innocently.

'Effie she calls herself, works in the grocer's shop in the main road.'

'I'd be grateful for any help you can give me. I really need to find him. I'm a friend, and it's his family, you see. A quarrel. Now

302

they want to put things right.' He spoke conspiratorially, getting her on his side, and he was invited in for a cup of tea.

'Thick as thieves they were,' she told him. 'Although I don't think he was as keen as her, if you know what I mean. Dug her claws into him, that's my suspicion.'

'You're a good judge of character, Mrs Davies. Not many would have noticed that. I suppose it's because of the work you do, caring for people and making them feel that this is their home. It's a rare talent.' He allowed his eyes to wander around the old-fashioned wallpaper that had probably been there for twenty years, and the worn linoleum. 'A real homemaker, that's what you are.'

He stayed an hour and learned all he needed to know. Ivor and the woman called Effie were now sharing a single room. The implications were clear, but how could he tell Marie.

He called at Badgers Brook several evenings each week and sometimes took a rabbit or a pheasant he had bought from a farmer when he went on his weekly round delivering paraffin. Marie welcomed him and the boys enjoyed talking to him. After weeks had passed, even Violet stopped talking about Ivor.

Jennie was sometimes there when he called, and she looked so different, he asked

Marie if her sister were ill.

'Between you and me, Geoff, she's dreadfully unhappy. I don't think Ernie is a very caring husband, and you remember how lively Jennie used to be.'

'Perhaps it's taking a time to adjust,' he said, uneasy about discussing a marriage.

'What puzzles me is that Ernie knew her well – after all, she'd worked for Thelma until she died, he'd seen her dressed up, dancing, having fun – so why did he marry her and expect her to change?'

'Love doesn't have to be reasonable or logical or even hold out any hope of fulfilment, does it?' He looked at her quizzically and she turned away, afraid of what she might see in his eyes. She was fond of Geoff and was grateful for his generous friendship and support, but she would never love him.

'In spite of all he's put us through, I still love Ivor,' she said softly. 'So I know what you mean.'

Contrary to her previous unwillingness to help, Jennie offered to stay with Violet while Marie went out. Their roles were reversing, Jennie rarely going further than Badgers Brook, and Marie, free from the confines of her family, meeting her friend Judy Morris, who still worked at the gown shop for Mr Harries, to go to the pictures, or simply to a café to talk. Neither was keen on dancing, so there were few places to go, and one day

Judy suggested they went to Swansea. 'There's a train that goes all along the sea-front, to the village of Mumbles, right to the pier. Violet would love it.'

Having planned one day to go to Swansea to find Ivor, now the opportunity was there Marie panicked. What if she saw Ivor with another woman? Even if he were alone, what would she say to him? Would she show her pleasure and relief, or turn away from him? In her heart she couldn't imagine being able to turn away. She'd make a fool of herself, run to him, he'd be embarrassed, having to explain that he didn't want to go back to her, that he was content in his new life.

'No, Lucy, I can't. How can I go to the very place where I might bump into Ivor?'

It was Jennie who persuaded her, reminding her that Swansea was a large town with many areas, each with its own centre, and the likelihood of walking through the very one where Ivor lived was extremely remote.

'Promise me that if you see him you'll guide me away and not tell me,' Marie said, although she was already dreaming of seeing him, and listening to him explain the reasons why he had left and how he longed to return. In her mind's eye she saw his dearly loved face and the dream of him returning to Badgers Brook made her glow.

Jennie joined them and one Sunday they all went by train to the seaside town that from the centre appeared to be in the mountains, with hills almost all around. A short walk took them to the beach and at one of the stops they clambered aboard the Mumbles train, the first passenger railway train in the world, and, crammed in with the other excited passengers, made their way around the huge sandy bay to the village.

Pushing and shoving was part of the fun as they made their way along the narrow strip of beach, the almost full tide making them jump away from its creaming surf. They wandered past boats both on land and bobbing in the sea, which was turbulent at the top of the tide. They stopped to queue for ice-cream, then walked up to the Norman castle on its hill that looked down benevolently on the village spread out below.

The beautiful place relaxed Marie and she lost the fear of seeing Ivor and having the children upset and her own emotions thrown into turmoil. Their picnic was eaten as they rested against the ancient walls. The boys played a few games of hide-and-seek with Violet, then they went to explore the shops. Behind the shops and houses of the village were lanes where deliveries were made and the ash cart collected from the houses.

It was as they were wandering along Chapel Street, heading towards Gower Place, that Marie saw Ivor. He came out of

306

the lane behind the shops and he and Marie stared at each other. The twins and Violet were a long way ahead of her with Rhodri, so it was only Marie and Jennie whom he faced. The meeting she had imagined and hoped for so many times was nothing like her dream.

'Marie,' he murmured, his face gradually losing its colour. She turned and stumbled away across the road, ran into Gower Place and out of his sight.

Ivor began to run after her, but his legs were weak, and although he called, shouted, the pleading in his voice ending with a wail of despair, she didn't turn around.

'What have I done that he can treat me like this?' she sobbed. Jennie led her into a lane that led back to the main road, where they were hidden from the rest of the family, and held her close.

'I don't know, and until he decides to tell you we never will.'

'There's someone else. It has to be some-one else. He stole from us not because of his gambling or to help poor Rhodri, but to set up home with another woman. What a fool I've been, waiting for him to return, believing that he still loved me and it was only guilt keeping him away.'

'Fools you and me both,' Jennie said. 'Love made a fool of you and I fell for the dream of an easy life with a sugar daddy.'

★ ★ ★

Effie was cleaning the cramped room when Ivor burst in, his face ashen. She asked what was wrong but he didn't reply. He took the suitcase from under the bed and began packing his clothes into it. The task calming him, he slowed down and packed neatly, folding his clothes as carefully as usual before closing the case and putting it near the door. Staring with eyes wide with alarm Effie watched, convinced he would stop, calm down and unpack, then explain what had happened to make him panic.

'I'll pay a month's rent,' he said. 'That'll give you time to find somewhere else. This will be too expensive for you on your own. Sorry it didn't work out.'

'You're going, just like that?'

'I'll be in touch, but I can't stay here with you. Sorry.'

'No explanation?'

'Sorry,' he repeated, shaking his head but not looking at her.

'Running away is what you do, is it? Running away from home, then from Marie, and now from me.'

'Don't talk about Marie in the same breath as yourself, Effie. Marie is different. Leaving her was the one thing I will always regret.'

She tried again to explain her actions on the night he had slept in his clothes, but he refused to listen. As the door closed behind him, Effie's face lost its pleading, sorrowful expression and a hardness tightened her lips. He wasn't leaving her. She wouldn't let him. It mustn't happen. No one would walk away from her ever again. He'd beg her to take him back.

She'd make sure he never found happiness with anyone else, or, like the man whom she had truly loved and who had betrayed her, Ivor would be punished one day.

Ten

Ivor didn't know where to go. He wanted desperately to go home, back to Marie and the children, but he couldn't. After she had run away from him like a scared child, making clear her unwillingness to talk to him, there was even less chance of returning to them than before. Why hadn't he stopped her? Made her face him? He wasn't a criminal, he was just a man who had tried to reinvent his past. But that was impossible, he knew that now. Life is a mirror, reflecting all you become, and also revealing everything you have been. Facts about his childhood and his parentage couldn't be pushed away like an unwelcome nightmare; they were only too real.

He found a room in a small hotel on the seafront and, after unpacking his clothes and sorting out those needing the attention of a dry-cleaning firm, he went to the office. At least there he had no need for pretence. What they saw was what they accepted.

With a reasonable wage, he had been able to find someone willing to tutor him to study previous examination papers in preparation for starting the accountancy course at night school in September. With nothing to do after work, no company and the need to lose his sorrows in something he worked even harder, enjoying the challenge ahead of him. His tutor praised him and assured him he would do well. It was little comfort when he had no one to please apart from the tutor and himself. He needed his family, and no matter how he tried he couldn't see a way back to them without telling Marie the reason he had left. That would be a warning for her to send him away again.

He usually went out at lunchtime and had a sandwich and a cup of tea in one of the cafés on the edge of town. It was as he was returning to the office at ten to two that he saw Effie. He wasn't surprised, although he was disappointed. He had hoped she would accept his departure as final.

'Where did you go?' she asked as she ran towards him. 'I searched for you until nearly nine o'clock, then I guessed you'd be in work so I went too, then at one o'clock I came back.'

'Why?' he asked coldly. 'Didn't you understand that I no longer want to share a room with you?'

'Where are you staying? I bet it'll cost more on your own than in our room.'

'It doesn't matter, I've found a place to

311

stay on my own.'

'You won't be able to send as much money to your Marie, will you?'

He put his hands on her arms to move her gently out of the way to go into the office but she held him. 'Please, Ivor, I think you misunderstood that night. I wasn't trying to get into your bed, I was just trying to make you more comfortable.'

'It doesn't matter. I need a place on my own and you'll be all right, the room is yours for a month, plenty of time to decide whether you want to stay or find somewhere else. Now, I have to go in, I have an appointment in fifteen minutes and I need to prepare.'

She stepped back and watched as he went inside, then turned away and hurried back to her own work. Her jaw was tight, her small eyes dark with anger. She walked with short, quick steps, pushing aside anyone who was in her way without a murmur of apology. This can't be allowed to happen. Not again. Even though the situation wasn't the same as the last time it was still rejection through no fault of her own, just someone else spoiling things.

That evening she went to see what was happening at Badgers Brook. She half expected to see Ivor there, welcomed back by his family like the prodigal son. Geoff was there. She guessed that from seeing his van parked at the end of the lane. Voices from the wood caused her to hide and she saw Marie and Violet running towards her screaming with pretend fright as they were followed by an elderly man wearing a head-dress of branches and making stupid howls. The twin boys followed behind, adding to the din, enjoying the brief return to childhood from the lofty age of fifteen.

Envy darted through her and left her feeling sad. She should have been a part of such scenes, surrounded by her family, laughing with them and joining in the fun.

Moving away from the game of chase she went further into the wood, walking slowly, aware of the increasing birdsong as evening lengthened the shadows and she moved further away from the house. A robin watched from a branch, his curiosity making him bold. A movement nearby made her turn her head in time to see the lovely undulating movement of a squirrel, disturbed at its feasting. Her sadness began to lift as the peace of the woodland surrounded her. She stopped and, leaning against the smooth trunk of a beech, stood hoping that more of the shy denizens of the beautiful place would appear.

Instead she heard more voices. Although Ivor was reticent in talking about his family, through the little she had gleaned from their conversations and her own observations she

313

knew most of them by sight. The woman coming through the trees about to cross in front of her at some distance she recognized at once. This was Jennie, Marie's glamorous sister. She couldn't immediately see whom she was talking to but it was a man. Not her husband, whom she knew to be much older.

The prospect of 'goings on', of seeing something she shouldn't, was exciting. She slid around the large trunk until she was sure she couldn't be seen, and waited until they had passed. Once she could get behind them she'd be able to follow.

They stopped, suddenly, and she almost revealed herself to them. The man leaned against a tree and the woman was wrapped in his embrace. A momentary glance and a chill of recognition: she knew the man was Bill.

Marie had been badly shaken by her unexpected sighting of Ivor. 'It was no more than that,' she told Geoff when he called at the house with a gift of illegal farm butter from one of his customers. 'We met at the end of a lane, Ivor looked shocked, as though he'd seen a ghost, and unable to decide what to do. I made up his mind for him, I turned and ran.' She was upset and trying to make a joke of it, failed. The day was gloomy, matching her sombre mood, rain pattering down the windows from a heavy sky. She had relived that moment so many times since. Every time it ended with her running towards him, almost melting into his arms, then stopping while he offered feeble excuses for why he couldn't come home to them, another rejection.

She went into the kitchen and filled the kettle noisily to hide her distress. Geoff waited until she came back then asked, 'Perhaps he feels too guilty to face you. I wonder if you might be wise to accept that he isn't coming back.'

'You know something, don't you? I can tell from your voice.'

'I don't know anything for certain.'

'Please, Geoff, tell me.'

'I went to try and find him and when I did he was with a young woman, no one I knew. They were coming out of the pictures, and they went into a boarding house together.'

'Then he did leave me for someone else.'

'I don't know. To be honest it appeared so, but there's often an explanation. Although, it's difficult to find one for this.' Having started, Marie was insistent that he told her the full story. 'I watched them, I know it wasn't my business and I've no excuse to offer, but I went on the same day the following week and the week after that. Each time they went to the pictures, once stopping to buy chips and walking through the streets, talking as they ate them.' He paused, not wanting to relate the rest, but she urged him on. 'Then for two weeks I didn't see them and I knocked on the door of the lodging house and asked to speak to him.'

'And?' she coaxed.

'He, that is they, had moved out. According to the landlady they were renting a single room which they were to share.'

'I see.' Marie's heart began thumping painfully and so loudly she thought it must surely be heard.

'I shouldn't have told you. I could so easily be wrong. I just didn't want you to live each day in the hope of him coming back. Whether I'm right or wrong, you have to stop looking for a happy ending and start building a new life. If he does come back it won't matter, if he doesn't then you won't have wasted part of your life.'

Geoff left soon after the revelation, even though he wanted to stay, help her by talking about what he had learned and perhaps think of a reasonable explanation. It was a Saturday evening and Marie had been sewing clothes for Violet's dolls. Roger and Royston were settled for the evening in the kitchen, playing cards with a couple of friends, and Rhodri was watching the card players and occasionally helping Roger, his favourite, to cheat. What on earth had possessed Ivor that he could walk away from this?

316

Jennie called soon after Geoff had gone. Her eyes were sparkling, her make-up less than perfect, and there was an air of excitement about her that Marie suspected was due to the company of a man. She hardly took in the implications, the shock of Geoff's news numbing her brain to everything else. She desperately needed to talk to someone and Jennie might be persuaded to listen, although she knew that was hardly likely.

At ten o'clock Marie offered to walk Jennie home. The rain was as relentless as earlier and they took a large umbrella, linking arms, Jennie laughing at the unexpected soakings as their unwary feet landed in puddles. Marie tried once or twice to tell Jennie what Geoff had told her, but Jennie was oblivious to her worries, chattering happily all the way. She gave up, knowing her story wouldn't have had a considered hearing. Sheltered beneath their large umbrella, protected from the downpour drumming around them, Marie began to enjoy the quiet isolation, finding it calming.

Unfortunately she walked in to trouble. Ernie opened the door before they touched it, and he looked anxious. 'Jennie! Where have you been? I thought you were going to see Lucy. I went round with an umbrella as it was raining so hard but she hadn't seen you.' He gave Marie a light kiss on her cheek and hugged his wife briefly.

'Oh bother,' she said, quickly inventing cover. 'I've been with Marie all evening. I completely forgot I'd arranged to meet Lucy. I'll have to go there and apologize tomorrow first thing.'

'But I don't understand, she wasn't expecting you.'

'She must have forgotten too.'

'Any chance of a cup of tea,' Marie interposed.

'Perhaps you'd make it? You know where everything is. Jennie, dear, you'd better get out of those wet things, look at you, your feet are soaking.' Fussing like an old woman he ushered Jennie upstairs and told her to find a pair of shoes to lend to Marie. 'Bill has been out all evening too,' he said when he came down. 'He came in a while ago and went straight to bed. They all left me on my own and we'd be glad if you'd stay a while, we both like a bit of company.'

Marie went into the kitchen and while she set the tray and dealt with the kettle, Jennie stayed upstairs. When she eventually came down carrying a pair of shoes, Marie looked again at her sister's bright eyes and glowing cheeks. Even if she hadn't guessed before, Marie would have known by her expression then that Bill had been the reason for that happiness.

Conversation was difficult. She felt acute embarrassment sitting with a cuckolded husband, her sister and Bill – the cause of it – having just stolen a few extra moments together.

'I'm going to see Judy Morris tomorrow, Jennie. I'm thinking of offering her a part-time job. I need an assistant but the business doesn't justify someone full time. D'you think she'll come? I would have gone tonight but then you came and put it out of my mind.' She was gabbling, afraid that if Jennie spoke it would ruin the fragile web of deceit they had woven.

With an expertise perfected by practice, and happy having so recently left Bill's arms, Jennie quickly accepted the lie, saying brightly, 'That's all right, sis. I'll come with you tomorrow, shall I? Together we'll persuade her.' They went into the kitchen to wash the cups, and in whispered bursts they exchanged details of their story, although they both knew that the less said the better. The fewer details offered, the less likely it was they'd be caught out.

There was no chance of Marie telling her sister what Geoff had learned about Ivor. Perhaps it was just as well. Better to sort it out in her own mind before allowing anyone else to add their opinion. She walked home, having refused a lift with Ernie, glad of the silence in which to think.

She still hoped that Geoff was wrong, that there was another explanation. Mistaken identity was a possibility, or spite on the part of the landlady. She had to believe in Ivor until he told her himself that he had left her for another woman, although his excuse that he'd been trying to help his father didn't seem believable, no matter how she tried to make the story fit the facts. He'd cheated her first by stealing and now by infidelity, how could there be an innocent reason for those things? And if there was an explanation, why hadn't he told her? After all, Rhodri was no longer a secret but very much a part of the family. Any shame he'd felt at having Rhodri for a father must surely have faded. The old man's odd behaviour had been accepted by all, and he loved Violet and she was fond of him. Any wounds must have been healed. So why didn't he come home? She couldn't think of a reason, unless Geoff was right.

Jennie called at the shop the following day to thank her sister for lying. 'I'm so sorry to have put you in that position. I promise never to do it again.'

'A few months ago I'd have been furious, all "holier than thou", but since Ivor left me, possibly for someone else, well, let's just say my moral stance is no longer certain.'

'I still regret you having to lie.'

'I'm considering applying for a divorce.'

'You and me both!' Jennie said gloomily.

'Seriously, I can't live this half-life. Being

widowed was hard, caring for the twins, not really belonging to anyone, but this is far worse. I don't want to be tied to a man who doesn't want me.'

Reacting late, Jennie said, 'What d'you mean? That Ivor left you for someone else? You said "possibly for someone else". What did you mean?'

'Oh, just a rumour, that's all.' Once more she felt unable to discuss Geoff's news with her sister.

'Probably rubbish,' Jennie said dismissively. There was no further reaction; true to form, she hardly heard her sister's whispered concerns, more interested in her own. 'Bill wants me to leave Ernie, go away with him and find somewhere we can live together. A fresh start among strangers; people who would accept us for what we appeared to be: a young couple recently married.'

'Don't go. I'll have no one if you leave.'

'There's Geoff. He's a good friend and he'd be more if you'd let him.'

'A friend, nothing more,' Marie said firmly.

'Then come with us. I'd be there to help with the kids and we'd find work easily enough.'

'I can't uproot Violet and the boys again. And what about poor Rhodri? I can't abandon him like his son did. Twice!' She turned to her sister and hugged her briefly in the hope of softening what she was about to say.

'You'll have to end it, won't you? Risking everything for the sake of a few stolen moments of passion – is it worth it?'

'How can I stay away from Bill? We live in the same house.'

'He'll have to leave. It's the only way. If Ernie finds out it would kill him. I know he doesn't behave like an ardent lover, but he's fond of you, in his way.' She looked at Jennie quizzically. 'Couldn't you learn to cope with that? It's what you promised in church.'

'Only if I never saw Bill again.'

'Then he *has* to leave. If he loves you he'll see it's the only way.' She hesitated then said, 'I don't want to alarm you, Jennie, but Violet saw you a few nights ago. She told us you and Bill were kissing. We tried to make a joke of it, telling her that as your stepson it was perfectly normal, but sooner or later someone else will see you and they might not be as easily persuaded of your innocence.'

Ivor had to see Marie. He began to think it was just possible that if he could talk to her and explain his fears she might agree to him coming home. That thought became a dream that he lived day as well as night, and eventually he found his way to Cwm Derw. He didn't go straight to the house, his nerve failed him. If she refused to talk he had shot his bolt and the chance of a further meeting would be low.

322

He went into the wood and walked as close to the house as he dared. He had to call when she was alone. Marie first. Then, if that went well once the full truth was told, they would talk to the rest of the family together.

Nervously avoiding making the final move, he walked into a dell where children picked bluebells and primroses in the spring, and it was as he stood there, dreaming, hoping, trying to pluck up the courage to knock on the door that had once, briefly, been his, that he became aware of someone watching him. Afraid at first to look up in case it was Marie, he slowly raised his head and stared into blue eyes so like his own. But these were angry eyes, and the face was scowling, the jaw pugnacious.

'Hello, Dad,' he said softly.

'Who are you? What are you doing here? Clear off, you're frightening the badgers.'

Rhodri was having a bad day, with his head filled with fears of being taken back to hospital.

'It's me, Dad, don't you recognize me?'

'Who are you?' A deep frown wrinkled the old face and then cleared. 'I know you! You're that doctor, aren't you? Come to take me back. Well I'm not going. Bugger off.' He clasped his face in his hands like a guilty child, then as he grew more confident he repeated the curse, saying it time and again, louder and louder, while Ivor backed away.

He left without trying to see Marie. What was the point? If she knew his father she would understand why he had to stay away from them; his future was written in the confused blue eyes. How could he put them through what was certain to come? He loved them too much to inflict that on them. He went back to his hotel room and sat unmoving, staring out of the window at the bleak grey sea, knowing that this was the best he could hope for for the years ahead: sitting alone in a silent room, staring into emptiness.

It was easy for Jennie to tell Bill she wanted to see him and to arrange a meeting place. Marie was right; they had to end their affair. Marie had agreed they could use a visit to her as an excuse, Bill pretending to help her with a repair to the house. They went to the park, where the gates and railings no longer barred access, the metal having been removed during the early years of the war for scrap, 'to build spitfires'.

They sat on a bench where bushes offered some shelter from the cool night air, and at once Jennie told him he had to leave. 'If you stay your father will find out and I don't want him hurt. He loves and trusts you and he's been kind to me. His generosity would be poorly paid if he found us together.'

He argued for a long time, trying from

every angle to persuade her to change her mind and go with him, but she was adamant. The clock was striking eleven when they parted, Jennie to go home and Bill intending to wait for an hour before following her.

They didn't notice the car parked on the corner with its lights out, and as they were switched on Bill and Jennie, wrapped in their final embrace, were caught in their beam. At once the lights were dimmed and the couple parted; Jennie ran towards home, while Bill stood there for a long time without moving.

He hardly noticed the sound of a car moving off, and the squeal of brakes in the next street seemed a part of a dream. It wasn't until he walked towards the house, intending to try to slip in unseen rather than wait out in the cold for an hour as he usually did, that the bundle in the middle of the road caught his eye.

Someone was standing over it, straightening it out, and he realized it was a body. With a wail of dread he ran towards it and the figure moved off, quickly swallowed up in the darkness. It must be a dream, it could not be happening to him again. He kneeled down beside the unmoving form, knowing even before he had looked that the unconscious woman was Jennie.

'Jennie! Oh, no! Speak to me, say you're all right! Jennie!' He found her pulse, hardly noticing that she had been arranged as though she were sleeping, her clothes carefully in place.

He knocked on the nearest door but there was no telephone. He persuaded the man to wait with Jennie while he ran to the phone box to call for an ambulance. No moving her this time, that lesson was still giving him nightmares. Having phoned he ran back and sat beside Jennie, talking to her, promising her that everything would be all right, that help was on the way.

The ambulance came and with it the police. They questioned him but he hardly remembered what was said. He went with her to the hospital and it was from there that he telephoned his father and Marie to tell them the awful news.

The night passed in a haze. The police had already called to tell Ernie and he had informed her parents, so they all met at the hospital, where officious nurses sent them to wait outside as there was 'no room for family reunions here!'

In an hour or so it was clear that Jennie's leg was broken and she had suffered other less serious injuries. She would be in hospital for a while and Bill knew that, in spite of their vows to separate, he couldn't leave.

The police questioned him and asked how he had happened to find her. The excuse that he had been walking home seemed to satisfy them but a day later he was reminded about the recent accident to his fiancée.

'The two accidents can hardly be connected,' he protested. 'One was my fiancée and the other my stepmother.' Again they seemed satisfied, but if just a small piece of his story was disproved they would dig until they uncovered the truth. He begged Marie to make sure she repeated her statement exactly. 'They mustn't find out about Jennie and me.'

Marie promised for the sake of her sister, but she was worried about what Violet might say. Like any child, she would enjoy the importance of the police questioning, especially if they flattered her, explained how much she was helping them.

In between hospital visits she and Ernie spoke about the accident and Marie suggested that she look after Jennie for a while.

'Thank you. It would mean I'd be on my own much of the time, but it would be better for Jennie.'

Better for you, too, if you but knew it, Marie thought. Violet might be persuaded to tell the truth about the time Jennie had arrived on the night of heavy rain. Or to boast about seeing them kissing. Kissing was something to giggle about when you were Violet's age. Like Bill, Marie knew the police only wanted a hint of an untruth to encourage more questions, start them digging until they had the full story.

She questioned Bill about the death of his fiancée, for which no one had been charged.

'You don't think there's a connection, do you?'

He frowned and shook his head. 'How can there be? A drunken driver who wouldn't stop in case he'd killed someone is the likely explanation, and that it happened twice only shows how dangerous these unlit roads are at night.'

'But weren't the clothes tidied, like the last time?'

'The police haven't mentioned that. I only told you.'

'But you should tell them. It might make a connection and help them catch the man who almost killed Jennie as Emily was killed.'

'Best not. I don't think it would help.' He couldn't tell her that it was himself and Ivor who had moved and covered the body of Emily. That would start unwelcome questions.

Did you use my car last evening, Ivor?' the office manager asked him the following morning.

'No, I didn't leave the hotel. Why?'

'Oh, nothing really. It was parked in a slightly different way, angled more towards the steps than I remember. I must have made a mistake. I asked because you're the only one with a key besides me.'

Ivor searched in his inside pocket and frowned. 'That's funny, I don't seem to have it. I've moved recently and perhaps it fell out in all the confusion. I'll have a proper search when I get back to my room.'

He went through all his things and remembered making certain that the pockets of the clothes he had sent to the dry-cleaners were empty. He was very thorough about such things. Perhaps he would have to go back to the room and ask Effie if she'd found it. It wasn't something he wanted to do but it was important not to allow his boss to think he was careless about such things. Important for him, too. He dreaded any sign he was becoming forgetful. That was the stuff that fuelled his worst nightmares.

Effie smiled widely when she opened the door to him. 'You've come back?' She stepped away to allow him to enter but he stood on the threshold like a stranger. 'It's such a lovely day today, nothing but good news and now you're back.'

'I'm sorry, Effie, but I'm not back. I just wondered whether you've seen a car key. I can't find it and I thought I must have dropped it when I was packing.'

The smile leaving her face she shook her head. 'You can come inside and look. I haven't done much cleaning since you went, it didn't seem important any more. You have

329

to have someone to please to make boring jobs worthwhile.'

He stepped inside and gave the floor a cursory glance. Effie dropped to her knees and urged him to do the same. 'Come on, Ivor, you won't find anything standing there like a handle without a brush, no use nor ornament.'

He kneeled down, carefully pulling up his trousers to save the crease, wishing he'd changed into older clothes. After feeling around under the couch and the chair and moving the folded table she gave a shout and held up the key. 'Here it is, aren't I clever? Don't I deserve a treat? What about taking me for a drink?'

'Thank you, I will, but not tonight. I'll arrange something soon.'

'That means never, doesn't it?' she said sadly.

He smiled and thanked her again and hurried from the house. He quickly forgot her disappointment. He was curious about the appearance of the key, which he had always kept in a buttoned pocket from which it was impossible for it to fall out. Had she taken it as an excuse for him to return? She certainly wouldn't have needed it. The car wasn't his and she had told him she couldn't drive.

Jennie's sojourn in hospital was really rather

pleasant. Ernie came for every visiting hour and brought gifts. Bouquets of flowers came for her parents, her sister and Ernie, and there was a home-made card to which Violet had added her childish scrawl. Bill sent a card too, signed with love and a solitary kiss. At least this disaster was giving them a breathing space, time to consider what was to be done.

When her parents came, Belle was very upset. 'We feel you should come home while you convalesce, dear,' she said. 'Marie tells us you're going there, but Dad and I want to look after you until you're really well again.'

'Mummy, I can't. You're all being kind and I love you.' She reached out and held Ernie's hand, and looked up at him adoringly. 'But I'm married now, remember, and I want to go home to Ernie.'

'Two visitors only at each bed,' the nurse called, and Ernie turned away and pretended to be visiting the lady in the next bed. At half time, 'like a football match,' Howard joked, the three visitors left to wait outside, while two more came in.

Marie and Violet brought fruit, a few home-made biscuits and *John Bull* and *Woman* magazines.

Because of the presence of her daughter, Marie couldn't talk freely. She still needed to tell Jennie all Geoff had told her and, ask her opinion – not with the expectation of sensible advice but more the opportunity to think aloud, clarify her own thoughts. Instead they listened to Jennie's amusing description of life in the ward with a dragon of a matron and nurses she could twist around her little finger. Marie was thankful when the bell went and she could go home.

When Jennie came out of hospital it was on crutches, and Ernie had arranged for a young girl to go in every day to attend to Jennie and prepare food. 'I have to confess it's a lovely life,' she admitted to Marie one morning. 'I hobble to the car in the afternoon and we go to the beach or the park for a sedate five-minute walk then back to the car to be fussed over like some hero awarded medals for bravery over and above the call of duty.'

'And Bill?'

'He's behaving like a gentleman.' She leaned closer to avoid anyone hearing and added, 'Something's bothering him, though. He keeps asking if my accident could be connected with that of his fiancée all those months ago. He said he had disturbed someone leaning over her trying to arrange her clothes. He didn't move me but there was someone bending over me as though they were about to do the same thing. Poor Emily had been lifted to the side of the road and laid out neat as neat. Strange, isn't it? Could it be a coincidence? Is it something people feel the need to do, make the victim respectable? I did wonder if it might mean it was a woman driving the car. She might have seen my clothes up exposing my legs and – no, it's nonsense. A drunken driver they suspect, and that's most likely to be a man. Oh, Marie it's so creepy.'

'No one was found for Emily's death, even though the enquiries went on for weeks,' Marie said.

'The police don't expect to catch the man who ran into me, either, if you ask me. No one's going to own up, are they? Knocking down a pedestrian, then leaving the scene of an accident, well, they obviously aren't the kind to feel remorse.'

'D'you remember anything?'

'Not really, except the sound of the car engine suddenly loud and close, not slowly approaching, but sudden. I haven't told the police that, though. It's more likely I'm remembering the moment of impact. The roar and the blow were instantaneous and I can't really remember any sound before that. It was as though the car started, revved and came straight at me, and I know that couldn't be the case.'

'Perhaps you should tell them, though. They say even small pieces of information help them to build an overall picture.'

'I just want to forget it now.' She pointed at the table. 'Pass me that knitting needle, will you, sis? I can't wait to get this plaster off. It's itching like mad again.'

'Go easy, you don't want it swelling!'

'Stop nagging, it's my itch!'

It was clear to Marie that any decisions about Bill leaving had been forgotten.

The James household had quickly reverted to its routine, with Ernie eating breakfast, reading the paper and going for a short walk in the morning. Lunch was followed by Ernie and Jennie going out for an hour or so, then Ernie would have his nap. It was during this time that Jennie and Bill talked.

'I can't tell you how much I long for that hour every day,' Jennie told her sister.

Jennie had booked a taxi when Ernie was attending a committee meeting at his club and they were sitting in the autumn sunshine in the garden of Badgers Brook. It was Marie's half-day closing, and she ignored the list of jobs she planned to do and listened to her sister.

'I worked in his mother's hairdressing shop for years, seeing Bill every day, but I hardly noticed him. Then he was horrible to me. He admits now that he was trying not to fall for me. He was afraid I'd laugh at him if he invited me out, him being older than my usual dates.' She laughed. 'He was right, mind, we did laugh at him, called him names. Now I'm married, we've realized how strongly we're attracted to each other.'

'It shouldn't have happened,' Marie admonished. 'I'm sure you aren't the first person this has happened to and you should have walked away before things went this far.'

'Me and Ivor both,' Jennie said sadly. 'I'm sorry, sis, you're getting both sides of an insoluble problem, aren't you? I shouldn't have confided in you, it was thoughtless and I'm really sorry.'

'It's all right. I don't know for sure that Ivor is with another woman. Until he tells me himself I won't believe it.' She picked up the sewing basket and began darning one of the twins' socks. 'I miss him, Jennie, and I want to believe in him. I can't relate what's happened to the loving, caring man I married.'

'Poor Ernie,' Jennie said softly, and once again Marie knew her sister hadn't been listening to what she had to say.

When Geoff called that evening he stayed for supper, and as Rhodri and Violet washed dishes with much hilarity, she asked him about the accident that had killed Bill's fiancée, Emily. 'I know it was in the paper and I read the account like everyone else, but she wasn't known to me except as a girl who worked with Jennie, and I didn't take it in. Can you remember the details?'

'Only that she was walking home through the lane and was hit by a vehicle. The driver disappeared but when the body was found it was laid neatly under the hedge, the clothes arranged and her arms at her sides, feet together, hair smoothed down around her face. He stopped long enough to do that but he didn't even phone for an ambulance in case the poor woman was still alive.'

'D'you think the same person hit Jennie?'

'It does seem possible but I can't think why.'

'They were getting married, so had there been a quarrel?'

'You don't think Bill was responsible, do you?'

'Of course not! But I wondered if there was someone out there who hates him seeing another woman.'

'There were rumours about another girl who worked at the hairdresser's shop before Jennie and Lucy, but I don't know for certain.'

'Tell me about her.'

'I can't remember her name, but she left suddenly and some said she was expecting a baby and was sent away from home. So far as I know she didn't die, though, just went away.'

'That can't have been Bill, or everyone would have heard. It isn't easy to keep a secret like that when the family is as well known as Ernie James's.'

'It was a long time ago.'

336

'Secrets can be buried deep but they never stay hidden. Something happens and up they pop. No, it can't have been Bill.'

'Odd though, all three working for Thelma James. And it's a strange coincidence, both women having their clothes straightened. D'you think the police know? About the first one?'

'Forget it, Geoff. They don't want any irrelevant information. It would only confuse things.'

'It would be wise to warn Jennie to be very careful, though!'

With the investigation increasing the chance of her affair with Bill being exposed, Jennie knew they couldn't see each other again. There was a serious risk of the police being convinced that the common factor was Bill. Besides that possibility, it was not certain that the accident had been deliberate and her life with Ernie was comfortable and easy: too good to risk giving up for love and less comfort with Bill.

She knew she was selfish and didn't think she would ever change. A gentle passionless life was not an appealing prospect, but an easy life as a rich man's darling had its compensations.

The romantic in her couldn't resist arranging one final meeting with Bill, to say their goodbyes. Ernie willingly drove her to wherever she wanted to go, and an afternoon at Marie's house seemed innocuous enough. He helped her into the house, where Rhodri and Violet were preparing tea while, outside, Geoff, Marie and the boys were turning the soil over and tidying up before the winter frosts.

An hour later Marie and the rest of the family left to go to the pictures and Jennie opened the door to Bill. They discussed the situation and Bill decided to accept Jennie's decision. 'I'll leave, find work in another town,' he said.

'I'm sorry it's you who has to move away but there isn't any other way to end it. I can't trust myself near you, and I have to stay with your father,' she said as he stood up to go.

Outside a car pulled up and Ernie walked down the path carrying Jennie's warm jacket in case she was cold. With the end of summer the evenings were decidedly chilly.

Jennie stood up and gave Bill one last, loving kiss and it was then that Ernie stepped into the room. He wasn't seen. The lovers were too engrossed in themselves to be aware of the slight gasp he made as he turned and left.

Bill left soon after and Jennie was tearful as she set the table for supper, after which Geoff would drive her home. The family burst in, talking about the film, arguing about which was the best part of the Abbot

338

and Costello comedy. Marie carried a steaming package of chips that were shared between the plates and eaten with bread and a scraping of margarine. Cocoa followed and Violet went to bed.

The boys went soon after and Rhodri put the dishes in cold water and went up to his room.

'Well?' Marie asked when the children were quiet. 'Did you tell him?'

'He's leaving. Going to start again in another town. He'll have no trouble finding work.' To put the others off the scent she pretended to talk about someone else. 'Electricians are in demand now, with electric cookers becoming popular and electric light replacing gas. Did you know,' she said, needing to talk but without saying anything important. 'Did you know these new prefabs have a fridge and the neatest kitchen, and electric light? Marvellous they are by all accounts.' She chattered on: silences had to be avoided or she would fill them with her tears.

'When is he leaving?' Marie wanted to know.

'Within the week. It has to be soon or we're both afraid we'll change our minds.'

Geoff said nothing. Better the sisters dealt with it on their own. He secretly thought Bill was a louse, but he didn't want to upset either of the women by saying so. He now

339

suspected that Bill was responsible for a young girl being sent away in disgrace some years ago, although he didn't know the outcome. Perhaps she had married, he hoped to someone more deserving of her than Bill James. He kept that opinion to himself too. He helped Jennie out of the van, sorted out her crutches and saw her to the door before waving goodbye and driving back to the shop.

Jennie looked up, expecting the door to open and her caring husband to be there, listening for the sound of the van and ready to open the door for her and help her inside. When the door wasn't opened she shrugged. He must be listening to something on the wireless or the gramophone. She turned the knob but the door didn't give. That was odd. They didn't lock the doors except just before they went to bed. She struggled with her stick and got her key out of her handbag. The key turned but still the door didn't open.

Unable to manage a torch, she limped cautiously on her crutches around to the back of the house, and at the kitchen door the same thing happened. She began to knock angrily, calling for Ernie to let her in. Although she knocked for several minutes the house remained silent. Bill wouldn't be home yet, as they had arranged, so there was only Ernie.

She began to worry. Why would he be out at this time, she wondered, as she made her way back to the front door. 'Ernie? Are you there?' Belatedly she began to wonder whether he was ill and needed help. She shouted through the letter box and peered in, trying to see, but the lights were all out. The place seemed devoid of human life.

Anxious now, she wondered who she could contact. The police? Ambulance? Bending again to shout through the letter box, she called, 'Ernie, dear? I'm going to call an ambulance, in case you've fallen and can't get to the door.'

A sound above her made her look up to see a window opening. 'I don't need an ambulance, Jennie. Go away. I never want you in this house again. Don't worry, I'll send your clothes to your lying sister.'

'Ernie? What's wrong?' she asked as dread chilled her. 'Are you ill?'

'Not ill, no, nothing that believable.'

'Then let me in, please, Ernie, tell me who's upset you.'

'Go away. Go back to Bill. I never want to see either of you again.'

341

Eleven

In sheer panic, Jennie called and called for Ernie to let her in. She pleaded and sobbed but the window didn't reopen and the doors remained firmly closed. After what seemed hours, when she became aware of the cold seeping up from the ground and chilling her and there was still no sign of Ernie relenting, she turned away, her sobs loud in the silence of the late hour. She went to call on Lucy. She would have a key to the door of the hair-dressing shop and from there she would be able to get into the main part of the house.

She gave a garbled explanation that was nothing like the truth. She'd forgotten her key and she didn't want to disturb Ernie, and could she borrow the one from the shop, was the gist of it. Not waiting to explain further and not caring whether or not Lucy believed her, she grabbed the offered key and hurried as fast as her injured leg would allow back to the shop.

Thank goodness Ernie hadn't thought of the shop. The key turned and she went inside. But as she opened the door to the rest of the house a light came on and Ernie stood at the bottom of the stairs. He guided her firmly back through the door.

'You can stay in the shop but only until tomorrow morning. Then I want you out of here.'

The words were spoken slowly and clearly but the sense of them hardly reached her brain.

'Ernie, what are you talking about? Has some gossip upset you? If it's unpleasant and concerning me it must be untrue, dear.'

'Untrue? I saw you with my own eyes.'

He stepped back into the hall, pushed the door closed and she heard keys rattle before one of them turned, locking her out.

'What am I supposed to have done? Ernie, please let me in.' Fear and panic turned swiftly to anger. How dare he treat her like this? She felt aggrieved, affronted, because what he must have seen was herself and Bill saying goodbye. In her recently renewed innocence, the unfairness made it automatic for her to put the blame for the whole situation on Ernie.

She picked up a towel to wrap around her for extra warmth and went out, slamming the shop door behind her. Her leg ached dreadfully and now she faced another long walk, but there was no alternative. She wasn't going to sleep in the hairdressing shop like a slapped dog. She made her way

343

back to Marie's house, and even though it was late a light shone in the kitchen. Thankfully, she pushed open the back door and went in, sobbing and begging for something for the pain in her leg.

The pain was genuine but the tears were not. She was past the time for tears. Marie made the inevitable pot of tea and listened to her sister's story without comment. When the words of outrage ended and only tears remained, she said, 'You must stay here tonight, and tomorrow I'll come with you and we can hopefully sort this mess out.'

'You don't understand, Marie. I'll never go back to him. Not now. He didn't even demand an explanation, he saw us together – nothing happened apart from a kiss – and he locked me out. I was tried in my absence, found guilty and sentenced without me saying a word. How can you expect me to go back to a man like that?'

'I can't give you a bed but you can share mine if you like,' Marie said, afraid to comment, not wanting to have her words thrown back at her at some later date when things had settled.

'Aren't you going to say anything?' Jennie demanded.

'Tomorrow. We'll talk it through tomorrow. Come to the shop at lunchtime and we'll go to a café and talk about what you should do. Right?'

'Wrong! I can't believe this. I've been thrown out like some abandoned animal and you're going to work tomorrow as though nothing has happened?' She gathered the coat she had thrown off and headed for the door.

'Jennie, sit down.' Marie tried to stifle an impatient sigh. 'Where d'you think you're going at this time of night?'

'Mam and Dad will take me in. I'll get some sympathy there.'

After trying and failing to persuade Jennie to stay, Marie put on her coat. 'If you insist, I'll come with you. But you shouldn't be walking any more today. That leg isn't fully mended.'

'Damn my leg. It's my heart that's broken, sis. I'm so sorry I've hurt Ernie. He didn't deserve any of this. His wife letting him down and his son.' Jennie seemed genuinely upset. Then remorse vanished as she said angrily, 'But he shouldn't have locked me out. That was the act of a spoiled child not a grown man!'

'Come on, stay here and we'll go to see Mam and Dad first thing, before I open the shop.'

Suddenly overcome with tiredness and the realization that tomorrow the town would be buzzing with gossip, she sat down and agreed. She needed a bolt-hole for a few days and it would be better to tell her parents later, when she had prepared her story. The truth of her own stupidity was not what she wanted them to hear.

It was October and the hours of daylight were few. Taking advantage of the dark streets the following evening, hoping to avoid meeting anyone she knew, Jennie knocked on the door of the house that had been her home. Ernie answered and stood firmly, preventing her from entering.

'Ernie, dear, we have to discuss this. I think you've got hold of the wrong end of the stick,' she said, an attempt at a smile resulting in a quivering lip and a nervous tic on her cheek. He was standing in front of the light from the hall, so she couldn't see his expression. The harshness of his voice was enough for her to guess it wasn't welcoming.

'I have seen my solicitor and he will be contacting you with details of our separation. I have told him to address the letter to your sister, as I imagine you'll want time to decide what you will tell your parents.'

The door closed as she took a breath to argue.

Two more days passed and Jennie stayed at Badgers Brook. Sometimes she was bright, with anger being the strongest emotion, and at other times she was unable to hold back tears. She'd been such a fool, losing a comfortable and easy life for a passion that now, in retrospect, in the chaos of the remnants of her marriage, seemed almost childlike. But gradually she relaxed, the calm of the old house working its magic and easing away her tension. She slept and awoke rested and peaceful.

There was no news of Bill. 'I doubt that he'll be at home,' Jennie told Marie. From Ernie's angry mood he wouldn't be forgiven any more than she would, even though he might have received some sympathy. People automatically blamed a woman, particularly other women, believing that it was the woman who needed to be strong in these circumstances, the man being less able to control his urges. 'Old fashioned,' she mused sadly, 'but still endlessly repeated.'

Instead of waiting for Marie to bring a cup of tea each morning, then sitting while her sister prepared breakfast, she rose at the same time and lit the fire while Marie dealt with the early cups of tea and began to prepare food. She helped Violet to find her clothes and her school books and seemed to enjoy being a part of the busy household. Marie said nothing, afraid a wrong word would restore her sister to her previous spoiled self.

Rhodri and the children accepted her unexpected appearance without too many questions and she began to help more and more with the household routine in a way that surprised and pleased Marie. There had been no gossip so far as Marie knew and, apart from Geoff, she had told no one. Their parents would have to know but until other people began making comments and asking questions, she and Jennie had agreed to say nothing.

It was on the fourth day, when Jennie was half seriously discussing her need for money, that the idea came to Marie.

'I'll have to make some decisions fairly soon,' Jennie had said. 'I need to find out what my financial situation is, and until I hear from the solicitor – oh how serious that sounds – I have no idea how I stand. No money and no job, and with no word from Ernie, I don't know how to deal with that problem.'

'I could go and see Ernie on your behalf,' Marie offered. 'He wouldn't be rude enough to refuse to see me.'

'No, not yet. I don't think he'll talk to you in any useful way, but he doesn't appear to have told anyone what happened, so there's no fear of people gossiping about me – I couldn't stand that, Marie, I really couldn't. So long as no one knows what happened I can cope. I need to get a job, though.' She looked hopefully at Marie. 'I know you haven't really got the room, but can I stay for a few weeks, until I've got something sorted? Perhaps, if I can earn a good enough wage, I can persuade Lucy to share a flat with me again.'

Marie looked hesitant. Was this new character for real or was it only a matter of time before Jennie reverted to her usual demanding self?

'What is it, do you know of a job going?' Jennie asked.

Her mind made up, Marie said, 'There is something you might consider. I was planning to ask my friend Judy Morris if she would leave old misery Harries at the dress shop and come to work with me but I've done nothing about it. I doubt whether I'd persuade her, I can only offer a part-time post, less money than she's earning at present, and she's unlikely to consider that. The thing is, I need an assistant, so would you like the job?'

Jennie leaped out of her chair, said 'ouch' as the sudden movement caused a pain to shoot through her leg, then hugged her sister repeating 'thank you', over and again. 'Thanks, sis, that really would be perfect.'

'You'll have to work, though. It isn't a hideyhole while the gossip comes and goes,' she warned.

'I'll even wash the front step, there, how's that?' Jennie grinned. 'So long as no one's looking, of course! I have my reputation to keep!'

Marie marvelled at how much her flighty sister had changed. Just weeks ago she wouldn't have considered employing her for a moment. The previous Jennie would have stipulated all the things she wouldn't do, complained loudly and left the boring tasks to someone else. She'd have expected her to cheat on any work she deemed arduous, refuse jobs she disliked. But the end of her marriage to Ernie and coming to live in Badgers Brook had changed her. The mellow house had that effect, even on visitors, calming them in some inexplicable way, making them happier people.

Telling their parents was the most dreaded result of the separation and Jennie and Marie agreed that Sunday tea-time would be the best time to break the news.

'We can't wait much longer, someone is bound to find out and tell them. They have to hear my version before one larded with innuendo and spite,' Jennie said. 'Most people can't help enjoying a story like this and adding a few embellishments to make it more spicy – well, I've done it myself, haven't you?'

'Few of us can deny the pleasure of being first with news, pleasant or otherwise,' Marie admitted. 'Although lately we've been the subject more often than most, haven't we? Ivor leaving me and the children and now you leaving your husband after only a few months of marriage. We're a gift to the gossips.'

'And we're always being accused of pretending to be better than everyone else,' Jennie added, a smile widening on her face.

'Well, we are,' her sister replied and they both broke into nervous laughter.

Belle and Howard took the news surprisingly well. Belle told them she was relieved that her darling daughter was no longer with that sad old man and Howard asked her amiably if she wanted any changes made to her bedroom before moving back in.

Jennie glanced at Marie, and after a nod of agreement said, 'Mam, I won't be coming back. Not yet anyway. Marie has a spare room and I like living there on the edge of the wood.' The expression on her parents' face was so comical both sisters laughed. 'Yes, I know, countryside, long walks to the bus stop and no shops, feeding birds and looking for badgers and foxes, it doesn't sound like me, does it?' She looked thoughtful then went on, 'The strange thing is, I love living in Badgers Brook. I feel safe there, and when I walk along the lane and get my first sight of it, solid and strong and welcoming, I – I feel a sense of peace coming over me.' As though embarrassed by her words she thumped Marie's arm and said, 'There, now I'm sure you think I've gone daft.'

'I don't,' Marie said. 'That's exactly how I feel about Badgers Brook, and when we moved in, and faced all that filthy mess, I knew even then that underneath the chaos there was a happy home. I still feel that, even though Ivor no longer lives with us. I feel sure that one day, when he can talk about what worries him, he'll be back and the house will perform its magic for him, too.'

'And what about his father?' Belle asked, somewhat embarrassed by the strange conversation. 'Is he keeping well?'

'Rhodri's happy, although he does get a bad day occasionally when he is confused. It's noticeable when he goes to the hospital for checks and sometimes an overnight stay. Then he shakes and shivers and can hardly hold a conversation, yet as soon as he gets back to the house he's fine. I know it sounds daft, our Mam, but Badgers Brook has an atmosphere of such tranquillity that troubles are eased away.'

Lightening the strange mood, Jennie said brightly, 'Now, what's to eat, Mam? We're starving.'

If Belle noticed the 'we', when Jennie normally only spoke for herself, denoting a togetherness her spoiled daughter rarely showed, she said nothing, but she was humming happily when she went into the kitchen to bring in the sandwiches and fatless sponge cake she had prepared.

'That went well,' Jennie said as the sisters walked back to Badgers Brook in the gradu-

352

ally deepening dusk.

'Only because you didn't tell them the full story,' Marie replied. They joked about the various ways they could have imparted the news about Jennie's affair with her stepson and their parents' imaginary responses and arrived home with laughter in their eyes, their faces glowing with good humour.

Jennie became easily accustomed to walking along the quiet lanes, the darkness no longer held fears for her. For a while after being knocked down she had been afraid of a repeat, with Geoff and Marie voicing suspicions that the so-called accident had been deliberate. Now the accident was far from her mind, and when it was suggested that she took extra care she laughed away any concerns.

She was walking home alone one evening, when Marie had arranged to call on Nerys Bowen, and experienced a sudden return of the fear. The night was very dark, with no moon, myriad stars like pinpricks in the velvet sky not giving a glimmer of light.

She didn't bother with a torch apart from shining an occasional beam to make sure she was far enough away from the ditch at the edge of the grassy path. The car, parked in a lay-by on the narrow lane, was invisible at first, then the dull gleam caught her eye and she became aware of the low murmuring rhythm of its engine.

Her legs weakened, her heart raced and a fear she thought forgotten roused her to the pitch of wanting to scream for help. Why hadn't she waited for Marie? She slowed her steps; there was a worsening of the ache in her damaged leg – a reminder of what had happened.

She stood there wondering what to do, trying to remember how far away she was from a house. The properties along the lane were few and it was impossible to relate to them in the dark. Then she heard footsteps and cried out in relief. 'Hello?' she called. 'Is that you, Marie? Come quick. Please hurry.'

She heard a woman's voice and faster footsteps, which were drowned by the sound of the car accelerating fast, its lights appearing over hedges until it was lost from sight. She stood, sobbing nervously, and when a neighbour came and introduced herself as Kitty Jennings, Jennie explained briefly what she had feared.

'I'll walk the rest of the way with you,' Kitty said, putting a comforting arm around her. She waited until Roger opened the door. Jennie's sobs brought Rhodri to see what had happened and Kitty smiled and said, 'Hello, Rhodri. How are you?'

Jennie didn't wait to hear any more. Thanking the kind neighbour, she ran to her room and sat tearing at a handkerchief until she felt calm enough to go back down, by which time Kitty had gone.

'It was probably a courting couple and I ruined their evening,' she said after telling Marie what had happened.

'In future we'll always walk home together,' Marie promised. 'You're probably right and it was nothing to worry about, but we won't risk upsetting you again.'

The following evening, Kitty called to ask if Jennie was recovered and, when she came in, she at once began talking to Rhodri. 'I knew them both years ago,' she explained as she was leaving, 'long before he became ill.' She asked about Ivor and Marie told her the truth. It was common knowledge anyway so there was no point being coy and inventing a more acceptable story. To her relief, Kitty was sympathetic and didn't apportion blame.

Effie was curious. She couldn't understand what had happened between Jennie, Ernie and Bill. It was several days, watching and following the sisters, before she worked out that Jennie was living with Marie at Badgers Brook and was working with her at the small clothes shop in Steeple Street. She and Ivor rarely shared a conversation, even though she often contrived to be passing when he left work or when he reached his lodgings.

'Your father was busy helping Geoff clear the overgrown bushes yesterday,' she called one morning as he was about to go into the office. At once she regretted saying it. She didn't want him worrying about his father living with Marie and the children. The last thing she wanted was for him to be sufficiently concerned about them to go home. 'Only visiting, mind,' she added. 'He was helping Geoff burn all the branches they'd removed. Having a good tidy-up they are.'

'Was Violet with him? Near the fire?'

'No, she was watching from inside and Rhodri went in to watch with her once Geoff and Marie had the fire going.' She tilted her head on one side and asked, 'What are you worried about? I thought it was your mother who was the fire raiser?'

'It was, but having seen the result of setting a building on fire, the speed of the destruction, how quickly it becomes out of control, I've always been a little afraid.'

'They work well together, Marie and Geoff. Lucky she is to have him, eh?'

He was turning away and she called, 'Fancy coming for a meal tonight? I've made a rabbit stew and I've even got some dumplings made with a gift of suet from a friendly butcher.' He thanked her but declined.

That was a setback. She had hoped to borrow his car keys again, but when they had met by chance, once in a café and once as they went into the pictures, she'd had no opportunity to reach into his pocket and retrieve them.

Borrowing someone else's car turned out to be easier than she'd expected. It was a quiet neighbourhood with few cars. Men often left them in the street or parked on waste ground not far away. They were never locked and it was not unusual to find the keys still in them. So few people could drive, mostly the higher paid or reps and travelling salesmen who needed transport for their job, or those who worked a long way from home and could afford one. There wasn't much risk of them being stolen.

She drove off in a Morris Minor, slowly at first until she accustomed herself to the slight differences, then as confidence grew she picked up speed so she didn't attract attention and headed for Cwm Derw.

Jennie had been determined not to see Bill again. Her brief affair had caused so much distress both to herself and her family and to Ernie, who really didn't deserve it. She had no idea where he was but presumed he was somewhere in London as he had once planned. A note came from him, the postmark confirming that he was indeed there, and she handed it to Marie to burn unopened. A second came and they wrote 'please return to sender' before slipping it back into the post box, and hoped that would end it.

When she left the shop to take some letters

to the same post box, Bill was standing in front of it. At once she turned to go back to the shop, but he ran across the road and held her arm.

'Wait, Jennie. I understand you don't want us to meet, but I need to talk to you. It's about Dad. He won't talk to me and I'm worried about him.'

It was the only thing he could have said that would change her mind.

'What d'you want me to do?' she asked sadly. 'I'll do anything to make him forgive me. Anything.'

'I feel the same, but we need to discuss it all and work out the best thing to do.'

They agreed to meet that evening at the end of the lane leading from the road to Badgers Brook, and it was there that Effie saw them.

They walked close together and at the end of their conversation they wrapped their arms around each other and kissed.

'Another goodbye,' Bill said sadly.

'We were seen last time by your father,' Jennie said with a shiver of apprehension. 'Surely we can't be unlucky enough to be seen again?'

They looked around as though a silent watcher would reveal himself, before surrendering to a final slow, loving kiss.

'This really is goodbye,' Jennie said, moving away from Bill's persistent embrace. 'We can't meet again. If we're to persuade your father what he saw was innocent, we'll have to avoid each other permanently.'

'That's why I took the job in London,' Bill said.

'It seems so far away, but making it final is a good thing I suppose.'

'I'm working on one of the big London stations. It's interesting, and having a new job and a new neighbourhood to explore should occupy my mind and ease our parting.'

'We have to try and convince your father he was mistaken,' Jennie said. 'I hate the thought of him being hurt.'

'All right, we'll prepare a story on the lines of what I've already tried to tell him, that I was upset after my girlfriend told me she didn't want to see me again. You were listening and comforting me.'

'True in a way.' Jennie smiled ruefully.

Bill stood and watched as Jennie went back to the house, and for several minutes he didn't move. He appeared to be expecting her to change her mind and run back to him.

Effie stared in disbelief, talking to herself tearfully as she started the engine. 'This shouldn't be happening. It's all over, they shouldn't be doing this. Why are they still together? Why didn't she die when that car hit her? Why?'

When Ivor left the office the following day

she ran up to him and said, 'I saw your Marie yesterday. Did you know Jennie is living there? She's been having a ding-dong with Bill James, would you believe. Married to the father, staying at Badgers Brook and having a ding-dong with the son. What a carry-on, eh?'

Ivor's first thought was not what Jennie was doing, but why Effie was interested enough to get to Cwm Derw and back just to report on his family.

'I'm sure there's a better explanation than Jennie and Bill having a "ding-dong",' he said, to give himself time to think. 'Perhaps the house is being decorated and both Ernie and Jennie are staying with Marie. Because you didn't see Ernie doesn't mean he wasn't there. Or Jennie might be planning a surprise for her husband.'

'Shock more like,' Effie said. 'As if there haven't been enough shocks in that family: Bill's mother dying of a heart attack, then Bill's fiancée knocked down and killed, now this mess. D'you think he should be told? Ernie, I mean, in case he doesn't know?'

'No, I think it's best not to interfere.'

He tried to edge away but Effie touched his arm, tightening her grip as she said, 'Geoff is at your house quite a lot.'

'Good. Marie needs all the help she can get, working all day, running the home and

360

trying to deal with the garden.' Every word seemed like a dagger in his heart. Instead of idling his life away, filling in hours walking aimlessly, reading or watching boring films, he should be with Marie, helping her, taking care of them all.

'Don't worry about the garden,' she said airily. 'Roger and Royston are working hard with Geoff's guidance and it's looking great. They still go fishing to help out the food ration but they're proper licensed now. Geoff sees to that for them. Good boys they are by all accounts.'

'I didn't think the boys were interested in gardening.'

'Oh, they seem to like it. Royston is building a sort of greenhouse with windows taken from a bombed house that's been left in ruins since the raid that all but flattened it. Geoff's encouragement again, I suppose.' She turned to him and asked, 'Why don't I cook us something and I can tell you all that's been done. Very observant I am.'

Almost unconsciously he followed her back to the room he had once shared and he sat on the solitary chair while she chattered and prepared a simple meal of tinned oxtail soup and meat paste sandwiches.

'Tell me, Effie, why do you go to see what my family are doing?'

'Concern for you, of course,' she said, biting enthusiastically into a sandwich. As

361

she chewed, she spoke in disjointed sentences, explaining that she knew he was worried and her observations were intended to reassure him.

'It's a long way to go, Effie.'

'Not really. There's a bus to the Graig and another to Cwm Derw then it's only a short walk.'

'Still, it takes a lot of your time.'

'I don't mind. I wish I could drive, though. It's only about twenty minutes in a car. Not that I could afford a car. After paying the rent of this room and buying food, there isn't enough money to save up, or even run a car. Poor me, eh?' There was no criticism in her tone but he winced just the same. Another woman whose life he had messed up.

He left after he had eaten, vaguely agreeing to Effie's suggestion that they meet again soon. He was puzzled by Effie's interest, but something was not adding up. She obviously hoped that they would become more than friends, even though he had done nothing to suggest it – apart from his stupidity in agreeing to share a room. That had been a serious error. If word of that got out he'd be found guilty without trial. Anyone hearing of it would automatically believe they had been sharing a bed. How could he have been such an idiot?

Twice during the following week he saw Effie waiting outside the office, and each time he waited until she had gone, hiding like a child in the dark office until he felt it was safe to leave. He would have to find the words to tell her kindly and firmly that they had no future apart from friendship, and even friendship was at risk if she persisted in forcing herself on him. No! That wouldn't do! But how could he word it to sound strong and at the same time let her down gently?

Sometimes, after staying late to avoid her, he didn't go back to his lodgings but went to the pictures instead, staring at the screen with no attempt to follow the story. When he came out into the dark streets it was too late for supper, which was served at nine thirty. He wasn't hungry anyway.

Most of the cafés were closed by five thirty, and the only one still open served unappetizing, and often stale, food. If only he could go home, back to Marie and the children. A bus came along, and in the same unthinking way he had gone back with Effie a few days previously he got on and made his way to Cwm Derw.

Approaching the end of October the woods smelled of dampness and that evocative, earthy scent that accompanies the approach of winter. In several places there was the cone-like shape of a bonfire in preparation for Guy Fawkes celebrations just over a week away. The thought of fires

363

reminded him of his childhood: the fearsome memories of a school burning, and the attempt by his mother to set fire to the house of a neighbour who had offended in some way. Bonfire night was not something he enjoyed. The reminder of his mother's mental state was always with him but never more so than on the night when people commemorated the attempt to blow up parliament in 1605. His mother's penchant for starting fires in retaliation for some offence and his father's inability, his unwillingness even, to stop her was why he was living alone, outside his family, hoping and praying that whatever madness he had inherited would not develop or, worst of all, reveal itself in his beloved daughter, Violet. Staying away was the only way he could help, a faint hope that not seeing his decline might make her own less likely. Foolish, unfounded, but it was all he could do.

Unclear why he was there and not knowing what to do, he stood just within the wood for a while, taking in the moist earthy scents of the late evening, feeling the chill melancholy of the dying summer, imagining the warmth just yards away from him inside the house where all his doubts and anxieties had been so cruelly revived.

Until he had learned that his father was living in the vicinity he'd been able to pretend, convince himself that he was nothing to do with him, that he had no connection with the behaviour that had ruined his childhood. On realizing that he could deny it no longer, he had done the cowardly thing and walked away without any explanation, leaving his family hurt and confused and in financial difficulties; their misery caused by him.

The chance to tell Marie had been when their darling Violet was born. But how could he explain why he had feared for the baby? Tell her the illness that had tainted his childhood might come back to haunt him anew, revived in the innocent child? For almost ten years he had watched Violet develop into a wonderful, bright and happy child, but seeing his father had wiped away his confidence and he could no longer pretend the fear wasn't there. He had reasoned that if he were to leave them, somehow the danger would be eased. If he had shown signs of illness such as his parents had suffered it might be contagious, like measles, and just having him there would be a catalyst and cause it to happen.

The curtains were drawn across the windows and only once, when one of the twins opened the door to take in a bucketful of coal, was there any sign of life. In the cold air a thread of smoke rose from the chimney, increasing into a sudden cloud as fuel was added to the fire within. His memory was touched by the smell of toast, a favourite bed-time snack, for which the children would be clamouring once the fire had taken up the fresh fuel and burned to a steady glow. He could picture it all so clearly. The warmth of it touched him and became almost real; sights and smells tormented him and the pain of being there made him turn and hurry towards the bus stop.

A bus loomed into view almost immediately, and as he jumped on a car passed him, the driver illuminated briefly in the light from the bus. A fleeting glance only, but the way she sat forward showed her clearly, her thick hair falling in curls around her face, and he was left in no doubt. It was Effie, who had told him on several occasions that she couldn't drive.

Jennie received a letter asking her to attend a solicitor's office the following week. She tried again to talk to Ernie. But even when she went into the hairdresser's shop she found the house locked and there was no reply to her desperate knocking. She had told Lucy most of what had happened, but Lucy was careful to avoid too strong a comment; she wanted to keep her job now she had been made manageress.

Jennie tried to persuade her friend to give Ernie a note. There had been no reply to previous letters so she thought that if Lucy handed it to him he'd have to at least admit to receiving it.

'Don't ask me to get involved, Jennie,' Lucy pleaded. 'Whatever happens between you, I'll be able to keep my job if I stay well out of it. My loyalty is to you, but it wouldn't help either of us if I lost my job, would it?'

Jennie felt a worse rejection than Lucy realized. They'd had so many friends until she married Ernie and now there was no one. So she asked Marie to go with her to hear what Ernie had decided to do.

With the owner's permission the shop was closed, and Marie dressed in a good quality mid-calf-length skirt and a jacket with padded shoulders in a soft green fabric, which she had bought for the occasion. Jennie dressed smartly but not outrageously, and her wild blond hair was pulled back and calmed with a green felt hat.

When they got off the bus, Jennie caught hold of the bus stop pole and bent over.

'Marie, I feel awful. I'm shaking so much my legs won't hold me. I think I'm going to be sick.'

'Nerves, that's all,' Marie comforted, leading her to a seat. She watched as the colour returned to Jennie's face. 'We're early so you can sit for a while. This is quite an ordeal for you. Hardly surprising that you're upset.'

'It's the embarrassment that'll be the worst. If it ends in divorce the papers will be splashing the story all over the town.' She protested that she couldn't go and begged Marie to telephone to tell them she was ill, but Marie persuaded her.

'It's only a few steps and we're there, and today could see the end of the worst of it. Come on, get it over. I'll be there and we'll all help you.' Slowly Jennie stood and walked arm in arm with her to the office of Harold J. Howells, Solicitor.

Ernie was sitting in the outer office, and she smiled and said, 'Hello, dear,' to which he gave the slightest of nods.

She only half heard what the solicitor said, waiting for the chance to say her piece. When he paused, she asked in her sweetest, most childlike voice, 'Can I tell you what I think happened?. My husband refuses to listen.' The solicitor glanced at his client but Jennie didn't give him a chance to refuse.

'Bill's girlfriend, of whom he was very fond, had told him she didn't want to see him any more. He was devastated, and, being in love myself,' she glanced coyly at the stony-faced Ernie, 'I perfectly understood how he felt. I listened to him, offered sympathy, and,' she paused theatrically, 'I kissed him and told him his father and I would do all we could to help him get over it. It must have been this that Ernie saw and misunderstood.'

'And that was all there was to it?' The

solicitor looked surprised. 'No long-term, er, affair? Forgive me, Mrs James, but I have to ask – there was no adultery?'

'There was not! I'm a happily married woman, Mr Howells! Or at least I was, until someone spread unkind rumours and upset my Ernie.'

Mr Howells coughed and said, 'Mrs James, would you be kind enough to wait in the outer office? Miss Griffiths will make you a cup of tea.'

A few minutes later, after several biscuits and a cup of weak tea, Ernie came out and said, 'You'd better come home with me. We have to sort this out.'

'No dear. I'll stay where I am for a while, just until you're quite sure you don't have any doubts about me. An affair indeed. And with your son. I don't know whether I can forgive you, Ernie, I really don't.'

'Have you ever thought of acting?' Marie said as they were leaving the austere building that held the offices of Mr Harold J. Howells.

Jennie threw off the hat she was wearing and pulled her hair out of its restraining clips. 'I don't know how I managed not to laugh,' she said, her eyes shining with humour. 'Poor man, he didn't stand a chance of getting rid of me, did he?'

'When will you go back to him?'

Jennie frowned as she concentrated. 'In

good time for my birthday I think, don't you?'

They returned to reopen the shop, singing 'They say that falling in love is wonderful', cheerfully unaware of the irony of their situation in which love had been far from wonderful, bringing them nothing but sorrow. Marie thought it was a long time since she'd been as happy as since her sister had come to stay.

Ivor was puzzled by the obvious lie, when Effie again told him she was unable to drive. He knew she had been brought up on a farm, and one day he mentioned that many farm-workers learned to drive a tractor long before being allowed to drive on the roads.

'My father wouldn't let me, even though I pleaded to try,' she replied to the remark. 'If I had a child I wouldn't hold them back from doing anything they wanted, so long as it wasn't dangerous, of course,' she added.

'You did have vehicles though?'

'A boyfriend I once had promised to teach me,' she said. 'But he left me for someone else when things became, you know, complicated, and I lost my chance.'

'How complicated?' he asked. He saw the frown of concentration cloud her eyes and she shook her head.

'It's all so long ago and I've forgotten,' she said unconvincingly. 'I hope he hasn't forgotten though. He doesn't deserve any luck after what he did to me.'

'Let you down badly, did he?'

'Us! He let *us* down badly – there was a baby.'

She said nothing more and Ivor wasn't interested enough to encourage further talk.

'I understand that Jennie is still with your ex-wife,' she said one day when she went into the café where he was eating lunch.

'Ex-wife? Marie and I are still married,' he said with a frown.

'Then why was she going to see a solicitor a few days ago?'

'What d'you mean?'

'She and Jennie had an appointment with that Harold Howells near the town hall. They came out laughing like children, so whatever they had gone there for the result must have been good news.' She didn't mention the presence of Ernie; that would have spoiled the story, given it a completely different slant.

Twelve

Kitty Jennings called to ask about Jennie and Marie invited her in. 'I'm sorry we haven't met properly,' Kitty said, accepting the offer of a cup of tea. 'I've been neglectful of you, I usually welcome new people to the lane but, well, I wasn't sure of the situation and didn't want to appear nosy.'

'It's been a difficult time,' Marie replied.

'I knew Ivor when he was a child.' Kitty looked at Marie hesitantly, wondering whether to go on. 'We all lived in a different neighbourhood then, and moved here around the same time. His parents were wonderful people, friendly and kind, always ready to give help when it was needed. His mother did some lovely watercolours of woodland scenes. They were so happy, until Rhodri suffered so badly during the First World War. Then everything changed for them.'

Marie stared at her. 'I know nothing about this. Rhodri doesn't talk about his life, and Ivor didn't tell me anything about his family.

372

But I understood that Rhodri's always been ill and that his mother, was, well – she had problems too.'

'The fires you mean?'

'I don't know anything except rumours,' Marie said defensively.

'My husband is retired now, but he was the policeman who arrested her, after a neighbour's house was nearly burned down, closely following the fire that almost destroyed the school where Ivor was a pupil.'

The defensive shield fell and suddenly it was a relief to talk to someone about Ivor. 'I wonder sometimes whether Ivor believes that the mental illness his father suffers is something he can inherit.'

'Nonsense, but if that was the case how would running away from you help?'

'I don't know. I don't understand any of it. We were so happy – at least I thought we were – then he met up again with his father, my life fell apart, and I don't know why.'

'His father was a lovely young man. His confusion started when he narrowly escaped a horrible death, and saw many of his comrades suffer an end that was truly terrible. Trapped and burned to death they were, in a building hit by incendiaries. He tried to get them out but was beaten back by flames and smoke. His comrades had to hold him back when he wanted to try again. Poor man. He never got over it.'

'What about his mother? She didn't fight, or see anything terrible. Why was she so obsessed with fires?'

She looked away and went on softly, 'You'd better ask my husband about that.' She seemed unwilling to say more. Marie showed her around the house, introduced her to Roger, Royston, Violet and a rather unwell Jennie, who was resting on her bed. Rhodri didn't appear to recognize her but proudly allowed her to inspect his cosy room before she left.

When she had gone, Jennie left her bedroom and came downstairs but she looked pale and wanted nothing to eat. 'I think I've got a touch of flu,' she complained. 'Either that or the fish we ate yesterday was off. It did taste a bit funny, didn't you think?'

'It was fine, you're just a bit bilious, that's all. Probably the shock of facing Ernie with that story of yours,' Marie said teasingly.

'I think I'll just try a drink of fizzy lemonade,' Jennie said, ignoring the jibe, which would normally have had her returning a cheeky response.

Marie was confused. She was certain that Ivor's parents' problems were the reason for him leaving, but why? If Rhodri's mental illness was due to his having been injured during the First World War, Ivor could hardly believe he would be tainted with the same condition. Trauma couldn't be inherited. If

374

only she could ask him. Again she felt that searing guilt. He'd been unable to talk to her; she had displayed something, an intolerance maybe, that made him unable to confide in her. She'd let him down and he had turned to someone else.

November 5th was the day jam rationing would end, Guy Fawkes would be celebrated, and it was also Jennie's birthday. It was then Jennie planned to return to Ernie, having decided he had suffered enough for not believing her lies. Marie laughed at her sister's crazy logic and helped her plan her birthday party, to which she intended to invite Ernie. 'I'll be generous and forgive him, and allow him to persuade me to go home with him,' Jennie told her happily. 'I expect to enjoy a bit of spoiling for a while.'

'As ever!' Marie replied.

Jennie woke one morning a week before her birthday and was immediately sick. Suspicions dormant in Marie's mind came to the fore. 'Jennie,' she asked as they walked to the shop, 'are you expecting a baby?'

'Oh, Marie, don't say it! I can't be. Life wouldn't be so cruel!'

'If you are, that's something you won't be able to lie about. You can hardly insist that Ernie's the father if what you told me is true.'

'It is true. If I am having a baby there's no

possibility of it being his. Even I couldn't invent a story to explain this. Oh, Marie, what can I do? He'll never forgive me. Bill's gone and in any case I couldn't marry him. I'm married already, and to his father. What a mess. If it gets out that the child is his I'll be shamed, a mother without a father for her baby.'

Marie had already suspected the possibility and thought about it. She said, 'It will only be Ernie who knows the truth and I think he'll keep quiet. He wouldn't want anyone to know the truth or admit he couldn't father a child, even at his age, so that's one thing you don't have to worry about. He'll want to cover up the truth for his own vanity. And Mam and Dad will believe the child is your husband's – why should they think any different? So you have to face Ernie with the terrible truth, and there's Bill, and whether or not you tell him.'

She raised a tearful face to her sister. 'Oh Marie, what can I do?'

'The hardest thing and the best thing would be to go to Ernie straight away and confess.'

Expecting Jennie to protest, Marie was surprised when she said, 'I think you're right, but I can't go alone. Will you come with me?'

'You'll really do it? Now? Tell Ernie you're expecting Bill's child?'

'I have to. There's no chance he'll stand by

376

me. He has no moral obligation to do anything for me, but I have to tell him, and before I tell anyone else.'

'Even Bill?'

Coldly, calmly, Jennie said, 'Bill? I expect he's already found himself a new love, and has promised *her* it will be for ever.'

Marie hugged her sister and promised to help in any way she could. 'For a start, and only if you are sure, we'll go and talk to Ernie as soon as we close the shop.'

Jennie decided not to announce herself or knock on the door like a visitor. After all, Ernie had admitted he wanted her back, so she could walk in without any concerns about her welcome. She went in through the back door with Marie following, and walked straight to the living room.

He was reading his evening newspaper, and the table was set for one, with a quarter of a tablecloth across one corner. She felt a surge of pity for him. He was alone and it was entirely due to her. Bill would have still been there, she would have been sharing his meal and he wouldn't be sitting beside that pathetic table set for one.

'Ernie,' she said, walking towards him, pushing aside his paper and hugging him.

'You're coming home?'

'Maybe,' she said and gestured to her sister to wait outside the door. 'First I have something to tell you, and afterwards you might not want me near you.'

'I'll wait in the hall,' Marie said, making her escape. She had brought a magazine, but although she stared at it and turned pages nothing went into her brain, she was listening to the low murmur of voices coming from the living room.

Jennie didn't hesitate, she made no attempt to edge her way towards what she had to say. 'Ernie, I haven't seen a doctor to confirm, but I think I'm going to have a baby. And as it can't possibly be yours, I have to tell you that it's Bill's child.'

'What did you say?' Ernie spluttered to give himself a moment to get over the shock. Whatever he'd expected it was not this. He stood up from his chair, leaning on it and staring at her. His face was a sickly white, his eyes wide with disbelief.

'I'm so desperately sorry, Ernie. I'd give anything for it not to be true. I know you won't forgive me, not for this, and I'll do whatever you want me to. It's probably best if I go away somewhere straight away, so no one knows. Just tell me what you want and I'll do it without question. I'm so sorry.'

When he spoke it was the voice of a stranger, faint and breathless. 'I'd like you to go now and let me think about this. I can't believe how badly you've treated me when all I wanted was your happiness.'

Jennie could no longer hold back her sobs.

'I'm so ashamed, Ernie,' she said and ran from the room. She pushed her way back through the hall and Marie stood to follow her. Ernie stood in the doorway to the living room, stooped and looking far older than his years, and Marie stopped briefly and said, 'Ernie, I'm so sorry, you don't deserve any of this.'

'She lied you see, that's what I dislike the most. In front of the solicitor she lied, pretended there had been nothing between them, and now, when I thought everything would soon be all right, this happens. You can't lie about a child growing inside you. Not even Jennie could explain that away.'

'I have to go after her,' Marie said, touching his arm, wanting to stay and comfort him but knowing Jennie was her priority at that time. 'If there's anything I can do, you only have to ask. I feel for you, I really do.'

'You can tell that sister of yours I wish I'd never clapped eyes on her.'

'I think she must know that.'

Bill found out about Jennie's predicament within days of her telling his father. Jennie told Lucy she was expecting a child and told her she was not pleased. Lucy confided in a customer who was a friend and the friend's brother was in touch with Bill. His reaction was immediate. He took a couple of days off work and went home.

His father was just setting out for a walk and at once told him to leave. Bill was shocked at how unwell he looked and persuaded him to go with him to a café and sit where they could talk.

'You've heard, I presume?' Ernie said, refusing to look at his son. 'That's why you're here, to meet up with Jennie and discuss your plans?'

'I've heard. I presume the baby is mine and I want to know what you want me to do.'

'Jennie wants to know that too. Everyone seems to be waiting for me to make up my mind. No one has an idea of what to do. The truth is there is nothing anyone can do. My wife is expecting your child. How can I find a way out of that situation?'

'Isn't the answer for me to wait for a divorce and marry her?'

'Where does that leave me? A joke on everyone's lips, that's what.'

'While if you and Jennie were together, pretending the baby was yours, everyone would think you were a hell of a man, fathering a child at your age,' Bill said slowly.

'Take her back you mean? How dare you suggest such a thing?'

'The only gossip would be good gossip. Jennie would never tell anyone the truth.'

'She already has, or you wouldn't have heard. As for the truth, Jennie wouldn't know the truth if it came up and bit her.'

'The few who know about this believe the child is yours. Only I knew at once that it couldn't be.'

'Oh, go away. I can't bear to look at you.'

'You have my address and I'll agree to whatever you decide.'

Before returning to London, Bill was unable to resist seeing Jennie, and the next day he stood near the bus stop at the end of the lane leading to Badgers Brook. Darkness was falling and he was hidden by trees on the grassy verge. He guessed she and Marie would be on the bus soon after five thirty and planned only to watch them as they walked home. He had no intention of talking to her, or letting her see him, but the car driving straight at them changed that.

He didn't take any notice of the low purr of its engine as it approached from behind, his attention was on the two figures walking in the middle of the road. But when it picked up speed and appeared to be aiming straight towards the two sisters he was close enough to run and grab them both and throw them into the ditch as the car hit him, caught his overcoat and dragged him along the road for several yards.

A couple came out of the nearest house having heard the racing engine and the squeal of brakes, and, having assured themselves that the women were shaken but unharmed, helped Bill into the house while someone ran to telephone for help.

'Did you recognize the car?' the man of the house asked. 'The police will be glad of any help. There's a mad man out there. This has happened twice before, a woman run down and the driver not stopping. Whoever he is he has to be caught.'

'I don't remember the make of the car, but I do know it wasn't a man driving, I'm sure of that,' Bill said slowly. 'I'm absolutely certain it was a woman.'

The car stopped half a mile further on and the driver ran off. It was very dark and on the little-known road the ditch that became the woodland stream called Badgers Brook was a hazard that was unavoidable. The muddy drop into the shallow water sent the figure sprawling and all the weight of the body went on one ankle. The trousers and jacket were smeared with mud. It was imperative to get away and, dragging one leg painfully, the driver made a path through the sedges, across the strip of water and on to the field beyond. It took a long time but eventually a road was reached and a van stopped and the driver offered a lift.

'Hello,' he said with a smile. 'What are you doing out here? Don't tell me you're walking home from a date that went wrong?'

'No, the evening was a reasonable success,' Effie replied.

The police asked Marie, Jennie and Bill endless questions but none of the three could throw any light on the reason for the deliberate attack. No one could decide who had been the intended victim, although with Jennie being hurt previously, she was afraid she was the most likely target. The reason was a mystery she couldn't fathom.

Bill was treated for shock and bruises but was released on his insistence the following morning. Jennie and Marie weren't harmed apart from muddy grazes and a few bruises from landing in the wet ditch.

Jennie told the nurses about her possible pregnancy, which the doctor confirmed. Her anxieties were calmed and she was reassured that the baby was unharmed, although she was told to rest for a few days.

Jennie told Ernie what had happened and he went to the hospital to be told that Bill was on his way back to London. 'You'd better come home with me,' he said gruffly. 'She's been staying with her sister,' he explained to the nurses standing near. 'I think you need to be looked after, especially as you're carrying our child.' He looked at her as he said it and tears welled in her eyes.

Jennie didn't know what to do. She couldn't just walk back into Ernie's house.

Apart from those words for the benefit of the nurses, nothing had been said to make that easy. Instead she went back to Badgers Brook and for two days she rested on the couch near the fire, warmed by its cheerful glow as well as the heat it produced. Both she and the roaring fire were tended by a concerned Rhodri.

On the third day, after Marie had left for work, she took the next bus into Cwm Derw. It was no use trying to hide and that was what she had been doing, using her pregnancy as an excuse to avoid people and their comments. She was helping Marie to redress the window when Ernie walked in. At once Marie stopped struggling with the display of autumn dresses and left them alone, going into the only available place, the tiny fitting room.

Jennie sat on one of the two chairs, inviting Ernie wordlessly to do the same.

'I think it's best if you come home,' he said.

'You mean you'll let me stay, me and the baby? I thought you only meant a few days while I recovered.' She spoke more sharply as she added, 'I won't part with it you know, so don't think it.'

Marie stifled her nervous laughter. Even at such a moment as this, Jennie had to make the rules.

'Come this evening after the shop closes and we'll talk about what's to be done,' Ernie said. 'I'll make us something to eat.'

'Thank you, Ernie dear.' Jennie looked up with blue eyes filled with remorse.

Marie almost choked. Could that submissive voice belong to her sister? What an actress she was. But when Ernie left and she went out into the shop she saw that Jennie was crying and the tears were genuine. She hugged her and tried to reassure her that everything would turn out for the best. 'Things usually do for you,' she said cheerfully. 'I don't know how you do it, but you come up smiling every time. Even after a disaster like this.' There was only a slight hint of envy there as she saw, fleetingly, how badly her own life had turned out. She wondered what she had done to deserve such heartache.

Ivor watched as a group of boys struggled to build a bonfire. It was situated on a piece of waste ground where once a house had stood, before bombs had destroyed it. There was plenty of space in what had once been the garden for people to gather as they enjoyed the fun. Although the scene as the children prepared was filled with shouts and bursts of laughter, he felt sad. Fires, even for a happy occasion like bonfire night, reminded him of his mother and her attraction to their destructive power. Turning away he went into a pub and ordered a drink.

A man sitting in a corner looked vaguely familiar and he frowned as the man nodded his head. He knew him, but from where? The man stood, and, carrying his pint glass, he approached. 'Ivor? Ivor Masters?'

'Yes, but I don't remember...' Ivor paused for the man to help him out.

'I'm retired now, but I was PC Jennings, the policeman who – er – dealt with your mother's case all those years ago.'

Ivor didn't know what to say. It was a most peculiar introduction and one he certainly didn't want to continue. 'As you say, a long time ago,' he said, preparing to move away.

'I see your father is living in Badgers Brook. He's very happy from what I can tell. Really contented. Thanks to your kind-hearted wife. My wife Kitty and she are friends.'

Still Ivor tried to get away. He didn't want to talk about his parents. Not even now, when the reflection of his past was glaring persistently at him from the mirror of the present, a view he was trying so hard to forget.

'I knew him when we were young,' Mr Jennings went on, standing to prevent Ivor moving. 'A well-liked and talented young man. He sang, and played several instruments, and your mother was a fine artist. So sad, when everything changed for them'

'I don't want to discuss it. Can't you see

that?' Ivor said, his head lowered, his eyes staring at the floor. 'I don't remember what he was like before the illness began.'

'The illness?' Bob Jennings queried, pretending ignorance of his wife's suspicions. You don't think it's hereditary, do you? His "illness" as you call it was the result of his suffering during the First World War.'

'That was when it revealed itself, but it was lying dormant, waiting to strike, and I know it will happen to me, one day soon. I've always know what was coming to me – I don't need you or anyone else to remind me.'

'You're so wrong. You can forget all that nonsense, wherever it came from. Your parents will have passed on to you only good things.'

'Stop this. You might be trying to make me feel better but it isn't helping to pretend.'

Bob Jennings sighed. 'I can see I won't be able to persuade you different, but talk to a doctor. The specialist who treated him is still alive. Retired now, like me, but he'll remember.' He took out a piece of paper and wrote down a name and address. 'Talk to him and you'll wonder why you didn't talk to him before.' Taking his still unsampled pint, he walked back to his seat.

Effie didn't go into work for a few days. When her landlady called to ask if she was all right she was surprised to see Effie using a broom as a makeshift crutch to support a bandaged ankle. Since the fall, after leaving the scene of yet another accident, she had avoided seeing a doctor and hoped the sprain would heal without medical assistance.

'How did you hurt yourself, dear?' her landlady enquired.

'I slipped off the steps at work when I was reaching to the top shelf for a new order book,' she lied. Her ankle was very painful and, as she remembered the way she had dragged herself across those cold dirty fields, she swore that this was something else Jennie would pay for.

It had been a surprise to see Bill. She had understood he was London, yet there he was, close enough to Jennie to pull her away from the wheels when she had tried again to kill her.

Marie made the boys promise not to start the Guy Fawkes bonfire before she was home. 'And I don't want it so close to the house,' she added as Roger began gathering thin branches for the pile.

'It's not fair,' Roger complained.

Marie laughed. 'It's a long time since you've said that.'

'Well it isn't. Violet can't stand too close, yet when we start building it near the

388

window where she'd have a good view you say we have to move it.'

'Violet is allowed outside, of course she is. In fact she's looking forward to eating the potatoes we'll cook in the ashes, but you have to be careful, that's all. Fire can be very dangerous, remember.'

'Grandfather says fire is beautiful,' Violet told them.

'And so it is, as long as it's under control.'

Marie had bought a box of fireworks and these she had kept hidden, in case the temptation to set a few off before the actual night was too strong. This night of the year was something everyone looked forward too, especially since the war years when they hadn't been allowed. But safety was paramount.

Effie was obsessed with thoughts of Jennie. When she had aimed the car at Emily, hitting her, running the wheels right over her, she had been killed, so why had it failed – twice – with Jennie? If she and Bill were still seeing each other she had to die. Bill's happiness couldn't continue. But now her thinking was beginning to change. Making Bill suffer by losing Jennie in the same way he had lost Emily was no longer her main desire. She now wanted to kill Jennie because in her twisted mind she was the cause of all her own unhappiness.

Confusing the time in between she believed Jennie had stolen Bill from her. Jennie was the reason Bill had abandoned her and sent her away to have their child alone. Jennie was the reason she had lost her child, having it taken from her without even being allowed to cuddle it.

After contriving three car accidents she knew she had to try another method to get rid of her. But what? The car accident had almost been successful and no one had suspected her. No one knew she was able to drive and the chances of the police questioning her were remote. Yet getting away with it three times must have added to the risk of discovery. She had to think of another way. Trying a different method had its dangers and she didn't want to end up in prison for killing someone who didn't deserve to live. She had to deal with Jennie and somehow get someone else blamed.

No one knew her in Cwm Derw and certainly no one in the lane on which Badgers Brook stood. Ignoring her still painful ankle, and with a notebook and fountain pen in her hands, she knocked on the door one afternoon and, when Rhodri answered, she asked if Jennie was in.

'Working,' Rhodri said abruptly, and began to close the door.

'Or Marie? I have a message from Ivor, you see.'

'Ivor?' The old man frowned and stared at her. 'Ivor?'

'Is she here? Marie, is she at home?'

'Working.' This time he succeeded in closing the door, and Effie walked back down the path. A neighbour was at the gate and Effie asked, 'D'you know where I can find Mr Ivor Masters?'

'Gone away. Can I help? I know the family quite well.'

'I'm from the hospital and I have to check up on Mr Rhodri Masters. His son is away you say? Then who's looking after him? He needs constant care, doesn't he?'

'Marie is wonderful to him. The hospital keeps a regular eye on him, and there's no trouble with the fires, not for a couple of years, since his wife died.'

'Wasn't it his wife who started the fires?' Standing only a few feet from the door of Badgers Brook, Effie pretended to look through notes.

'From the hospital you say? Then I would have thought you'd have known.'

Again Effie thumbed through the notes, then looked knowingly at the neighbour and said, 'I'd like you to confirm what we have on record. About the fires,' she coaxed. 'What have they to do with Rhodri? It was his wife who went to prison for setting fire to the school and houses, wasn't it?'

'Well, that's the official story, but it was

really him. That's what most of the people involved believe anyway. His wife covered up for him, even going to prison. He was so ill, you see, and she knew he wouldn't be able to cope.' She frowned. 'I thought the hospital would have known that, even though the police didn't have the evidence. The psychiatrists would have put that forward as a theory at least, wouldn't they? She was charged with causing the fires but everyone knew it was really Rhodri. He's fine now, though. Seems the obsession with fires ended when he lost his wife.'

Effie snapped the notebook closed and, thanking the woman, walked briskly back to the bus stop. The sooner she got away from here the better. One nosy neighbour was more than enough. From now on she must make sure she wasn't seen by anyone in the area. She took off the clumpy shoes, the stolen mackintosh and the old-fashioned hat and threw them away. The glasses, which she only used for reading, went into her handbag; twice they had threatened to tip her into the ditch again.

Inside the house, Violet showed Rhodri the drawing she had made of the woman who had stood outside talking to Mrs Jenning.

'I wonder why she was wearing glasses, Grandad? She wasn't wearing them when she came into the shop. Nosy-parkering, Mam said she was, not intending to buy.'

She copied the drawing but this time left off the glasses and added curling hair, which she coloured with a red pencil, instead of the awful hat.

The words of Bob Jennings echoed round and round in Ivor's head. Could what he'd said be true? That his father didn't have a hereditary illness? He fingered the piece of paper on which Bob Jennings had written the name and telephone number of the doctor who had treated Rhodri. The next afternoon he rang and arranged to see him. They were to meet on Wednesday morning, November 5th, Guy Fawkes day. The significance didn't fail to register.

The doctor confirmed everything Bob Jennings had told him. He also learned that the fires had been his father's doing and his mother had protectively taken the blame. Ivor's first reaction was shame. If only he'd known. If he had stayed at home for a few more years his mother would almost certainly have explained. Such love, for her to go to prison to save Rhodri from suffering.

Running from home at the age of twelve he'd been too young to be trusted with such a secret. His mother would have known that pride alone would have persuaded him to boast. Pride in his mother for such a heroic act. And his attempt to end the merciless teasing and bullying he suffered would have made telling his tormentors the truth irresistible. Then her sacrifice would have been for nothing. His father would either have been sent to prison or to a hospital for the dangerously insane.

He didn't know what to do. He didn't feel capable of walking back into Marie's life and explaining he'd made a stupid mistake. How could he expect her to listen to him, let alone forgive him? He went to see Geoff.

Effie had been aware of the approach of bonfire night for several weeks. Beside the growing piles of wood and rubbish built ready for the bonfires, there were a few fireworks set off in the street; in fact, a group of boys threw a 'jackie jumper' on to the pavement near her feet and caused her to jump with shock as it followed her around as she tried to escape. The boys laughed but she pushed one so fiercely and unexpectedly that he fell into the road. The laughter stopped abruptly and the boys hurried off. She stood glaring at them, and as they turned and saw her watching they increased their speed until they were running, laughter restored, jeering calls reaching her as they disappeared around a corner.

She walked home noticing the large number of huge piles prepared for burning, wood and a few unwanted household items collected in every available space. There were dozens of cardboard boxes, many filled with newspapers, all waiting for November 5th. It was then that she remembered seeing the early preparations for a fire in the garden of Badgers Brook.

A night filled with flames, and a man known to enjoy destruction by fire. If she thought this out with care she could have a method for getting rid of Jennie and someone to take the blame. Bonfire night. An old man obsessed with burning. Perfect.

When Ivor had explained his fears to Geoff, they both went to the ladies' clothes shop to see Marie. Jennie was there, and before either of the women could say a word Ivor pleaded with Marie not to send him away until she'd heard what he had to say.

She picked up a dress on which the hem had fallen and began sewing, even though her hands were shaking so badly that she knew she would have to undo every stitch she made. It was only the second time they had met since he had left her and his unexpected appearance had confused her. Her heart was racing and banging so painfully in her chest it threatened to explode from her body. She was so afraid of what he was going to say, trying to stop her ears from hearing the words, trying to think instead of other things, mundane things like whether he would want a cup of tea, convinced she was about to be asked for a divorce.

'I think you might be in danger tonight.'

Marie almost laughed, the words were so unexpected, so ridiculous.

'My father was the one who almost burned the school down and set fire to a neighbour's house. My father. Not my mother.'

'Rhodri? He's no danger to us. He's had plenty of opportunities to set fire to the house but he's shown no interest in fire except to keep the house warm. You must be wrong. Now go away and tell your stories to—' She was unable to complete the sentence. How could she refer to the new woman in his life? Mentioning her would give her credence, would make this whole sorry mess a reality.

'It's true.' Geoff spoke for the first time. 'Please listen to Ivor, Marie. We both think you should keep away from Rhodri, for his own safety. In fact, for tonight at least, he should be locked in where he can't do any damage. We think you should call the police.'

'No, I won't do that. If what you say is true – and I seriously doubt it – he needs us to trust him.'

'Close the shop and come with us to find him. At least do that,' Ivor said pleadingly. Pride, that sometimes foolish emotion, made her shout, 'I don't want to go anywhere with you, Ivor Masters.'

Geoff added his concerns. 'This isn't the

time for arguments and recriminations. We need to find Rhodri.'

'I'll come with you,' Jennie said. 'If it's only for tonight, there'll be plenty of us to watch him. I'll phone Ernie and he'll come too. We can make sure everything is all right without him knowing we're concerned. Tomorrow it will be back to normal.'

Seeing from Ivor's and Geoff's faces that they were seriously concerned, Marie nodded. 'Violet will be home from school soon.'

'Perhaps we should meet her.' Ivor suggested.

Believing that his appearance was only temporary, Marie shook her head. 'I think it's best she doesn't see you at all. She's slowly getting over your leaving us and it would be cruel to revive an interest you don't intend to prolong.' She was switching off the lights and picking up the door keys as she spoke, and didn't see the look of pain that crossed Ivor's features.

Ivor and Geoff went straight to Badgers Brook and Jennie went with them. They called first to leave a message for Ernie to follow them.

'The first thing is to find Rhodri, and from then on we don't allow him out of our sight,' Ivor said anxiously.

There was no possibility of Ivor avoiding being seen by Violet, and as she and her mother reached the gate and saw him with

Geoff, searching the sheds and garden, she ran to him and hugged him and chattered excitedly about all that had happened and how glad she was that he was back home. Holding her in his arms he looked at Marie and shrugged an apology, his eyes filled with unshed tears.

'There's no sign of Rhodri,' Geoff said. 'We've searched the house and garden.'

'He often goes to sit by the brook, watching the birds. Perhaps he's there,' Violet suggested. 'He feeds the foxes most evenings too. He'll be frightened for them with the fireworks going off tonight. Perhaps he's there, feeding them before the noises stop them coming. He's been very upset at the thought of the noise.'

At the edge of the wood, dressed in drab brown coat and unsightly hat, Effie watched them. She felt an increase in her heartbeat as Jennie walked down the path to greet a new arrival. It was Ernie. What was he doing here? The last she'd heard they were living apart, Jennie staying with her sister. She watched in disbelief as the couple walked arm in arm up the path, and felt the pain of jealousy as Jennie stroked her slightly swollen belly. She was going to have a baby! That gesture of pride and protection left her in no doubt! Her arms ached as she felt the ghostly weight of a child. She hadn't even held her baby and here was Bill's father proudly escorting Bill's latest secret love, who was going to have the joy of mother-hood, something of which she, Effie, had been robbed.

There was a discussion going on and she watched as Ivor and Geoff set off for the woods, while Jennie and Violet and Ernie went into the house. Marie stood at the door for a while and the twins came along the road from the direction of the bus, arriving back from work. The twins went to where the fire stood ready to ignite. Marie's voice calling to them, a warning not to light it until everyone was present, came clearly in the evening air. She saw Marie's arms beckoning to the boys to go inside.

Effie knew she had to get them all out of the house, except for Jennie, but how was she going to arrange that? With darkness falling and everyone busy with their own fire, she took a risk and went to the bonfire and lit the paper someone had stuffed in its heart. She hid in the shadows as the flames leaped, and smiled as Roger ran out, shouting, 'It isn't fair.' He was followed by the others, Marie carrying a bowl filled with potatoes to cook in the ashes.

Effie ran into the house, and called softly in a sing-song voice, 'Violet, come and find me. I bet you can't find me. Shhh, don't tell the others. There's a present if you find me first.'

399

Violet choked back a chuckle in her excitement and ran up the stairs, following the tantalizing voice. She ran from room to room, and when she went into the room where she slept she heard tapping and went to the heavy oak wardrobe. Opening the door she was startled in an enjoyable way as Effie stepped out with a finger to her lips to request silence. She handed Violet a shilling.

'Well done, Violet! I didn't even hear you coming. Now, if you can hide in the wardrobe for ten whole minutes without a sound, while I catch someone else, I'll give you *ten shillings*. She held a note temptingly in front of Violet's face and at once the girl stepped into the wardrobe and allowed Effie to turn the key on her with only the slightest qualm. Then the door opened and Effie said. 'Better idea. First call to your Auntie Jennie, then go and hide.'

'Still for ten shillings?'

'Of course.' She handed the note to the overjoyed girl.

Looking over the banister, Effie almost shouted in her delight when Jennie came into the hall alone. The night was chill and she had obviously decided to come inside to warm up as she went straight to the fire and held her hands close to the flames.

'Jennie, come here, quick,' Violet called. Then, giggling, she ran into her room and stepped into the wardrobe. Again Effie

400

closed and locked the door.

Jennie went up the stairs and looked in her niece's bedroom but it was empty. She was smiling. Violet loved playing hide and seek. Behind her the door closed and the key turned, and on the landing Effie opened a bottle containing petrol.

With no sign of Rhodri at any of his usual haunts, Ivor, Geoff and Marie returned to the house. Ernie and the twins were feeding the fire with the pile of wood the twins and Rhodri had collected, hoping to keep it going into the evening for the promised supper of baked potatoes.

'There's no sign of Rhodri.' Marie sounded worried. 'Where can he be?'

'And you were told not to light the fire until we were all ready,' Geoff said to the boys.

'We didn't. Someone else did. It's not fair,' Roger complained.

'Where's Violet?' Ivor asked then.

'In the house with Jennie,' Ernie told her. 'They were feeling cold.'

They all went inside, surprised to find the room empty. Upstairs Effie held off from pouring the petrol and unlocked the bedroom door, behind which Jennie was banging and calling. 'Damn,' she muttered. 'Why did they have to come back now?' She needed a few minutes for the fire to take hold if her plan was to work.

In the living room, as Jennie joined them explaining that the bedroom door had stuck, Ivor saw the drawing Violet had done of Effie.

'How d'you know this woman?' he asked Marie. 'What's her picture doing here?'

Marie looked at it and smiled. 'Violet is good at getting a likeness, isn't she?' She held the sketch for Jennie to see. 'That woman comes into the shop occasionally but she never buys, just looks and chats and leaves.'

'There are a few who do that. Nosy-parkering, we call it.'

'I know this woman and I don't think she was interested in clothes,' Ivor said.

'Your new love, is she?' Marie hissed, hoping the twins wouldn't hear.

'You're my only love. And this woman is seriously – perhaps dangerously – odd.'

Quietly, so as not to alarm Marie, Ivor whispered to Geoff to go and telephone for the police. She might be a harmless unhappy woman, but her lies about her ability to drive and her inexplicable interest in his family came to the fore and he felt a chill fear envelop him.

Jennie explained about the aborted game of hide and seek and both Marie and Ivor began calling Violet's name, running through the house into every room. But in the wardrobe Violet covered her giggles with her hands and pressed the ten shilling note against her face.

They all went outside, calling Violet with increasing alarm, except Jennie, who decided to stay in the house in case either Violet or Rhodri came back. This time it was Effie who called her, a whisper that could have been the voice of a child. 'Auntie Jennie, come and find me.'

'Come on, Violet. This isn't the time for games. We're all worried about your grandfather. Come out and we'll play later, after we've seen the fireworks.'

As if on cue, the sound of distant fireworks filled the air. There had been a few spasmodic bursts, but suddenly the sky was illuminated with a moving picture of bright colours and the display intensified as more and more filled the night air with colour and sound as garden parties joined in. The sharp cracks and loud bangs, the sibilant hisses, the wails and whooshes of the varied displays, and the accompanying shouts of entranced children broke the silence of the night. Children squealed in delicious alarm as the entertainment increased, looking around them, convinced they were at the very centre of the annual extravaganza.

Locked in the wardrobe, Violet heard the excitement and, aware that she was missing the display, she began knocking on the wardrobe door, demanding to be let out. Holding the ten shilling note in her hand, she called to her captor, offering it back to be allowed to take part in the fun. Hearing her calls, the voice raised in alarm, Jennie ran to the bedroom, and at once Effie closed and locked the door.

The petrol dripped faster and faster on to the landing floor where she had thrown a few screwed-up pieces of paper, and slowly edged towards the bedroom door. Throwing down the empty bottle, Effie took out a box of matches.

Outside, Ivor looked around in agitation. 'Where is she? What has Effie done?'

'Where are the police?' Geoff muttered anxiously. 'I'll go and call them again.'

Unaware of the urgency of the search for their sister, Roger and Royston carrried out potatoes and pushed them into the edges of the now fiercely burning bonfire.

Jennie saw the stream of liquid moving inexorably closer, creeping under the door towards them as she struggled to release Violet from her prison. There was no sign of the key and she tried to force her fingers into the edge of the door, but to no avail. There was a washstand with a bowl and jug on its marble surface and she smashed the jug, using a broken edge to try to break open the door.

Failing to force the wardrobe door and with Violet beginning to panic, her shouts turning to screams, Jennie threw the bowl at the window. It was Roger who heard the smashing sound, which, on such a night, might have gone unnoticed if he hadn't been directly below and seen the missile land near his feet. He looked up and saw Jennie at the window. He called Ivor, who ran at once and looked up at the window where Jennie was shouting for help.

'There's petrol! And I can't open the wardrobe door,' she screamed. Before Ivor could ask why she needed to she added, 'Violet is locked in there. Get us out quick!'

Ivor told Marie to get wet blankets and ran up the stairs. There, on the landing, stood Effie. She held a match in one hand and she struck it as Ivor was halfway up. In her haste she snapped it and, drawing another, she held it close to the box.

'There's nothing you can do. Your child and Jennie's child have to die. I had my baby stolen and it was Jennie who stole Bill from me. You didn't care. You'll all suffer like I did. Then you'll know.'

Ivor had stopped just a few feet from her. His only chance was to talk her out of striking the match. Below, Geoff had returned from the telephone box and had seen what was happening. He climbed a ladder and entered the bedroom where Jennie and Violet were held. He tried to open the wardrobe door with tools he carried and the sound reached Effie. As she scraped the match against the rough side of the box the sound seemed inordinately loud in the chaos of the evening. There was a momentary hesitation as she glanced back at him, and Ivor leaped at her, the match mercifully failing to create a flame.

To the accompaniment of the continuing fireworks display, a police car arrived and four constables got out. Subduing Effie was easy. Ivor had held her face down close to the petrol with which she had planned to kill his daughter and Jennie, her arms crossed behind her back, and he hadn't allowed her an inch of movement. He was panting not with exertion, but with imagination racing to what might have happened, and also how he might have avoided it.

'It was Rhodri who did it,' Effie kept repeating. 'He's mad. He burns buildings, not me. He planned this and I was trying to save them.'

Over the following days they learned that Effie had intended for Rhodri to be blamed for the fire – but he had an alibi. Fearing that his weakness might render him unable to resist the one night of the year when fires were permissible, he had signed himself into hospital for safety.

Jennie went home with Ernie, who had arrived in time to see the police arresting a still protesting Effie.

'I'm so thankful that you weren't harmed,' he said. 'You'll have to see the doctor immediately though, to make sure no harm was done to you or the baby.'

'I don't know what will happen to me, Ernie,' Jennie said tearfully, 'but I do know that I want this child. To have coped with so much and still be there makes me realize how badly she wants to be born. If that sounds like fanciful nonsense I don't care. I want this child, whatever you decide.'

'I want it too. I'm looking forward to caring for her, giving her my time, which was something I couldn't do for Bill.'

She held her breath, waiting for the rest of his words with anxiety.

'In public we'll be the devoted, happy couple but in private we'll be polite and pleasant to each other but nothing more. Do you understand? I can never forgive you for the way you behaved. And I don't want Bill to have anything to do with either of us. Or the child.'

Assuring him she understood, she risked putting her hand in his and was relieved to feel his fingers grasping her own. His attitude was understandable, she had hurt him in such a terrible way, but she had the feeling that it wouldn't last. 'I do know how lucky I am, Ernie, dear. I'll never do anything to make you regret taking me back. I could have died in that house and it's as though I've been given a second chance. From today, I'll do everything I can to make every moment of your life a happy one.' She felt his fingers tighten around her own and knew that, despite all that had happened, they would be all right.

No one wanted to sleep at the house, where the smell of petrol pervaded every room and they had put the fire out for fear of the fumes igniting. Marie and the three children went back to Geoff's shop. Ivor stood and watched them all go before settling to sleep on the couch with the doors open and the fire reduced to wet ashes. It was an analogy for his life, he thought, staring at the sodden coals and dead ashes.

The following day he went to work, and after leaving the office at five thirty he went to see his father. Rhodri was free to leave, but until the police had finished their examination and Badgers Brook had been properly cleaned Marie felt unable to return to the house where attempted murders had taken place, so he had been invited to stay with the others in Geoff's storeroom.

'I've been very stupid, Dad,' Ivor said, as he walked Rhodri to where a taxi waited for them.

'I'm stupid,' Rhodri said amiably, 'but not all the time, only now and again. Just now I feel happy to be going home to Marie and the boys and Violet.' He turned to face his son and said, 'Why don't you come with me? Geoff's always got room for one more.'

Although it was not what he had intended, Ivor got in beside his father, who looked out of the window, pointing to things like an excited child. There was no hesitation as Geoff invited them inside.

'There might be a bit of a squeeze if you want to sleep here, mind,' he said to Ivor. 'Although you could sleep on a chair in my room.' He stared at him as he spoke, as though wanting to say more. Perhaps to tell Ivor he slept there alone, in case he was still in any doubt.

'I'd better get back to my room. I brought nothing with me and I'll need a change of clothing for tomorrow.'

Geoff smiled. 'Marie's always telling me how particular you are about your clothes. Never the same shirt twice and all that.'

'I never had to worry about clean clothes. Marie made sure they were always there when I needed them. Now I use a laundry and she wouldn't be impressed.' He looked at Geoff then. 'I've been so rigid about so many things, and in most of them I've been wrong.'

'Not about clean clothes though?' Geoff

grinned.

'No, but just everything else.' Half turned away from the man who had been such a good friend, he said, 'It's impossible to explain how worthless and unlovable a childhood like mine can make you feel. You have to experience it to know. I sound self-pitying but I wasn't like that. I refused to accept the life I'd been given and fought against it. As a twelve-year-old, coping with it the only way I knew how, I ran away. I invented a past and built the kind of life I imagined I'd been born to, pretended my parents were not really mine, that I was adopted, or stolen, anything to free me from the anguish of my situation.'

'And Marie? Didn't she deserve the truth?' Geoff asked softly.

'By then it *was* the truth.'

Marie came out and invited him to stay and share their meal. 'It's baked potatoes,' she said. 'After the disappointment of yesterday's bonfire, that's the only thing I can put right.'

After a questioning glance at Geoff, he agreed.

'The rest will settle,' Geoff said, 'once the house is cleared of the smell. I'll help clean it, buy a new wardrobe for Violet, a new rug to freshen it up.'

'I don't think Badgers Brook wants any of us to go back there,' Marie said. In surprise

410

Ivor asked, 'Not for a while? Or not ever?'

'Not ever.'

'If it's because of me, I promise I'll stay away. I don't want to – I want to come back more than you'll ever know – but if it helps I'll stay away.'

Geoff coughed to remind them he was there, then he said, 'I'll see to our supper but I think you two ought to go somewhere and talk.'

It was to Badgers Brook they went, to the house that once again looked sad and unwelcoming. The warmth that had been nothing to do with the amount of heat had gone. They stood in the cold room where Ivor had spent the previous night, and when Marie shivered Ivor took off his coat and wrapped it around her. He didn't take his arms away but tightened them around her until she raised her face to his and they began to smile. A tentative smile at first but relaxing into an acceptance of their reviving love.

'What do you want me to do?' Ivor asked softly.

'Talk to me. Tell me your thoughts, your fears, your hopes and dreams.'

Guiding her to the settee he sat beside her. 'To begin with, I love you. I've never stopped loving you for a moment. I left because I believed it would protect you from an illness threatening me. If my health didn't deteriorate in front of you there seemed a slight chance that what you didn't know couldn't harm you or affect our darling Violet. I thought that seeing me becoming sick would somehow be a catalyst. Oh, Marie, I was so afraid for Violet.' His arms tightened and he pulled her closer. 'After meeting my father again, I saw the past as though through a mirror and feared what I saw there. Believing it would all recur unless I left you and kept you in ignorance of it. My mother's apparent fascination with fire and my father's confusion. Running away seemed the only protection I could offer you.'

'And now? Have we a future?'

'Will you forgive my stupidity?'

Marie stood and walked around the room, touching the walls, feeling no comfort. The coldness and the dank, unloved atmosphere made her feel like a stranger there. 'I think the house has had enough of us. It was a haven when we needed one but now it's worked its magic, we've sorted out our problems and Badgers Brook wants us gone.'

'There'll be other houses.' He stepped towards her and she didn't move away, or resist as his arms claimed her, holding her close.

'It seems we're on the move again,' he whispered. 'But as long as we're together, all six of us, it doesn't matter where we live.'

There was no response. 'Are we?' he asked, touching her cheek with his lips. 'Are we together?'

'For always.'